Pra

"A fast-paced read with humor and mystery blended together to create the perfect story."
Socrates Cozy Cafe

"Playing With Poison is a fun cozy mystery that will keep you laughing and on your toes all the way to the nail-biting end."
Dorothy St. James, author of *The White House Gardener Mysteries*

"Jessie is a fantastic character, I loved the inside look at her writing life, and I found myself laughing out loud at some of her antics."
Melissa's Mochas, Mysteries and More

"A little mystery, suspense, and romance makes *Playing With Poison* a 'break' out debut!"
Tonya Kappes, bestselling author

"I definitely can't wait to read more books in this series to find out what's in store for Jessie and Wilson!"
Cozy Mystery Book Reviews: Keep Calm and Read a Cozy Mystery

"Plenty of quirky characters ... If you enjoy your mystery peppered with humor and romance, Cindy Blackburn has the balls racked and ready for you to play."
Linda Lovely, author of *The Marley Clark Mystery* series

"Jessie Hewitt seems prepared to handle anything life throws her way."
Joyce Lavene, author of *The Missing Pieces Mysteries*

Also by Cindy Blackburn

Playing With Poison
Double Shot

Three Odd Balls

by
Cindy Blackburn

A Cue Ball Mystery

Three Odd Balls
Copyright © 2012 by Cindy Blackburn
Published by Cindy Blackburn
www.cueballmysteries.com

This is a work of fiction. Names, characters, places, brands, media, and incidents are either the product of the author's imagination or are used fictitiously. Any resemblance to actual events or locales or persons, living or dead, is entirely coincidental. The author acknowledges the trademarked status and trademark owners of various products referenced in this work of fiction, which have been used without permission. The publication/use of these trademarks is not authorized, associated with, or sponsored by the trademark owners.

All Rights Reserved.

No part of this book may be reproduced in any form or by any means without the prior written consent of the publisher, excepting brief quotes used in reviews.

ASIN(Kindle):
ISBN-13: 978-1480222519
ISBN-10: 1480222518

For my sister Sharon, who learned to hang ten
at age fifty-four. You go girl!

Acknowledgements

I could not have written *Three Odd Balls* without gobs of help from gobs of people. Thanks to everyone who offered me their support, encouragement, and time. I am bound to forget someone, but here goes: Jean Everett, Anne Saunders, Sharon Politi, Jane Bishop, Joanna Innes, Bob Spearman, Kathy Powell, Megan Beardsley, Betsy Blackburn, Martha Twombly, Karen Phillips, Shari Stauch, Teddy Stockwell, Sean Scapellatto, Carol Peters and my friends at the LRWA. Special super-duper mega thanks to my husband John Blackburn, my technical guru extraordinaire and my hero.

Chapter 1

"I'm loving it, Babe!" Louise shouted into the phone. "Love, love, loving it!!"

I held the receiver a foot away from my ear and wondered why my literary agent even bothered using a telephone. Geez Louise Urko speaks so loudly, and with so many exclamation points, I would have heard her if she had simply opened her office window and bellowed out. Never mind that she works in Manhattan. And I live in North Carolina.

The reason for her excitement? *My South Pacific Paramour*, my alter ego Adelé Nightingale's next novel. Adelé was venturing into new and untried territory with this one. Instead of placing her energetic and altogether over-sexed lovers somewhere in Europe, sometime in the sixteenth century, Adelé had Delta Touchette and Skylar Staggs seeking adventure and discovering romance in a tropical paradise.

"In the nineteenth century no less!" Louise was shouting. "It's, like, practically a contemporary, Jessica!"

I shook my head at Louise's math. "Maybe by Adelé Nightingale standards," I said. "But the sixteenth century was starting to bore me."

"Oh, absolutely! All those lords and dukes and earls, with their castles and turrets and dungeons? They were getting downright dreary."

"And this new setting makes sense." I winked at my cat Snowflake. "What with Wilson and I heading to Hawaii tomorrow for seven days of sun and fun."

"You'll be inspired, Jessica! A vacation is just the ticket!"

Speaking of which, I remembered the task at hand and returned to packing. "Heck," I said as I dropped a tube of sunscreen into the suitcase on my bed. "I may even be able to write off part of this vacation as a research expense. The IRS doesn't need to know I never bother with anything so tedious as actual research, do they?" I rummaged around in the closet for the ridiculous pair of daisy-adorned flip flops I had purchased for the trip. "But no." I stood up, flip flops in hand. "I'm far too law-abid—"

"Oh my God!" Louise interrupted. "I just had a fantastical idea, Jessica! I mean, beyond fantastical!"

"Oh?" I tossed the new shoes onto the bed, where Snowflake took immediate interest in the fake daisies.

"I'm coming!" she shouted.

My face dropped. "Excuse me?"

"To Hawaii! With you! And Wilson! What an utterly fantastical idea! I'll meet you there!"

My face dropped a little further with each new exclamation point, and I struggled to find my voice as Geez Louise continued on her merry and insane way.

"I need a vacation," she shouted. "And I've never been to Hawaii! And I've never met that hunky heartthrob of yours! The man who inspired Adelé Nightingale to new heights of sexual fantasy? I am dying, dying, dying to meet Wilson Rye the mystery man for myself. I must meet your paramour, Jessica! Must, must, must!"

"But now?" I squeaked. "During my vacation?"

"Yes, now! Of course, now! I can help you with him."

"Help?" I took the sandals away from Snowflake and hid them in the suitcase.

"Yes, help! I'll help you uncover the mystery man's deep dark secrets! You know how you've been wondering about his past, Jessica? Well, just leave it to Louise! By the end of this vacation, all will be revealed. Every single, scintillating detail. The man will be an open book, I tell you. Oh! And that gives me another idea, Jessica!"

"I think I need to sit down," I said.

"The plot for *My South Pacific Paramour*! I'll help you with that, too! No more plot plight for Adelé Nightingale. We'll lounge by the pool, sip silly drinks—you know, the kind with little umbrellas in them—and brainstorm together. I can't wait! Can't, can't, can't!"

I sat motionless and blinked at the cat.

Louise cleared her throat. "Now then," she said, all business-like. "Tell me your exact travel plans."

I was so stunned I actually did so.

Snowflake was still staring at me as I hung up the phone. "Wilson is going to kill me," I told her.

The cat did not argue.

***

"Oh now, Honeybunch, you and Wilson just go on and have a grand time," Mother said. "I don't want you to worry about me even for one minute, do you hear?"

My mother might not have the lungs of Louise Urko, and she definitely needed the aid of the telephone, but I heard her loud and clear. I again cringed at the cat and wondered why I had ever chosen to answer my phone that day.

"No, Mother," I argued as I arranged a stack of shorts into suitcase number two. "I cannot go off and have this grand time you're insisting on, knowing you'll be alone for Christmas. Why aren't you going to Danny's? Wasn't that the plan?"

The fact is, I had never, in all my fifty-two years, spent a Christmas away from my mother. So when Wilson and I planned our Hawaiian vacation, I took pains to be sure she could visit my brother Danny and his family for the holiday. But, as Mother was now informing me, Danny's wife Capers had decided otherwise.

"Capers says she needs a vacation, too," Mother explained. "They're taking the twins to Saint Martin for the holiday."

"And they just informed you of this today?" I gave up on packing and plopped down on the bed.

"Oh, Jessie, please don't be mad at me."

I hastened to tell my mother that I most certainly was not angry with her, but with my hapless brother and his inconsiderate wife, who lives to make my life difficult. Of course, Capers wouldn't tolerate me, Jessica Hewitt, enjoying a fun-filled tropical vacation if she couldn't do so herself. So of course, she made these last minute plans. And of course, she thought nothing of leaving my eighty-two-year-old mother in the lurch.

"The Live Oaks is planning a very nice Christmas party for us residents," Mother was saying. "I'm sure it will be lovely."

She was putting up a brave front, but I knew she wasn't looking forward to spending Christmas without any family, even if she did have lots of friends at The Live Oaks Center for Retirement Living.

I pursed my lips and made an executive decision. "You'll come with us," I said. I ignored Snowflake's shocked expression and headed toward my desk.

Mother started protesting, but I was already getting online to see about her plane tickets on such short notice. While she repeated over and over that she wouldn't dream of interfering in my vacation, I played with the internet and made her reservations. The Hawaiian gods were smiling on me—there was even space available at the resort where Wilson and I were staying.

Interrupting a rather involved description of the elaborate Christmas Eve dinner The Live Oaks was promising, I gave my mother her flight information. I had gotten her on the early morning flight from her home in Columbia, South Carolina to Atlanta.

"Wilson and I will meet you at the Atlanta airport," I said. "And from there, the three of us can fly together." I tapped on the keyboard some more. "Believe it or not, they even had a last minute cancellation at the place we're staying. Soooo," I hit the enter key, "I've just booked you a bungalow at The Wakilulani Garden Resort. Wilson keeps calling it the Wacky Gardens. Doesn't that sound fun?"

"Jessica Hewitt!" she scolded. "You are not listening to me. I will not be ruining your vacation with that darling beau of yours. I will not be a third wheel, so you just cancel those reservations this minute!"

"Non-refundable," I argued. "And besides, you won't be a third wheel, but a fourth. Louise Urko is meeting us there, too."

Mother skipped a beat. "Geez Louise is coming?" she asked, her tone considerably brighter. "Well then, I'd better start packing, hadn't I? What should I bring, Jessie?"

I told her to remember a bathing suit and hung up.

Snowflake was watching me. "Wilson is going to kill me," I said quietly.

Once again, the cat did not argue.

***

"You're gonna kill me," Wilson informed me the second he made it through the door of my condo. He's a big guy, but even he was struggling with everything he was lugging. He turned around and gestured to the bottle of champagne he had tucked under one elbow, and I grabbed it before it fell.

"Hopefully that will keep you in a good mood, despite my news," he said as he set down his luggage and the huge cat carrier he was holding. He bent over to open the door and glanced up. "Ready?"

"Of course we're ready." I offered an encouraging nod to my cat. "We're looking forward to seeing our new friends, aren't we, Snowflake?"

She yowled and jumped to the top of the refrigerator.

Okay, so maybe not. But Wally was banging his skinny black body into the door of the cage, and Wilson did the honors anyway. Out Wally popped, and right behind him came Wilson's other cat, an enormous calico named Bernice.

She took a moment to glower at Snowflake, yawned dramatically, and found a corner of my couch for her next nap. Meanwhile, Wally had located a jingle-bell ball under the coffee table and started flicking it across the floor and going for the chase.

Wilson sat down with Bernice. "You still think this will work, right?"

I sure did hope so. I poured the champagne and reviewed our cat-care plans. My downstairs neighbor and good friend Candy Poppe had volunteered to look after our pets while we were away. So far, so good. But her offer rested on all three cats staying at my place for the week. And what if Wally and Bernice didn't like my place? Or what if Snowflake wasn't the most gracious hostess?

With the what-ifs in mind, we'd been practicing for days, and Wilson had been bringing his cats over for play dates. Thus far, no one had actually played together. But then again, no one had started fighting either. I decided to take that as a positive sign.

"Our cats are not going to kill each other," I reassured everyone. I took a seat beside Wilson and handed him a glass. "But you may kill me."

"Why's that?"

"Well, umm, Louise called this afternoon," I began in the breeziest voice I could muster. "She's very excited about my new book."

"Isn't Geez Louise always excited?" He clicked my glass. "To Hawaii."

"In fact," I continued, undeterred, "she became so enthused with the tropical paradise theme Adelé Nightingale is planning, that you'll never guess what she's decided to do." I tilted my head and waited for him to guess.

His face dropped. "You're kidding, right?"

I grimaced. "She's meeting us in Hawaii! Please don't kill me." I grimaced again and kept going. "Louise has no family at all, Wilson. She considers me her family. And it is Christmas. And she wants to help me with my book. And—" I stopped and tried to think of more excuses. "And, umm—" Nothing more was coming to me, but when I hazarded a glance sideways, Wilson was actually grinning. Indeed, he seemed altogether disinclined to kill me.

"Are you feeling well?" I asked and then repeated that Geez Louise Urko would be joining us on our vacation. "She pulled a few strings and booked herself a last minute bungalow at the Wakilulani Gardens and everything."

He kept grinning.

I eyed him suspiciously. "What exactly is the bad news you have for me?"

***

Whatever it was, Wilson's news would have to wait—Bernice was on the move. She hopped down from the couch, yawned expansively, and in typical Bernice-fashion, sauntered past several cat toys, ignored Wally's invitation to play, and found the food dish. Snowflake's food dish. Wilson and Snowflake were on it in a flash.

While Snowflake scolded her guest, Wilson spoke to me. "This will be the issue while we're gone." He pointed to Bernice, who was involved in an intense stare-down with my cat. "It's the reason she's so fat. She steals food. She eats Wally's all the time."

I shifted my gaze to Wally. But he had discovered one of Snowflake's catnip mice and was completely unconcerned about the food-dish showdown. I shrugged and reminded everyone Candy had been apprised of Bernice's dietary regimen. "She promises to make sure everyone eats only the food allotted to them."

"Good luck, Candy," Wilson mumbled. He picked up Bernice—no easy feat—and returned to the couch.

"Your bad news?" I asked.

He cleared his throat. "You know Chris?"

I blinked twice. "No," I said. "I do not know Chris. Your son refuses to meet me, remember?"

"Well, he's changed his mind. He's tagging along."

"With us!?" I jumped and would have spilled my champagne if Wilson hadn't caught the glass.

"The ski trip to Vermont with his buddies fell through," he explained and quickly put the glass back in my hand. "His roommate Larry broke his leg."

"Excuse me?" I shook my head in dismay. "That's what happens while one is skiing, not before."

"Maybe. But Larry was cramming on his way to his chemistry final and wasn't watching where he was going. Bumped into a brick wall and fell backwards down a flight of stairs."

I groaned and took a gulp of my beverage.

Perhaps I should mention that Christopher Rye is a junior at the University of North Carolina. And yes, I had never met the guy. This, despite the fact that I had been dating his father for months, and despite the fact that Chapel Hill is quite close to Clarence, where Wilson and I live. Apparently Chris chose to hate me, sight unseen.

"Larry will be fine," Wilson was saying. "But it ruins the ski trip. Chris sounded pretty disappointed."

"So you asked him to join us."

"He's meeting us at the Atlanta airport. I can't stand the idea of him being alone for the holidays, Jessie. The kid's pretty independent, but." He caught my eye. "You okay with this?"

I considered the news. "Maybe. But I thought he hated me?"

"Well," Wilson sang. "Maybe he's changed his mind."

"Maybe? Chris has never even given me a chance."

"So here's your chance. What do you say, Jessie?"

I had to say I was quite curious to meet the Rye offspring. "Who knows?" I said. "Maybe I'll win him over, and he'll tell me all your deep dark secrets." I raised an eyebrow. "Unless, of course, you'd like to do that yourself?"

Wilson kept his gaze steady and said nothing.

I sighed dramatically. "Okay, so Chris is unlikely to tell me anything of any use," I grumbled. "But will he at least be civil to me?"

"Absolutely. But I doubt we'll see much of him. I booked him his own bungalow at the Wacky Gardens. And if I know my son, he'll spend the week surfing and chasing bikinis."

Thinking the matter settled, he leaned back and relaxed. But that would just not do.

"Umm, Wilson?" I said soothingly. "Going back to the idea—your idea—that no one should be alone for the holidays? There's one more teensy reason you may want to kill me."

He blinked at the index finger I was holding up. "What's that?"

"My mother."

"Your mother, what?"

"She's coming with us!" I blurted out and quickly dived into the whole spiel about Danny, and Capers, and the twins, and Saint Martin.

But Wilson stopped me before I had gotten very far. "Tessie Hewitt goes Hawaiian." He offered one of his signature grins. "This, I have got to see."

I reached out and squeezed his hand. "Mother is right about you, you know?"

"She thinks I'm darling."

Testimony to our whimsical and flexible natures, we toasted our impending vacation and vowed to have a fantastic time, despite the three odd balls who were tagging along, and the three odd cats we were leaving behind.

It was only later that night, as I was tossing one last bathing suit into my suitcase, that a thought occurred to me.

I shooed Snowflake away as she tried to join the bathing suit and spoke to Wilson. "I wonder why the Wakilulani Gardens had so many last minute cancellations during the holiday week. I mean, isn't it interesting that everyone got their own private bungalow? On such short notice?"

Wilson looked up from pushing Bernice out of his suitcase. "Interesting," he agreed.

"Downright wacky," I said and closed my suitcase.

Chapter 2

"I would have recognized you anywhere," I said as we shook hands. A bit of an exaggeration, but Christopher Rye did look a lot like his father. Tall, dark, and handsome, he was a younger, slightly slimmer, brown-eyed version of Wilson. He even had Wilson's frown. I wondered if he might also have his father's grin, but as the frown evolved into an all-out scowl, I concluded that the younger Rye was not much for smiling.

I told myself that a crowded corner, at a crowded gate, at a crowded airport during the holiday travel rush probably isn't the best place to meet anyone, stepped over my carry-on, and introduced him to my mother. At least we had found Tessie a seat, and at least Chris seemed genuinely pleased to meet her.

Indeed, there was that Wilsonesque grin. Chris pumped Mother's hand with far more enthusiasm than he had mine. "Dad's told me all about you, Miss Tessie. Are we gonna have fun or what?"

"Or what!" she squealed in reply, and Chris asked if she had ever surfed.

Of course the answer was no, but ever-ready to give me heart palpitations, she professed a burning desire to learn.

"I'll teach you!" he said, and with that he kicked over his carry-on and hopped on.

While Chris pretended to ride imaginary waves, and while my mother and Wilson asked far too many questions as to how one keeps one's balance and so forth, I called Candy. Chris had launched into a detailed explanation of things called point breaks versus beach breaks when she answered.

"Have they killed each other yet," I asked.

"Umm, not exactly."

"What does that mean?"

"They could be so cute together if they tried," Candy said, not exactly clarifying things. "You know, Jessie? With

Snowflake all white, and Wally all black, and Bernice all mottled-like."

I interpreted the report. "So they're not playing together, but they aren't fighting either. Is that it?

"They're doing both, actually."

"Candy!" I said, and a few people around me jumped. "Please tell me everyone's getting along."

"Okay, okay." She tried to calm me down. "Puddles and Wally really like each other, okay? They're chasing each other all over the place."

Puddles, still in the throes of puppyhood, is Candy's Poppe's poodle. If Adelé Nightingale possessed half of that dog's energy, she could write a book a day.

"Your condo is great for chasing games," Candy was saying. "Lots of open space, no extra walls. It's almost as good as Round Robin Park."

As if verifying Candy's assessment, I heard Puddles bark in the background. "What about Snowflake and Bernice?" I asked.

"They're the ones kind of fighting."

"You mean, they're actually swatting at each other?" I looked to Wilson for support, but he was still paying rapt attention to his son's surfing advice. "Has anyone drawn blood?" I asked Candy.

"No, nothing like that. They're just staring at each other and hissing. And their tails are, like, really bushy. Is that normal?"

I groaned. "Cats do that when they're mad."

"I figured. But don't worry. If worse comes to worse, I'll bring Bernice and Wally downstairs to stay with Puddles and me. No one will get hurt, okay?"

I groaned again and thanked my valiant friend for her efforts. "I hope all this cat sitting won't ruin your holiday, Sweetie."

"Gosh, no. Puddles likes the company, and I bet the cats will be best friends by the time y'all get back."

"I'll be happy if they'd just tolerate each other for a few days."

"No, Jessie. You and Wilson are destined to be together forever. So your cats have got to be best friends."

"Forever?" I glanced skeptically at Wilson. My mother had stood up, and he was holding one of her hands aloft as she suitcase-surfed on Chris's carry-on. I tried not to notice how the crowd was encouraging her.

"Like, duh!" Candy sounded exasperated. "I'm sick of reminding you how much you love the guy, Jessie. Which reminds me—what's his son like?"

As if he had heard the question, Chris took a hiatus from smiling at my mother in order to frown at me. I held his gaze.

"He and Mother seem to have hit it off," I said and hung up as Tessie toppled off the suitcase into Wilson's arms.

"Now then, Chris," she said as she sat back down. "Explain to me what hanging ten is?"

Chris glanced at his father. "I took them off for TSA, so why not again?" He tore off his sneakers, and much to my mother's delight, demonstrated hanging ten over the edge of that poor suitcase.

Mother clapped in glee. "Do you think I'll be able to hang ten?" she asked.

Lord help me, Chris was actually giving her eighty-two-year-old, one-hundred-pound frame an appraisal and considering the possibility. He must have seen me flapping my arms and shaking my head from the sidelines, but he ignored me. "We'll get you out on the waves," he told her. "I promise."

Mother giggled and twisted around to face me. "Me, hanging ten, Jessie. Can you imagine such a thing?"

Unfortunately, yes. I turned to the complete stranger next to me and asked if he happened to have an Advil in his carry-on.

***

No, but the flight attendant took pity on me. And with my headache averted we soon—or rather, eventually— found ourselves in a taxi and at the gates of The Wakilulani Garden Resort. Can you say "Ahhh?"

"Welcome, welcome, welcome!" Louise shouted and waved an enormous sunhat from across the sun-drenched patio.

"No!" She ran to meet us as we climbed out of the cab. "A-lo-ha, a-lo-ha, a-lo-ha!"

"A-lo-ha, a-lo-ha, a-lo-ha!" we all shouted back, and a few of us did a little dance of joy.

As Wilson, Chris, and the cab driver unloaded the luggage from the back of the van, Mother and I hugged Louise and looked around, astounded and amazed.

Beautiful? Oh, my Lord.

"Even the parking lot is beautiful," my mother concluded in wide-eyed wonder.

"It's why I picked the Wakilulani," I said. "Not the parking lot, necessarily, but the gardens. The pictures on Google were remarkable, but this—" I waved a hand, trying to think of an adjective to do it justice.

"Fantastical!" Louise helped me out. But Louise wasn't interested in the garden—she was staring at Wilson with unabashed curiosity. "And here he is!" she exclaimed. "The mystery man! Jessica Hewitt's paramour!"

"Paramour?" Chris glanced up from pulling his surfboard out of the van.

Wilson put down the suitcase he was holding. "Wilson Rye," he said and held out his hand to Louise. But Geez Louise had other ideas. She handed me her hat and opted for a bear hug instead.

Wilson flapped his arms and appealed to me for help. I shrugged and introduced him to my agent. "Isn't she everything I said she would be?" I asked him.

"And more." He gave up and hugged her back, and Geez Louise emitted another fantastical.

Eventually she freed the poor guy from her firm embrace and held him at arm's length for another assessment. Wilson mumbled something about how nice it was to meet her.

"Nice!?" she shouted for the whole island to hear. "I cannot believe it! Wilson Rye! In the flesh! Oh, and Jessica, what fine flesh it is!"

She let go of Wilson and set her sights on Chris. But the younger Rye was faster than his father. He held up his surfboard for self-protection.

Never one for a lengthy attention span, my agent dismissed the possibility of any further groping and spun around to take my mother by the hand. "Wait until you ladies see the beach!" She reclaimed her hat, and with a fantastical here and a fantastical there, led us ladies down the garden path.

Mother and I were content to take in the exotic scenery while Louise talked nonstop. "I do not understand why the place is so deserted," she said as we passed by several bungalows that did indeed look unoccupied. "Other than the guy on staff, I've been the only one here all afternoon. It's been so lonely!"

She put an arm around my mother. "I'm so happy to see you! How have you been, Tessie? It's been, like, forever since we last saw each other. I think we should meet in Hawaii every year, don't you?"

Mother giggled but had no time to respond before we reached the beach. We stopped short and beheld the Pacific Ocean looming only a few yards away. To Louise's credit, she actually shut up for a full ten seconds to let us soak it in.

But Geez Louise was soon interrupting the soothing sounds of the waves crashing onto Halo Beach. "Wilson Rye." She sounded almost forlorn. "Isn't he the absolute, most perfect man for Jessica?"

"He is darling," Tessie agreed.

"They make a fantastical couple!" Louise continued. "Romantic, majestic, statuesque—"

"Statuesque?" Mother was studying me as if she had never seen me before.

"Okay, so I'm tall," I told her and turned to Louise. "But if you call Wilson Rye statuesque to his face, he's apt to arrest you."

"He's off duty," she reminded me. "And about four thousand miles out of his jurisdiction. Therefore, he cannot arrest me. Isn't that right, Tessie?"

"Wilson almost arrested Jessie once," Mother mused.

I rolled my eyes and tuned out any further discussion of the darling and majestic Wilson Rye. I breathed deep of the sea air. "Aloha," I whispered.

"Aloha," Wilson whispered back.

I jumped and turned, and noticed Mother and Louise had conveniently disappeared.

"Aloha," I repeated. I was giving my beau a kiss worthy of Adelé Nightingale when Chris ran by, surfboard in hand.

"Didn't you guys get a bungalow for that?" he called over his shoulder.

***

If only it were that easy. But checking into our rooms at the Wakilulani Gardens proved far more challenging than booking all our last-minute reservations. The person in charge of this seemingly impossible mission, a big thirty-something Hawaiian guy, tapped at his keyboard, clicked his mouse, and furrowed his brow, while Wilson and I watched and waited. And waited.

"Where'd you get your shirt?" Wilson asked him eventually.

The clerk stopped clicking and tapping to glance down. But his Hawaiian shirt, in a brilliant and downright blinding pattern of yellow and orange Hibiscus flowers, must have startled him. He dropped his mouse, and it dangled forlornly off the edge of the desk while the men discussed the shopping options along Halo Beach.

Wilson Rye discussing clothing stores? I chalked it up to jetlag and leaned on the counter for a short snooze.

"Shynomore Shirt Shop has the best selection," the clerk was saying as I opened my eyes.

Wilson, apparently in all seriousness, asked if the Shynomore Shirt Shop was close by.

"Yes, sir! It's just down the beach. You can even walk there if you want. I'll point you in the right direction. Most anyone can point you in the right direc—"

"Our reservations?" I said loudly and directed everyone's attention back to the computer screen, which of course, had gone completely blank.

That spurred the clerk back to action. He picked up the mouse and began clicking at a furious and alarming pace.

I swallowed a groan. "Is there a problem, Mr.—" I squinted at his name tag. "Palakapola? Did I say that right?"

"Almost. But I'm Mr. Okolo. Palakapola is my first name."

He must have seen my alarm. "Everyone just calls me Buster," he said. "Me and my brother are the new owners here." He offered a big happy smile, which soon disappeared as he returned to the problem at hand. He banged at the keys and slapped the side of the monitor with the palm of his hand. "Three bungalows?" he asked for the tenth time.

"Is that a problem?" Wilson asked.

"Oh no, no, no." Buster continued abusing the keyboard. "No problem. No problem whatsoever."

Reminding myself that patience is a virtue, I stepped away from the counter while Buster Okolo attempted to solve the no problem whatsoever. We were in "The Big House" as the sign out front had informed us. More specifically, we were standing in the expansive lobby with whitewashed, rustic wood walls and a high, bare-beamed ceiling. The restaurant and bar to our right boasted huge windows overlooking the ocean. And to the left, with views of the gardens, were the library and game room.

Wilson must have seen me staring at the pool table. "Shoot me a game?" he asked.

"Maybe later," I answered. "After we've settled in." I emphasized the after for Buster's benefit, but he didn't take the hint.

"I don't play very well, myself," he said. "But the pool table was my idea. It's brand new. What do you think?"

Wilson said he thought Buster should concentrate on checking us in. Buster cleared his throat and returned to his arduous task.

I continued nosing around the lobby. The upstairs, a loft with a wrap-around balcony, seemed interesting. The empty bird cage up there in the corner was especially intriguing, but a chain across the narrow stairway informed me that the upstairs was "Private."

"Where's the bird?" I asked and raised my eyes to the rafters overhead. Sure enough, a big green bird was perched up there. Some sort of parrot. I whistled, and to my delight, the bird responded in kind and swooped in for a landing on the counter.

"Darn it, Ki!" Buster exclaimed.

"Darn it, Ki!" the bird repeated.

"Is this Ki?" I smiled and reached out to touch him, but thought better of it when I saw the size of his beak. I pulled back my hand.

"That's Bee Bee," Buster said.

"Bee Bee," Bee Bee repeated and waddled over to me. He seemed to expect a pat on the head.

I again reached out a tentative hand. "Does he bite?"

"No way. He loves attention."

Thus I patted Bee Bee's head and told him what a beautiful boy he was.

"You can have him if you want," Buster said. "Ki hates him."

Wilson mumbled something about Snowflake as he stroked one of Bee Bee's wings with the back of his index finger. "Who's Ki?" he asked.

"My brother—the one with all the computer smarts." Buster took another swat at the computer. Some paperwork on the desk jumped, but the machine in front of him remained unfazed. He whimpered slightly. "I begged him not to, but Ki installed all these updates when we got the place. Update this, update that. It's impossible!"

"Impossible!" Bee Bee hopped onto the desk and started shuffling around the disarray of papers. He knocked a whole stack on the floor, but the hapless Buster took no notice.

I gently suggested that perhaps Ki might check us in and glanced around in search of the computer whiz. "Perhaps he's upstairs," I said, eyeing the "Private" sign. "Do you guys live up there?"

Buster kept his eyes trained on the computer screen. "We have an apartment upstairs. But Ki's never here, no matter how much I beg him." He bent down and yanked the computer plug from the outlet. "I give up," he concluded and folded his arms across the sea of hibiscus flowers.

"Give up," Bee Bee agreed. He stuck out a claw and deftly opened the top drawer of the desk. Wilson and I watched in fascination as the bird ducked his head in and came out with a large old-fashioned key ring hanging from its beak.

Buster took the keys and handed them to Wilson. "Your friend—the lady who got here earlier—took Blue Waters bungalow. Other than that, they're all free." He turned to me. "Walk around, take a look, and take whichever ones you want. How's that?"

Wilson and I shrugged at each other. Fine with us.

"Welcome to The Wakilulani Garden Resort!" Buster said, rather belatedly. "I hope you like it here! I've been sprucing up the place. New curtains, new linens, new beds, even. I built them myself. The wood's from koa trees. Hawaiians used to make canoes out of koa trees. You'll see koas everywhere around here—"

Wilson interrupted by jiggling the key ring.

Buster stopped and blinked at the keys. Then he pointed us to the doorway. "Make yourselves at home and enjoy!"

The parrot looked up from where he was more or less eating some of the papers that had not yet landed on the floor. "Enjoy!" he told us.

Chapter 3

"So much for security," my beau the cop mumbled as we walked back outside. My mother and Louise were nowhere in sight, and presumably Chris was hanging ten out in the waves. But the huge pile of luggage awaiting us on the patio was not so easy to avoid.

"Let's settle Mother first." I pointed to the bungalow closest to us. "Right there. She'll be close to the restaurant, the office, and the parking lot—less walking over all these bumpy footpaths."

Wilson grabbed her two larger suitcases, I took her carry-on, and we managed the short walk to Seagull's Roost bungalow. We climbed the steps to the porch and turned to admire the beach. Chris was still surfing out there. And unlike dry land, the waves seemed populated with human life.

"What did I tell you?" Wilson said. "Chasing bikinis already."

I took a closer look, and sure enough all of the surfers surrounding Chris were female. "Maybe watching your son surf will satisfy my mother," I suggested. "Maybe she won't insist on trying it herself."

Wilson told me to keep dreaming and unlocked the door. He arranged Tessie's luggage at the foot of her bed while I surveyed the accommodations. Altogether charming. The bungalow was small, but had the same whitewashed wooden walls, high-beamed ceiling, and white tile floors as The Big House. A Buster-made four-poster bed built from tree trunks took center stage, and the quilt on the bed and the curtains on the windows were indeed a fresh, crisp chintz, just as promised.

"She'll love it here," I concluded and followed Wilson outside to find a room for Chris, who, he was sure, would also want a beachfront bungalow.

We wandered past the Misty Breezes and Sandy Feet bungalows, and Wilson chose Surf's Up for his son. "This is good," he said. "He's got the ocean, but won't be too close to Tessie to bother her."

"Chris won't bother my mother. They like each other." I was going to mention Chris didn't seem all that crazy about me, but Wilson was already scooting across the patio to collect more luggage.

He came back with a carry-on and small duffle bag and tossed me the key ring. I opened the door, and he unceremoniously dumped the luggage inside.

"He didn't pack very much," I said.

"Bathing trunks, hiking boots, and a surfboard. What else does he need?"

Ah, to be young. And male.

We walked back to the patio and faced our own substantial pile of junk. "Let's decide on our bungalow and come back for it," I suggested. "It's not like it's in anyone's way."

We agreed we wanted a garden-view bungalow and set out to explore. Garden views would be easy. But choosing which garden view would be the difficult task. The Wakilulani was veritably drenched in foliage and flowers.

"It's like the Garden of Eden," I said as I stopped to admire a particularly lovely thicket of flowering somethings near the swimming pool.

"And you, Jessica Hewitt, are the epitome of Eve!" Louise called out. "A big, blond, beautiful, slightly menopausal Eve!"

I looked up the hill and saw my agent and my mother sitting on the porch of Blue Waters bungalow, admiring the blue waters of the swimming pool below them, and sipping some sort of pink drink decorated with tiny gold umbrellas.

"Eve?" I said skeptically as we took a few more steps in their direction. "Exactly what's in that drink, Louise?"

"Who knows? But they're fantastical!"

Mother giggled. "They are delicious, Honeybunch. Y'all should join us." She took a rather large drag from her straw to demonstrate and waved down toward the tiki bar located next to the swimming pool. "Davy will be happy to mix up another batch, won't you, Davy?" Mother fluttered a few fingers at the bartender.

"Davy's a genius!" Louise added. "Genius, genius, genius!"

We approached the bartender. "I take it you're the genius?" Wilson asked.

"Davy Atwell," he answered, and they shook hands. "Can I get you guys something?" He turned to me and winked. "Everyone likes my punch. I call it Pele's Melee."

"Pele, as in the Hawaiian volcano goddess?" I asked.

He winked. "Hot and feisty—like all women should be."

"Feisty." Mother giggled from above us and considered her beverage. "These Pele's Melees do have a certain zing to them, don't they?"

"Zing, zing, zing!" Lousie agreed.

"Zing-zing!" Bee Bee screeched from overhead and flew in for a landing on Louise's porch railing.

Mother and Louise took it in their stride, but Wilson seemed as startled as I. "He's allowed outdoors?" he asked the bartender. "Won't he run—I mean fly—away?"

"Why would he do that?" Davy said. "The Wakilulani has been Bee Bee's home for decades."

"Decades?" I said.

"Oh, yeah. Bee Bee's an Amazon. He's about thirty now. But he'll live at least as long as you and m—"

"Jessica and Wilson!" Louise had moved to her porch railing to give bird the attention he deserved, and to scold us with a bit more vigor. "Get yourselves some pink drinks and come join us!"

"Later," Wilson said.

"Soon," I promised. And as everyone, including the bird, reminded us how fantastical the Pele's Melees were, we continued onward and upward in search of our bungalow.

"Privacy," Wilson reminded me as we got out of earshot of the others.

"Garden of Eden," I reminded him.

And thus we found Paradise, the most remote of the bungalows, tucked away in the farthest corner of Eden.

"Perfect!" I said and raced Wilson down to where our luggage awaited.

"We'll have a view down to the ocean from the bed," he called out just as we jogged past Blue Waters.

I heard my mother giggle from behind us. "If he weren't so darling, I'd be scandalized," she told Louise.

***

Okay, so the pink drinks really were fantastical.

Our entourage, plus Bee Bee and minus Chris, had reconvened at the poolside tiki bar before dinner. My mother, Louise, and I had lined up our lounge chairs with views out to sea, and Bee Bee was perched on one of Louise's ankles. Wilson was perched on a barstool close by and was interrogating Davy the genius bartender about hiking trails on the Kekipi Crater, our very own friendly neighborhood volcano.

I studied my beau. "If all his deep dark secrets are as scary as that shirt he's wearing, maybe I don't want to know about his past," I mused.

Louise tore her gaze from the Pacific to assess Wilson's attire. "It's not every man who can wear fuchsia butterflies and get away with it, Jessica."

"Who knew he even owned a Hawaiian shirt? Or flip flops for that matter."

"That goes for you, too." Mother pointed to my own flip flops. "I haven't seen you in sandals since you were ten. Have you been saving those all these years?"

They were brand new, but Tessie did have a point. Adorned with ridiculous fake daisies, my sandals might well have been exact replicas of a pair I had worn in grade school. And considering my general aversion to open-toed footwear, on myself or anyone else, my new flip flops were indeed the first pair of sandals I had owned in decades.

I mumbled something about when in Rome.

"Trust me, Babe," Louise said. "No Italian woman in her right mind would be caught dead in those."

"But they're perfect for Adelé Nightingale," my mother insisted as Bee Bee leaned over to take a gentle poke at the daisy petals. "Just her style. Speaking of which, Louise and I have been discussing *My South Pacific Paramour*."

"Excuse me?"

"Don't you remember, Jessica? Tessie and I are here to help you." Louise waved her glass on front of her eyes as if conjuring up a plot. "Delta Touchette and Skylar Staggs are in for some fantastical adventures! Beyond fantastical!"

"You always think of such clever names," Mother told me. "And it's clever of you to try something tropical, what with us being in the tropics ourselves."

"Tessie and I are picturing a King Kong theme," Louise said.

"King Kong, King Kong." Bee Bee liked the sound of that.

"But with no King Kong," Mother elaborated.

"King Kong, King Kong."

"So let me get this straight." I scowled at the bird. "We have a King Kong theme, but with no King Kong?"

"Mm-hmm." Mother nodded. "But of course, we should begin with Delta Touchette, who has just arrived in the South Pacific at the behest of her spinster aunt. Auntie Whoever owns a large estate on one of the islands. She has lived there, without the benefit of husband or family, for decades."

"Delta has never actually met this Auntie person," Louise continued, and Bee Bee hopped over to the arm of her lounge chair to hear more. "She has, however, corresponded with her for years. Much to the consternation of Delta's frightfully conventional parents, Auntie Whoever is the girl's role model."

"Delta just adores her Auntie," Mother agreed. "The adventurous life she leads, far from the confines of stuffy old England, has always intrigued her." She jiggled the ice in her pink drink. "Delta has always dreamed of visiting her Auntie Whoever."

"And let me guess," I interrupted. "The last letter from Auntie," I hesitated, "Auntie Eleanor—hinted at some sort of danger on the island?"

"Exactly, Honeybunch! How did you know?"

"King Kong," I answered. "So Delta," I sat up a bit and got into the groove, "yearning for adventure, left stuffy old England behind and embarked on a journey to the South

Pacific. And at long last she arrived at the port of...the port of Mekipii Hui, on the island adjacent to Auntie Eleanor's."

I sipped my drink and contemplated Delta's dilemma. "But she had a most difficult time finding someone to sail her over to... to Ebony Island—that's her Auntie's island. Alas, all of the local skippers refused to assist her. They were vague as to why, but the lovely and courageous Delta surmised they were afraid of Ebony Island. Indeed, she even overheard the word monster mentioned once or twice!"

My mother and my agent shook their heads. "Amazing," they said in unison.

"Amazing," Bee Bee echoed the sentiment.

"But Delta finally did find someone to take her?" Mother asked.

"Skylar Staggs, of course." I glanced down at the Pele's Melee in my hand. "These drinks are starting to grow on me," I admitted.

Mother giggled. "They're a bit stronger than the champagne you usually have."

I cleared my throat. "Of course, there were instant sparks between Skylar and Delta on the journey over to her Auntie's island. All was going well until a terrible, terrible gale kicked up. Oh, it was treacherous, indeed. Our lovers were barely able to keep Skylar's boat afloat and were tussled about dreadfully." I sighed dramatically. "They fell into each other's arms just as the waters calmed. And of course, one thing has led to another." I stopped and let the imaginations of my literary agent and most loyal fan fill in the blanks.

"So there's your first sex scene!" Louise said.

"Sex scene!" Bee Bee shrieked, and Wilson and Davy glanced over.

"I write romance novels," I told Davy.

"Hot and feisty?" he asked with yet another wink.

Mother tapped her chin. "I don't believe Adelé Nightingale has ever put a love scene on the open water."

Dare I say, Tessie was right? Considering how Adelé's lovers had managed to get passionate in just about every corner of Europe, however unlikely the terrain, how could it be that not once had any of them made whoopee on the water?

"High time to rectify that!" I beckoned to Wilson. "More pink drinks, please," I asked, and the three of us held up our woefully empty glasses.

"But, Jessica," Louise said, "something has to happen to take Skylar away from Delta once they reach the shores of Ebony Island. Isn't that right?"

"That's the easy part," I said. "Skylar has to get back to Diamond Island because he's the only lawman of Port Mekipii Hui, and there's a dastardly villain on the loose. Someone who's taken to robbing every gold shipment right as it leaves port." I sat back and watched Wilson and Davy flip-flop over. "Let's make the bad guy a pirate-type, shall we?"

Mother said she'd always liked those pirate movies that are so popular.

"But the pirate is so charming and lovable in those movies," I reminded her. "*My South Pacific Paramour* will have a truly evil pirate. And Skylar the hero? He'll be a Tarzan-type."

Poor Davy seemed a bit perplexed. He set down his tray and handed a drink to my mother. "I hate to burst your bubble," he said as he handed me the next glass. "But I'm almost sure the South Pacific never had any gold."

"Davy, Davy, Davy," Louise scolded and reached for the third glass. "You simply do not understand the ins and outs of these things. If Adelé Nightingale," she pointed to me, "says there was gold in the South Pacific, then there was gold in the South Pacific!"

"My stories aren't exactly known for their factual detail," I explained, and Wilson harrumphed.

"But now, we can't get too fanciful," I continued after a long and thoughtful sip. "The King Kong thing will need a convincing explanation."

"King Kong thing?" the men asked and pulled up a couple chairs.

"Only rumors, of course." I waved a dismissive hand. "But our evil pirate villain guy will want to capitalize on those rumors."

"This is becoming a bit complicated, isn't it?" Mother asked.

"And that," Louise spoke to Davy, "is why Adelé Nightingale is a bestselling author. Her fans eat this stuff up!"

Wilson shook his head. "I can't believe I'm asking this, but what's the evil pirate guy's name?"

"Oh, Jessie!" Mother jumped. "Can I name your villain this time? Please let me try. I'm sure I can think of something good."

"Those things should unlock your imagination." Wilson pointed to Tessie's glass, and I took a moment to calculate just how many hours my jetlagged, elderly mother had been sipping Pele's Melees in the hot Hawaiian sun.

"How many of those have you had?" I asked her.

She removed the little gold umbrella and poked me in the arm with the tip of the tiny parasol. "I am of age, you know."

I confiscated the gold parasol, but otherwise decided to not worry about it. I mean, how much trouble could Tessie get into, surrounded by family and friends, and staying at what had to be the sleepiest resort in all of Hawaii?

Chapter 4

"The Hoochie Coochie Brothers have arrived!" Buster reported as he seated us in the dining room that evening. "They're unpacking, and then they promised to play!" He pointed to the small stage across the room and scurried away, still holding the menus he had forgotten to give us.

Wilson and I blinked at each other. "Hoochie Coochie?" we asked.

"Isn't it exciting?" Mother said. "They're ukulele players. Davy told Louise and me all about them while you were checking us in." She reached over and patted Wilson's hand. "Thank you for getting me and my things settled. You are such a darling."

He blinked again. "Did you say ukulele?"

"Mm-hmm. Evidently they stay here every year for the annual Yuletide Ukulele Jamboree. This year's the tenth anniversary. Can you imagine?"

I turned to Louise, who nodded ominously. "According to Davy, we'll be hearing ukulele music all week. The Hoochie Coochies like to practice a lot."

While I let that unsettling news sink in, my mother elaborated. "Well now, they'll need to practice won't they? What with the big competition on Christmas Eve." She clapped in glee. "I've never been to a ukulele contest before. Won't that be fun?"

Luckily, our waitress came by and saved us from answering. Young and enthusiastic, Bethany touted the dinner specials as she passed out menus. "The Wakilulani has a reputation for authentic Hawaiian cuisine," she told us. "And our new chef Makaila Isiano? Wait 'til you see. She's fantastic."

"She must be fantastical," Louise agreed. "Just look at all these people!"

I had to agree that the dining room of the Wakilulani was downright crowded. Buster was in the middle of the action, scurrying from table to table, pointing out the empty stage to one startled group of diners after another. He carried a stack of menus but was too excited about the

Hoochie Coochie Brothers' imminent appearance to actually distribute any of them.

Bethany shook her head. "You folks want something to drink while you decide?"

Bless his heart, Wilson suggested another round of pink drinks, and Bethany left to place our order with Davy, who now stood behind the dining room bar. He winked at me, or perhaps at my mother.

"He is quite handsome, isn't he?" she said as she fluttered a few fingers in his direction.

"Too young for us, Tessie," Louise said. "Not everyone has your daughter's luck at these things."

I rolled my eyes at Wilson. "Will I ever hear the end of the fact that you're five years my junior?"

"Five? I thought it was closer to ten." You guessed it— the ever-charming Christopher Rye had arrived. He smirked down at me and introduced his companion. "This is Emi Ulii," he said. "Can she join us?"

"Of course she can," several of us answered, and with a shuffling of chairs we added two more to our grouping. Wilson caught Davy's eye from across the room and held up two fingers.

"The Pele Melees are quite tasty," my mother assured Emi as everyone got introduced and situated.

"They sure are, Mrs. Hewitt." Emi smiled at Mother and explained that Davy's drinks were famous on Halo Beach. "I work down at the Cabana Banana, but our bartender can't compete with the Pele's Melees here. Davy keeps the recipe a deep dark secret."

"Some men are like that," I mumbled with a glance at Wilson.

"Are you a bartender, too?" Emi asked him.

"Dad's a cop." Chris frowned at me. "He doesn't tell his secrets to just anyone."

I thanked Chris for reminding me and was happy to see Bethany arrive with our beverages.

And Bethany? She was thrilled to meet Chris, but a bit less enthused by Emi's presence. Clearly the two young women already knew each other. "Are you still working at Bananas?" Bethany asked her.

Emi sighed. "Yeah, but I'm not getting the hours I want. The manager's kind of mad at me."

"More time for surfing, then." Chris flashed the Rye grin and looked up at Bethany. "I'm starving. What's good?"

Everything, apparently. With a lot of help from Bethany and a little coaching from Emi, we placed our orders for exotic-sounding fish, fruit, and vegetable dishes, which were, in fact, as delicious as promised. We had made it to dessert, and Louise was quizzing Emi about the macadamia nut soufflé Bethany had just placed in front of her, when Buster leapt onto the stage.

"The Hoochie Coochie Brothers!" he announced, and forks dropped all around the dining room. "Hal and Cal Coochie!" He pointed a menu-laden arm in their direction, and the Hoochie Coochies took the stage amid polite, if not enthusiastic, applause.

For some reason I had expected short, young Hawaiian guys. But the brothers were even blonder than I, almost as old, and at least as tall as Wilson. Their size was altogether incongruous with the teeny-tiny instruments they held. They bowed to their audience, sang a little "Aloha" ditty, and then asked for requests.

Everyone seemed stumped for ideas until my mother stood up. "How about Christmas carols?" she suggested.

"Christmas carols it is!" Hal, or maybe it was Cal, exclaimed, and the brothers delved into an off-key rendition of "I Saw Mommy Kissing Santa Claus."

When the Hoochie Coochies veered off onto a "Silver Bells" tangent, harmonizing about city sidewalks, Louise had a momentary spell of homesickness. "Ah, Manhattan," she said. "I know it's cold in December, but New York at Christmas is simply fantasti—"

"New York?" Emi interrupted. "Oh, my God! Are you from New York?" She blinked her big brown eyes at Louise. "I'm dying to see New York City someday! To live there, even! Take the subway to work, jog in Central Park, shop in Soho." She looked at Chris. "It's my dream for when I graduate."

"And what a fantastical dream it is!" Louise agreed and commenced an involved and detailed monologue on the joys of living in New York, especially the joys of shopping in New York.

"When you get there, go straight to Soho," she said. "It absolutely must, must, must be your first stop! The shoes? Oh, Babe!" She fanned herself with one of the little gold umbrellas that were accumulating on the table. "Beyond fantastical, I tell you! I myself could never live anywhere else. I mean, where would I shop?" Louise glanced around the table for alternatives, but none of us had any suggestions.

Wilson cleared his throat. "Speaking of shopping," he said, and I looked up from my mango brulee. Surely the man had not consumed enough pink drinks to care about designer shoes?

"Is Shynomore Shirt Shop the best place to get more of these?" he asked Emi and tapped on his chest. "That's what Buster says."

The poor girl somehow managed to tear her thoughts away from Manhattan long enough to regard Wilson's fuchsia-infused shirt. "Shynomore's the place," she said with only the slightest frown. "It's just down the beach. It's open twenty-four hours a day."

"How convenient," I mumbled as the Hoochie Coochie Brothers gave up on Christmas and commenced singing a song about coconuts. I tilted my head and double-checked. Yep. Coconuts.

Chris excused himself and Emi, and said he'd be walking her home.

"*My South Pacific Paramour*!" Louise exclaimed over the coconut chorus, and the whole restaurant turned to stare. Louise didn't notice, however, since she was busy getting my mother to her feet. "We need to be plotting some more complications, Tessie!"

"Let's put our thinking caps on and find a name for the pirate-villain person," Mother suggested as they tottered off toward the bar.

Wilson and I watched in dismay.

"They're great friends," I explained. "Ever since I signed my first book contract, they've been conspiring on ways to land me more bestsellers."

"They're a little scary."

I pointed to his shirt. "Almost as scary as you wanting more of those."

He grinned. "Take a walk with me?"

***

A tempest is what Adelé Nightingale would call it. Later that night it poured. Jetlagged and wide awake, I lay in bed and listened to the wind howl and the rain beat down on the roof of Paradise. I kept listening and could even hear the waves crashing on the shore in the distance.

Jetlag never felt so good, I thought to myself and snuggled a little closer to Wilson's sleeping-like-a-baby body. But I still didn't sleep. Eventually the rains stopped, and I decided it would be rather atmospheric to take a walk around the grounds at—I glanced at the clock on the nightstand—2:15 a.m. I slipped on my flip flops, ignored the fact that I was in my pajamas, and tiptoed down the garden path heading toward the ocean.

A light was on at Song of the Sea bungalow, where I assumed the Hoochie Coochies had taken up residence. At least they weren't practicing at that hour. I passed Louise's darkened bungalow, and the swimming pool. The tiki bar was closed, thank God. If it were still open, I could just imagine my mother, lounging on a deck chair, sipping yet another of her beloved drinks, and devising yet more improbable scenarios for Adelé Nightingale to somehow get down on paper.

I wandered along, admiring this and that tropical plant or flower. I recognized the bromeliads and gingers, and of course the roses, but failed to identify many of the more exotic species. "Puts my little rooftop garden to shame," I said to the wind and kept going.

Indeed, I decided a two a.m. stroll through the garden might become part of my regular routine during my stay at the Wakilulani Gardens. I was thoroughly enjoying the solitude, if not the quiet. Who knew how noisy a tropical wind could be?

I meandered my way toward the beach. The lights were out in Chris's bungalow, but a light was on at my mother's. Tessie's a night owl, and jetlag or not, ten pink drinks or not, I was not at all surprised she was awake.

I was deciding if I should disturb her when Mother dashed out onto her porch. Her gaze darted back and forth along the beach until she noticed me standing there in the foreground.

"There you are, Jessie," she said in a faltering voice. "I'm glad you're here, but maybe you should go get Wilson."

"Excuse me? It's the middle of the night, Mother. He's sound asleep."

She sighed. "Well then, maybe we should call the Hawaiian police instead."

My face dropped. "Why?" I sang.

"Because, Honeybunch, there's a dead man in my bungalow."

Chapter 5

"Maybe we should go get Dad," Chris said, and I almost landed on top of the dead guy.

I steadied myself on my mother's threshold and stared aghast. But it was rather difficult to decide what to stare at—the dead guy on the floor, the pool of blood he was lying in, or the bare-chested Christopher Rye, who had stepped forward from the corner of the room.

I chose Chris's chest. "What the hell are you doing here?"

"He's been stabbed, Jessie. We need to get Dad."

I raised my head and found his eyes. "I'm not leaving my mother."

He pushed me aside and jogged away into the night.

I was frowning at the tray of pink drinks on the bed when my mother tiptoed inside.

"Those are very flattering," she said quietly and pointed to at my pajamas. "Yellow suits you, Jessie."

I told her it's my favorite color and admired her own baby blue nightgown. And doggedly determined to avoid looking at the dead guy, we continued along this surrealistically odd tangent of conversation until Chris returned with his father.

I was relieved to see my beau the homicide detective, but Wilson reminded me he was off-duty and out of his jurisdiction. Then he glanced down at the body and started issuing orders.

"Get out," he told Mother and me in no uncertain terms. "And don't touch anything. Jessie, help her down the stairs so she doesn't have to use the railing. Go stand in the sand. In one spot. Do not wander around."

He turned to Chris. "You! Run up to The Big House. Tell whoever's up there, no one leaves. Buster can guard the parking lot. Tell him to bring the police down here when they arrive."

He turned again, and in one step, made it to Tessie's nightstand. Using the edge of the T-shirt he had thrown on, he picked up the receiver. "Move, people!" he ordered, and we did.

***

But Buster Okolo was not so adept at following simple instructions. He came back to Seagull's Roost with Chris, wringing his hands and sputtering out question after question about who was dead, how it happened, and how could something like this happen, anyway.

None of us had any answers, but Wilson still spoke with authority. He stood his ground at the top of the porch stairs and refused him entrance. Buster argued that he was the owner and needed to see what had happened. Wilson argued it was a crime scene and needed to be left undisturbed. Chris hovered at the bottom of the stairs telling Buster to listen to Wilson. I contemplated asking my mother where she had purchased her nightie.

Wilson again reiterated that someone needed to guard the parking lot. "There's been a murder here."

"Murder?" Buster squeaked, and the rest of us nodded.

He stood frozen while that horrid fact sunk in. Wilson again mentioned the parking lot, and Buster turned around and walked off.

Chris made as if to climb the stairs himself.

"No!" Wilson held up a hand. "Go stand beside Jessie," he ordered and then glared down at me. "And you stay," he said. "You, too, Tessie," he said in a much gentler voice and walked back inside.

"Yes, Wilson, honey," my mother answered to the empty porch. She squeezed my hand. "I guess he knows us, Jessie."

Yes, I guess he did. And considering the present circumstances, perhaps he had a right to talk to me in that bossy tone, since I have, in the past, on occasion, stuck my nose into his police business. One time I had even gotten my mother involved. Okay, so maybe that wasn't the brightest idea I've ever had, but this time I was behaving myself. I had not done anything whatsoever to get in the way and was obeying Captain Rye without question. This, despite the fact that he was off duty and out of his jurisdiction.

Chris also decided to listen to Wilson. He came over and stood next to me as directed.

"What the heck happened?" I asked.

"We need to wait for the cops," he said. "That's what Dad wants us to do."

"But surely we can tell Jessie what happened?" my mother said.

I smirked at Chris. "Surely," I agreed.

"I'm afraid it all started with weather." Mother pointed to her porch. "I was up there watching the rains come and go when Chris walked by on his way home from Emi's. I invited him to join me, and we've been keeping an eye on the storm all night. We've been getting acquainted, haven't we, Chris?"

I raised an eyebrow at Rye Junior. He shrugged, but said nothing.

"We stayed on the porch until it started raining that last time," Mother said. "And then we moved inside."

The tray of pink drinks I had glimpsed on my mother's bed suddenly registered. "Don't tell me you two have been drinking those stupid Pele's Melees all night?"

"Nooo." Chris finally spoke. "We didn't have anything until the rain let up again."

"But then we decided on a nightcap before the bar closed," Mother added. "It closes at two, you see."

No. I really, really did not see. But I only whimpered slightly as Tessie continued, "So I rang the bar and ordered one last pitcher of Pele's Melees."

I closed my eyes and prayed for strength.

"We ordered just a small pitcher," she said in her defense. "Davy offered to bring a tray down, but Chris said he'd run up to the bar and fetch it himself."

"It's only, like, ten steps away," Chris said. "When I got back, we decided to kick back on Tessie's bed."

I opened my eyes and glared. "And, of course, my mother just happened to be in her nightclothes, and you just happened to be half-naked?"

"It wasn't like that!" they both exclaimed.

"There's a perfectly good reason why poor Chris is half-naked." Mother patted his broad, bare chest. "The poor thing was soaking wet from the rain when he got back from Emi's. His tee-shirt is drying in my bathroom."

I was asking if there happened to be any Advil in that bathroom when we heard the sirens. A minute later two people, who I assumed were the Hawaiian cops, rounded the corner of Seagull's Roost. They were followed by a very nervous Buster, who was wringing his hands and sputtering inanities about how he did not understand how something like this could have happened.

Wilson welcomed them onto the porch, and as everyone filed into the bungalow, he issued yet another warning to us poor slobs down in the sand. "Stay!" he repeated. I saluted, and he disappeared through the doorway.

I cleared my throat. "So, let me get this straight," I said. "The two of you were lounging on the bed together, drinking Pele's Melees at two a.m., and some guy just happened to walk in and die right in front of you?"

"That's right," Mother said. "But I do believe it was closer to two thirty. And it wasn't some guy. It was Davy Atwell."

"Davy!?" I shrieked.

Chris shook his head at me. "You didn't notice?"

No, I did not. I said something about the body being face down. "To be honest, I tried my best not to look."

"I don't blame you," Mother said. "It's a bloody mess, isn't it?"

"In more ways than one," Chris mumbled, his eyes fixed on Seagull's Roost. "I bet I watched him mix his last batch of drinks ever," he said. "I bet I was the last person he ever talked to."

"What did you talk about?" I asked.

"He wanted to know which bungalow to charge for the drinks. I told him yours and Dad's."

***

"Let me get this straight," the Hawaiian cop asked me. "You just happened to be outside your mother's cabin when

David Atwell dropped dead? Because you just happened to be taking a midnight stroll." Captain Vega pointed at my pajamas. "In that outfit."

"It was closer to two thirty," I corrected him.

"What were you doing wandering around at that hour?"

"Insomnia," I said. "I'm jetlagged since we just got here this afternoon." I re-calculated. "Umm, yesterday afternoon."

And what a difference a day makes, I thought to myself as I glanced around. Our once sleepy little resort was now swarming with cops. Up in the parking area scads of them were combing the pavement, flashlights in hand. Captain Vega and I were outside The Big House, sitting at a table on the patio. And other cops, some uniformed, some not, dotted all the other tables. Each of them was babysitting one of us.

My mother, Chris, and Wilson had already been interrogated. And Louise, the two Hoochie Coochies, and Buster were waiting their turns after Vega got through with me. Apparently Bee Bee was the only resident of the Wakilulani Gardens not under suspicion.

"Your walk?" Vega reminded me.

"I ventured out after the storm."

"And while you just happened to be prowling around, did you see or hear anything out of the ordinary?"

"No," I said firmly. "The wind was howling, and the waves were crashing. Considering the hour, I just assumed I was alone." I pointed to my attire. "Hence the pajamas."

Vega waited for more.

"Really," I said. "I didn't notice anything unusual until I saw my mother."

"She's unusual, alright."

I folded my arms and glared. "My mother is amazing."

"And your amazing mother just happened to know you'd be outside her bungalow? So she just happened to step out to her porch to tell you about the murder?"

I stopped glaring. "Okay, so I know it's hard to believe, but you have to understand Tessie. She has this incredible intuition. Especially when it comes to me."

"What was your incredible mother doing in bed with Christopher Rye? You got an explanation for that?"

"They were getting to know each other." I heard what I had just said and sat up straight. "But it wasn't like that!"

"Well then, what was it like? They were drinking, and they were both half-naked."

"My mother was as fully-clothed as I am," I said indignantly, which did not exactly help the defense. "And Chris," I swallowed a groan, "was half-naked."

"Half-naked," Vega repeated and studied something on his notepad. "How long have you known the Ryes?" he asked.

"Why?"

"How long?"

"I've known Wilson for about five months. And I met Chris for the first time yesterday at the Atlanta airport. Why?"

"How'd you meet his father?" Vega asked, and I swallowed another groan. Why, oh why, did that particular question have to come up?

"I'm waiting, Ms. Hewitt."

I took a deep breath and explained, as casually as possible, that Wilson had investigated me for murder the previous summer. "He's a cop," I added.

"So I gathered."

What a surprise—Vega insisted on hearing the details of the Stanley Sweetzer murder investigation, and thus I summarized the whole sad story. "But it's ancient history," I insisted. "Wilson never did arrest me. I was innocent all along."

Vega stared at me for a good long time, but I refused to squirm. "How well do you know him?" he asked eventually.

I caught Wilson's eye from across the patio. He gave me a thumbs up, and I waved a few fingers. "We are very involved," I said.

"I'm not asking you about your sex life, Ms. Hewitt. I'm asking you how well you know the guy. What do you know about his character? About his past?"

I sat up even straighter. "What are you getting at?" I asked.

"Wilson Rye's character," Vega repeated.

"Is excellent," I said. "He's honorable, and honest, and a damn good cop."

"Yeah, and I'm sure you're an expert judge on that." Vega looked up from his notes. "What about his past?"

I blinked twice. "I don't know," I mumbled.

"What was that?"

"I said, I do not know about Wilson's past." That time I was loud and clear.

***

"We did promise we'd watch the sunrise at least one day while we were here," Wilson reminded me as we plopped ourselves down in the sand.

The entourage of cops had finally left, and my mother had been moved to Misty Breezes bungalow, where I hoped she was sound asleep. Chris and Louise, whether asleep or not, were also back in their bungalows. All of us had been ordered not to leave the island. Conveniently, we had no plans to do so.

"What do we do now?" I asked.

Wilson put his arm around me and rocked me back and forth. "We enjoy the sunrise, right? And then we sleep in late, and then we go about our vacation as planned. How's that sound?"

It sounded good. But I wondered out loud if we could do it.

"We have to," Wilson said. "Vega told me point blank he doesn't want my help."

"I don't believe Captain Vega likes you very much, Captain Rye."

"And he doesn't like how we—how I—handled things before he got here."

"What?" I protested. "We did a great job."

"Vega's not happy you guys got me involved before anyone called 911."

"But you're a cop!" I said. "Of course we got your help."

Wilson caught my eye. "Vega's not convinced I was asleep when Chris came to get me, Jessie. He suspects I was awake and prowling around the grounds."

"Well then, he should have asked me. You were sound asleep when I snuck out."

"Vega's not buying it. Especially since my stupid kid put those last drinks on my bar tab. I tried telling him Chris always sticks me with the bill. He's a college kid, for God's sake."

"And Vega's arguing that point?" I asked.

"Yep. No one can confirm it was Chris, not me, who ordered those last drinks. The entire staff had gone home by then."

I asked about Buster, but apparently he was already upstairs in his apartment by two a.m., and apparently that presented another problem. According to Vega, Wilson never should have gotten Buster involved.

"He didn't need to be guarding the parking lot so no one would leave," Wilson explained. "No one was still here."

"But you didn't know that," I argued. "How could you have known that?"

"Take a guess where the stabbing occurred."

I recollected all the cops combing the parking lot and muttered a four-letter word.

Wilson nodded. "Yep," he said. "With all the blood, they're sure it happened in the parking lot."

"Did they find the weapon? I assume it was a knife?"

"No weapon yet. But Vega let it slip that the knife likely came from the kitchen. One's missing from the knife block."

I pictured the layout of The Big House. Anyone could have had access to the kitchen from the dining room that night.

"Everyone and his brother had access to the kitchen." Wilson read my mind. "And the murderer must be thrilled I sent Buster out to the parking lot. He did a lot of pacing back and forth while he was up there. His footprints were all over the bloodstains."

I shook my head. "Thus destroying any footprints the murderer himself might have left."

"Vega threatened to arrest me for tampering with the crime scene."

"Come on! He can't really believe that? You were trying to do the exact opposite."

Wilson thanked me for my loyalty but suggested I try to think like Vega. "It looks like I sent Buster up there purposely to destroy evidence," he said.

"Oh, my Lord, Wilson. Are you actually a suspect?"

"Me or Chris." He took a few deep breaths. "You know about his shirt?"

I closed my eyes and prayed for strength. "You mean the one he wasn't wearing?" I asked. "The one drying in my mother's bathroom?"

"Evidence. Vega's claiming Chris and Tessie washed it out to get rid of blood stains."

"What!? So now my mother's a suspect?"

"You and I know it's absurd. But Vega's working on the assumption of some sinister conspiracy between us."

I muttered that four-letter word again, and we watched a few waves roll in.

"Okay, so does the brilliant Captain Vega have a motive for this sinister conspiracy?" I asked. "I mean, what possible reason could you, Chris, and my mother—my mother!—possibly have to kill Davy Atwell? We just met the guy, for Lord's sake."

"Bingo." Wilson grinned and squeezed my shoulder. "Vega can try to twist the circumstantial evidence any way he wants. But he'll be hard-pressed to stick a motive on it."

"So we can relax?" I was far from convinced.

"Let's take a lesson from Tessie and Chris. They're not worried."

"Mother does seem to be taking it in her stride," I said. "I think it helped that Chris was with her."

"And it will help if we carry on as normal, right?"

I sighed and leaned forward to scratch a picture of the sun in the sand. Wilson twirled his finger under my sun and added a few waves. Then we looked up from our artwork and watched the real sun rise over the Pacific.

"Chris wants to hike Kekipi Crater with me later today," he said. "Ironic, but Davy gave me lots of advice on trails. Come with us?"

I scowled. "Surely you jest?"

"Let me guess—too many bugs."

"I do not like the heebie jeebies," I clarified. "And trust me, Wilson. Anytime I have ever been stupid enough to venture out into the wilderness, I've been heebie-jeebied beyond endurance. Bugs!" I said with a dramatic shudder.

He chuckled and added what I think was supposed to be a palm tree to our beach scene in the sand.

"You go tackle the volcano," I told him. "Meanwhile, I'll be lounging by the pool and tackling a few scenes from *My South Pacific Paramour*. Mother wants to help me, which will be an excellent way to keep our minds off of what's happened."

"And we'll let Captain Vega tackle the murder, right?" In the growing light I couldn't help but notice the stern cop-like look Wilson was directing at me. "Right, Jessie?"

"Right," I said and crossed my fingers behind my back.

Chapter 6

Eleanor Touchette watched skeptically as her niece donned her first pair of trousers ever. Delta was bound and determined to wander out into the wilderness, but the dear girl seemed far less certain about those breeches. She wiggled and wobbled, and pulled and pried, unsure of how to get the things onto her curvaceous frame. She persevered, however, and eventually managed to maneuver the pants over her hips and into place. As she buttoned her fly—something else Delta had never before done—she assured her Auntie Eleanor that she did not believe in monsters, and was not afraid of the jungle either.

When reminded she had never actually been in a jungle, Delta stood her ground and insisted she would get to the bottom of the silly rumors that were causing her beloved Auntie and the inhabitants of Ebony Island such distress. She gathered the machete and canteen she had acquired from a villager the day before and announced she was "Ready."

Eleanor looked pointedly at the canteen, and Delta conceded that perhaps she was not quite prepared. She began struggling with the cap while the older woman continued to marvel. Her favorite niece certainly was a comely young lady—even more lovely than Marcus had implied in his letters. Indeed, in his most recent missive, Eleanor's brother had intimated that several wealthy and titled gentlemen were vying for his daughter's hand in marriage. But that, of course, was back in England. Stuffy Old England, as Delta had been insisting ever since her unexpected arrival at Emerald Estate two days earlier.

Eleanor stepped forward and demonstrated how the canteen cap operated. She filled the vessel from the water pitcher on the dressing table, and as she handed it back to her niece, she gently enquired about those would-be suitors.

Delta shook her head impatiently and insisted she had better plans for her life than to marry some dreary duke or dismal lord. She would see the world, or at least a goodly part of it, before settling down to the mundane existence her parents were forever touting. Demonstrating her resolve, she brandished her machete and promptly sliced the curtain hanging beside her in half.

Auntie Eleanor glanced askance at the damage, and with no further ado, escorted her niece outdoors and to the edge of the estate. She reminded her that dinner would be served at seven, pointed her in the direction of the deepest jungles, and waved encouragingly as Delta disappeared into a grove of pandanus trees.

Brave and plucky, our heroine set off with the utmost confidence, and maintained a swift and steady pace until faced with a rather daunting thicket of some such brambles she had never seen in England. She pursed her lips and glanced at the machete in her right hand. How exactly did one use the contraption?

The winds picked up while she pondered the dilemma, and Delta turned her sapphire blue eyes upward. Some rather large somethings swooped around in the branches high above her head. The somethings were striped and had tails. Inordinately long tails. She jumped when a bird—at least she hoped it was a bird—screeched in the distance. Reminding herself that she did not believe in monsters, Delta assumed a firm grip on her machete and started hacking.

**

"Jessie, honey, jump in here and help me," Mother said, and I looked up from my laptop. She and Louise were in the pool, where my mother was trying to teach my agent how to swim.

"I need help, Jessica!" Louise agreed. "And Tessie needs a break."

"And I can't wait to read what you have so far." Mother climbed out of the pool and took my computer from me.

I pointed to the screen and explained how I had delved into *My South Pacific Paramour* right in the middle of the story. "Delta Touchette has already arrived at Auntie Eleanor's estate," I said. "I'll go back some other time and fill in the details of her thrilling journey from dreary old England to Ebony Island."

"Don't forget her first encounter with Skylar Staggs," Louise reminded me.

"Or their first sex scene," Mother said. "Sex, sex, sex!"

"Sex, sex, sex!" Bee Bee repeated, and the Hoochie Coochie Brothers hit yet another sour note.

Indeed, Louise's swimming lesson had attracted quite a bit of attention at the Wakilulani Gardens. The parrot was coaching her progress from his perch near the shallow end of the pool. And perched a few yards uphill, on the porch of Song of the Sea bungalow, the Hoochie Coochie Brothers had also been offering encouragement—serenading us with a medley of old-timey tunes. Leaving the yellow rose of Texas behind, they headed to Louisiana. Susanna may not have been crying for them, but I do believe the rest of us were contemplating that option.

Mother tilted her head. "Don't you need a banjo for that one?" she asked.

I mumbled something about how a modicum of talent would also help and dived into the pool. I did some demonstrating and ended up in the shallow end with my arms under Louise's stomach while she tried again.

"I cannot believe I'm forty-three and still can't swim," she said as she paddled and kicked, paddled and kicked. "Anytime I try, I end up choking on water."

"That's because you're always talking," I said. "Shut up and swim."

"Easy for you to say."

I glanced up at my mother. "She can't drive either. Probably because she's lived in Manhattan her entire life."

"Born and bred! I love, love, love New Yor—" Louise choked on a mouthful of water and went under.

I lifted her up, and Mother reminded her to keep her mouth closed. "We could teach you how to do that, too."

"How to shut up?" Louise said. "I doubt it, Tessie."

Mother giggled. "No, silly. How to drive."

When Hawaii freezes over, I thought to myself. My mother has many talents, but trust me, driving is not one of them. I suggested we leave the driving lessons for another vacation.

"You're probably right," Mother agreed. "We won't have time, will we? What with Chris teaching us to surf and such."

I let go of Louise. "Excuse me?"

"Don't you remember, Jessie? He promised. We have our first lesson once he and Wilson get back from their hike."

I blinked twice, but had no time to react otherwise because Louise had actually made it to the opposite end of the pool. Needless to say, the crowd went wild. Bee Bee let out a cat call, the Hoochie Coochies played a few bars of "We Are The Champions," and Mother and I clapped. Louise waved to her adoring fans. But she quickly thought better of it and grabbed onto the edge with both hands.

"That was good!" I said. "Now swim back to me."

"Do I get a pink drink if I do?" she asked, and everyone frowned simultaneously at the bartenderless tiki bar.

"I suppose we shouldn't drink until after our surfing lesson." Mother sighed forlornly and went back to reading my book. "Delta is about to get herself lost, isn't she, Jessie?"

"About to?" I said as Louise managed one more lap.

She reached the shallow end, announced she could not survive another minute without talking, and climbed out. She gabbed away with my mother while I did a few laps myself.

"We have a name for your villain," Mother informed me when I climbed out of the pool. "Urquit Snodgrass. What do you think?"

"Urquit!" Bee Bee screeched. He swept over and landed on Louise's chair. "Urquit!"

I agreed that Urquit sounded perfectly sinister and stepped under the nearby shower to rinse off. My bleached hair would end up as green as Bee Bee if I let the chlorine from the swimming pool dry too long. As I toweled off I wondered out loud how our woefully lost damsel in distress would manage to come into contact with the repulsive Mr. Snodgrass.

Tessie and Louise regaled me with a plethora of ideas until I held up my hands and reminded them I had been writing for hours. "Enough of *My South Pacific Paramour*." I plopped into my lounge chair. "We need to talk about what happened last night instead."

Mother resigned herself to her fate and closed my laptop. "What would you like to know, Honeybunch?"

"I want to know what you were doing in bed with Christopher Rye." Louise winked at me. "In your nightgown, no less?"

"It wasn't like that!" Mother insisted. "I'm old enough to be the boy's grandmother, for Pete's sake."

I did the math. "Or great-grandmother."

"We were having a chat is all," Mother said. "Jessie and I always have our best heart-to-hearts lounging in bed together, don't we, Jessie?"

"What did you two talk about?" I asked.

"You and Wilson. I asked Chris why he doesn't like you. Surely you've noticed?"

"What did he say?"

"Well now, you know about Christopher's mother? Wilson's wife?"

"I know nothing!" Louise complained, and so I filled her in on the details. Lisa Rye had died of cancer when Chris was twelve.

"But how completely and totally awful! Poor Chris. Poor Wilson. Poor Lisa!"

I nodded. "Wilson doesn't like to talk about it."

"Both of the Rye boys were devastated for years," Mother added. "But things got better once Chris entered high school. And when he started dating, he convinced his father to give it a try also."

"But neither father nor son ever got serious about anyone," I explained. "Until Wilson and me, that is."

Mother cleared her throat. "I don't think you have the full story there, Jessie."

I tilted my head and contemplated Bee Bee. "Oh?" I squeaked.

He tilted his head. "Oh?" he squeaked back.

"Wilson had a lady friend when Chris was in high school," Mother informed us.

"Oh?"

"Oh, indeed!" Louise exclaimed. "At long last—the mystery man's deep dark secret!"

"Secret!" Bee Bee said.

"Deep dark," I elaborated and scowled at my mother. "Why haven't I heard about this mystery woman before?" I asked. "What's her name? Where is she now? What happened?"

"Her name is Dianne Calloway. But I didn't have a chance to find out what all happened between her and Wilson. When I asked last night, Chris said he needed a pink drink."

"No pink drinks yet," Buster called out. He was carrying a tray of food up the path to the swimming pool pavilion. "It's time for your lunch, and then we're decorating."

"Lunch?" Louise asked.

"Decorating?" Mother asked.

"Dianne Calloway?" I asked, but no one was paying the slightest attention to me, since Buster had set down his tray and was distributing plates of seafood salad sandwiches, replete with potato chips, pickles, and some sort of tropical fruit slices. Okay, so maybe I was hungry.

Mother asked Buster to join us, but he refused a seat and instead wandered around our chairs, picking up the occasional stray leaf or twig and scolding us for missing breakfast. "Breakfast is new here." He frowned at a fallen flower petal. "I thought the Wakilulani should give it a try. I make good pancakes."

"Pancakes!" Bee Bee said enthusiastically.

"Bee Bee never misses breakfast on the patio," Buster informed us. "He likes my pancakes."

"Your sandwiches are fantastical, too," Louise said. She tore off a corner of bread for the bird, and Bee Bee stepped over to share.

While Louise and the bird communed over the remnants of her sandwich, Mother and I made excuses for missing breakfast. Buster fretted, but eventually agreed we had needed to sleep in—what with jetlag, and murder, and cops, and not getting to bed until after sunrise.

He dropped his handful of debris and pointed down to The Big House. "But now that you're rested and fed, I need your help with the Christmas tree. I set it up this morning. And I bought all new ornaments this year. Come see."

"A Hawaiian Christmas tree!" Mother said. "Doesn't that sound like fun?" She and Louise stood up and donned their cover-ups, but I refused to budge.

"Dianne Calloway," I reminded them and turned to Buster. "We were kind of in the middle of something before lunch."

"Oh, Jessie," Mother scolded and gestured for me to stand up. "Surely that can wait until later? There's a tree to decorate."

"But what about Wilson's mystery woman?" I whined from my lounge chair. "What about his deep dark secrets?"

"Mystery woman? Secrets?" Buster bent over and stacked our empty plates back onto the tray. "Is this about last night?"

"Nooo," I said. "It is not."

"We are quite certain Jessica's paramour has an intriguing past," Louise said casually. "But we can worry about that some other time. There's a tree to decorate!" She gestured to Bee Bee, he hopped onto her outstretched wrist, and the two of them meandered away toward The Big House.

Buster looked at my mother. "Paramour?"

"Louise is just being silly," she assured him. "Wilson Rye is as darling and wholesome as can be."

Wholesome? I might have scowled at that assessment, but Buster didn't notice. He picked up his tray, offered my mother a cocked elbow, and they, too, began to wander off.

"Don't you be a Scrooge, Jessie," Mother called over her shoulder. "Come help us."

I gave up on pouting and was buttoning my own cover-up when I noticed the Hoochie Coochie Brothers waving their ukuleles at me.

"We'll play Christmas carols to get you in the spirit," Hal, or maybe it was Cal, said, and the two of them clamored off their porch toward The Big House.

I was about to follow, but the Song of the Sea bungalow suddenly captured my rapt attention. Hadn't a light been on at the Coochie cabin the previous night? When I was taking my walk? I tilted my head. When Davy Atwell was stabbed?

I glanced down at The Big House, where the first chorus of "Santa Claus is Coming to Town" was just getting underway. Santa was making a list of who was naughty and who was nice.

Taking a wild guess as to which category I fell into, I flip-flopped over to Song of the Sea.

Chapter 7

Bless their ukulele-playing hearts, Hal and Cal had neglected to lock their door.

I tiptoed inside and stood at the foot of one of the twin beds. Wilson and I hadn't spent much time checking out this bungalow when we were settling in the previous day. We had seen the twin beds and moved on without further ado.

"Time to rectify that," I whispered to myself and took a closer look around.

Two open ukulele cases were tucked away in one corner, and a stack of fliers advertising the ukulele jamboree was piled on a nightstand, but otherwise the place was neat and tidy. No murder weapon, no bloody clothes, nothing.

I walked into the bathroom. A couple of towels were hanging over the shower rack. But again, no blood.

I went back into the main room, where one of the dressers caught my eye. Reminding myself I was on the naughty list anyway, I opened the top drawer. Lo and behold, a wallet stared up at me. Reminding myself I was on the naughty list anyway, I picked it up and studied Hal Coochie's driver's license.

"Anything interesting?"

I jumped ten feet in the air. And Hal's wallet flew across the room and landed in one of the ukulele cases.

Once I was steady on my flip flops again, I hazarded a glance in the direction of the doorway. Wilson Rye. Frowning. His big, intimidating, cop-like frown.

"Umm," I said. "How was the hike?"

"What the hell are you doing?"

I had absolutely no idea.

"What are you doing?" I tried.

"Your mother sent me to look for you. They're almost done with the tree." He raised an eyebrow. "And you?"

"Almost done!" I jumped again. "Well then, I need help!" I dived into gathering up the contents of Hal's wallet, which were now scattered everywhere. But at some point I realized I was working alone. Wilson had not moved.

I looked up from the credit cards that had landed on one of the beds. "Help me!" I pleaded. "They'll be back any minute."

He stepped inside and finally, finally started to pick up a few things. "I cannot believe I'm helping you cover your tracks." He found the wallet and assembled the miscellaneous wallet-stuff from the other bed.

"Come on, Wilson," I said as I handed him the stack I had gathered. "It's not like I was going to steal anything. I'm not a criminal, for Lord's sake."

He stopped his sorting and stared at me. "Probably not," he mumbled after far too much contemplation.

We put the wallet back together as best we could, put it back where I had found it, and got the heck out of there.

**

Personally, I was ready to join in all that Christmas cheer happening down at The Big House. But as soon as we rounded the swimming pool pavilion, Wilson grabbed my elbow and held me back.

"Go ahead," I told him. "Get it out of your system."

He did so, and in hushed but stern tones, reminded me how we had agreed to leave things to Captain Vega. Then he moved on to the part about how I could have been caught pilfering the Coochie bungalow. He concluded with a scathing assessment of my questionable character and poor judgment. Yadda, yadda, yadda. Naughty about sums it up.

I waited patiently until he was quite through. "Dianne Calloway," I said, and it was his turn to jump ten feet in the air.

Thus I launched into a scolding of my own. Yadda, yadda, yadda. I commenced a lengthy rant, questioning why his deep dark secrets needed to be so very deep and dark, and why I was reduced to learning the vital details about his past from my mother of all people. "My mother!" I stamped my flip flop and offered an indignant huff.

"Tessie told you the details?" he asked.

"No!" I practically shouted, and we both jerked our heads toward The Big House. "She doesn't know the details," I said more quietly, and Wilson breathed a sigh of relief.

"Yet," I added ominously.

"Well then." He took another deep breath. "Let's get back to Vega, shall we?"

I folded my arms and glared. "Go ahead, Wilson. Change the subject."

Unfortunately, he did so. "I know it's hard to leave things to Vega." He was back to his annoyingly calm and sensible self. "It's hard for me, too. You get it?"

"Let me guess. It's out of our jurisdiction."

"Our?"

"Okay, your. It's out of your jurisdiction. But Captain Vega doesn't seem all that interested in what happened. He hasn't been here all day."

"What? No way."

"I certainly haven't seen him." I turned to face the Song of the Sea, this time from a safe distance. "They stay here every year, you know?

"The ukulele players?"

"They come for The Yuletide Ukulele Jamboree."

"And?"

"And therefore," I glanced back at Wilson, "both of the Hoochie Coochies must have known Davy Atwell. At least one of them could have had a motive."

"Such as?"

"Heck, I don't know. But they arrived just hours before the guy got killed. And their light was on when I walked by their bungalow last night." I shrugged. "It seemed suspicious when I thought about it, so I decided to check it out."

"What? In hopes of finding the murder weapon?"

"Exactly."

"You're a little scary. You know that?"

***

"Kekipi Crater rocks!" Christopher Rye announced the minute we entered The Big House.

"That tree rocks." I pointed to the huge Christmas tree, which now dominated a significant portion of the lobby.

"Rocks," Bee Bee agreed from his vantage-point up in the rafters.

"It's fantastical," Louise said, and Bee Bee agreed with her also.

Mother stood up from where she was hanging miniature leis on the lower branches. "Aren't these just darling, Jessie?" She jiggled a little orange lei. "Buster did a good job selecting ornaments, didn't he?"

Buster was wringing his hands as usual, but was clearly pleased with the results of his efforts. "We need to remember the season, no matter what happened last night," he said. "Ki would be very upset with me if the tree wasn't up."

"Your brother?" Wilson asked.

"He'll be here any minute. He has to help out now. You know, now that Davy's gone."

Everyone murmured inane sentiments about the recent tragedy. But lest the party become too morose, the Coochie brothers hopped up and delved into a rousing rendition of "Oh, Christmas Tree." Remembering the season, as it were.

"So!" I said loudly as the last chord was struck, or strummed, or whatever. "Speaking of trees, how was your hike?"

I had turned to Wilson, but it was Buster who answered. "It must have been great," he said. "They went up the Maka Koa trail to Flint Ridge. That's always been my favorite spot. Ki's, too."

"Flint Ridge rocks!" Chris said.

"But we never did find Pele's Prison," Wilson added.

"Excuse me?" I asked.

"It's a cave," Hal, or maybe it was Cal, Coochie said. "Locals know about it, but few tourists ever find it."

"Technically it's a lava tube," the other Coochie added and then explained the geological process on the formation of lava tubes. "Pele's Prison isn't the largest tube, but it is the most interesting."

"You guys like hiking?" I asked as the incongruous image of the Coochie brothers playing their ukuleles in a cave struck me.

"Oh yes! Kekipi Crater has some of the best trails on all the islands," one of the brothers informed me, as the other waxed poetic about the bird-watching opportunities near a place called Juniu Ledge. "We make a point of going up there every year while we're here," Coochie Number One continued.

"I'm sure it's beyond fantastical," Louise said. The hikers might have missed the sarcastic drip, but I noticed. Geez Louise is about as interested in wilderness exploration as I.

"No heebie jeebies?" I asked and began looking Wilson up and down for bug bites, rashes, and other assorted, jungle-related, red itchy spots.

Chris shook his head in disapproval. "I can't believe you're scared of the woods."

"Jessie isn't scared of anything," Wilson mumbled. "Unfortunately."

"It's not the woods, it's the bugs." Mother looked on as I lifted Wilson's arms and inspected them for any tell-tale signs of the heebie jeebies. "Jessie's hated bugs ever since she was two and toddled into an ant hill."

"But you must do some hiking while you're here," Buster encouraged me. "Some of the trails are very easy. I promise."

"Are there shoe stores on any of them?" Louise asked.

***

"I suppose I can't claim the ocean gives me the heebie jeebies," I said.

"Why do I know this will be completely and totally un-fantastical?" Louise said.

"This should be interesting," Wilson said.

"I can't wait to hang ten!" Mother said and scurried off toward Christopher Rye and the five surfboards he had lined up at water's edge.

Wilson patted my bottom and followed Tessie.

Louise and I continued staring aghast. "I barely know how to swim," she murmured.

"Chris knows that," I tried reassuring her. "Remember he said this part of the beach has the calmest waves?" I cringed as a rather un-calm wave crashed before us. "Something about an offshore coral reef," I added weakly.

Louise took a deep breath. "Whatever happens, promise me a bucketful of pink drinks afterwards?"

I reminded her the pink drinks were Davy's secret recipe. "We may never see another Pele's Melee."

"What!? After learning how to swim and surf? All in one day?" Louise snorted and started walking. "Trust me, Babe, there are pink drinks in my future. I'll make them myself if need be."

"Merry Christmas!" Chris called out as we approached. I do believe he was actually smiling.

And of course, my mother was positively aglow. She gestured toward the boards. "Chris rented these for the whole week. Isn't that a thoughtful gift, girls?"

"Thoughtful," Louise and I mumbled in unison.

Chris pointed down the beach. "The lady at Folly Rentals couldn't believe it when I told her how old you guys are. But I said we'd have some fun anyway."

"Fun." Louise and I blinked at the surfboards looming before us.

"She couldn't believe where we're staying, either," he continued.

I tore my eyes from the surfboards. "She heard about the murder?"

"She says it's gonna hurt Buster and Ki more than all the other stuff combined."

"What other stuff?"

"How should I know?" he said impatiently. "Something about a Rachel Somebody."

"Rachel Somebody Who?" I persisted, but Wilson came over and put his arm around me.

"Leave it, please," he whispered. He pointed to Chris's board and spoke up. "Why's yours smaller than the rest?" he asked. "Shouldn't Tessie's be the smallest?"

"These are long boards," my mother the would-be surfing expert stepped forward to explain. "They're what we beginners are supposed to use. Isn't that right, Chris?" She gave one of the boards an affectionate tap. "Can I have this one? It's so shiny."

I grimaced at Tessie's shiny surfboard and bit my tongue. The woman was a broken bone waiting to happen, but who was I to deny my eighty-two-year-old mother any joy, thrill, or adventure she wanted to try?

Chris assigned the rest of us our boards. We were then instructed to lay them in the sand, and to lie ourselves, stomach-sides down, onto said boards.

"And here I thought surfing involved water and waves and such," Louise whispered to me as we got into position. "This isn't so bad after all."

It got bad soon enough, however, when our lesson involved repetitious attempts to move from the lying-on-our-stomachs position, to the squatting-on-our-toes position. We were supposed to accomplish this feat all in one fell and graceful swoop. No, really.

"Do a push-up and quick pull your feet up underneath your hips. Like this." Chris demonstrated the maneuver several times. Mother smiled, Wilson looked mildly interested, and Louise and I frowned. Then we all lay back down and tried again.

Wilson got the hang of it pretty quickly, which I chalked up to upper body strength. But Louise, who is a little plump and not exactly the epitome of physical fitness, was also up and squatting soon afterwards. No offense to Louise, but that was altogether aggravating. Here I keep myself slim and trim, and do hours of yoga every week for strength and balance, and I was the one struggling alongside my very elderly mother?

For better or worse, Chris was a patient teacher. He had us two less-adept pupils stand up and watch again, and this time Wilson and Louise joined him in the demonstration. Indeed, the synchronized surfboard dancing was a rather entertaining spectacle. Mother and I tried again, and finally, finally, we sort of, kind of, got the hang of it.

Speaking of spectacles, Chris announced it was time to catch some waves. He tossed Louise a life jacket. "This will give you confidence," he told her. "And salt water is really easy to stay afloat in."

"And remember we have that nice coral reef to keep us safe," Mother added.

"Fantastical," Louise said. She donned her jacket, picked up her board, and stalwartly headed out to sea.

"You're next, Jessie." Chris waved toward the ocean in case I had forgotten where it was. I smiled wanly and took the plunge.

The first wave crashed over me, taking with it all the sunscreen I had so carefully been applying all day. But no, not all the sunscreen. A goodly portion of it ended up in my eyes. Semi-blinded, I reminded myself I had always enjoyed frolicking in the ocean. But then another wave landed on top of me, and my head hit my surfboard. Or maybe my surfboard hit my head. Frolicking, I reminded myself as I desperately tried to get the stupid thing underneath me.

Have I mentioned upper body strength? While I struggled solo to catch a wave, Chris and Wilson made valiant efforts to move my mother, Louise, and their surfboards out to the breakwater point. Eventually we were all out far enough to really injure ourselves.

We puttered about to no avail whatsoever as Chris demonstrated various positions and techniques. At least Wilson caught on to a few basic maneuvers. He had even managed the squatting position a few times when Louise screamed how tired she was getting. I turned and searched for my mother.

Bless her heart, Tessie was trying her hardest, but clearly the woman was tuckered out. I motioned to Wilson, he got his son's attention, and while the two of them worked to get her safely into shore, I helped Louise. The going got much easier once I mentioned a bucketful of Pele's Melees. We practically raced each other toward dry sand.

Chapter 8

I might have been exhausted from the late afternoon surfing lesson, but the Hawaiian shirt Wilson donned after our showers woke me right up.

"We need to go back to Shynomore and get more of these," he told my reflection as I stepped out of the bathtub. He pointed proudly to his chest, where a plethora of red, orange, and pink bicycles paraded about. "I can't believe I only bought two last night." He gave himself another admiring glance in the mirror. "What was I thinking?"

"Perhaps you weren't," I suggested.

I was slipping into my own evening attire, a sundress, which I do believe was the epitome of understatement, when my cell phone rang. A blast from real life, it was Karen Sembler, calling from North Carolina. Another of my neighbors, Karen had back-up duty in the cat care project.

"Girlfriend!" she greeted me. "How's Hawaii?"

"Beautiful except for the dead guy." I stretched out on top of the bed. "And if I have to endure another surfing lesson, I may end up joining him."

"Did you just say, dead guy?"

"Don't ask," I said and calculated the time difference. "How are the cats, Karen? Where's Candy? Is Snowflake okay?"

Karen reported that Candy was working late. "Be thankful you're not here, Jess. Tate's is having their annual blow-out bra sale. Kiddo bought me this hideous red and green thing last night and threatened to bring home the matching panties tonight."

"And the cats?" I asked. "Is everyone okay?"

"No one's dead yet," was Karen's less than reassuring answer. Then she filled me in on the details—Snowflake and Bernice had been hissing at each other since we left. "The little black cat isn't too worried," she said, "but it's starting to get to Kiddo and me. Any ideas what we should do?"

"I thought Candy was going to keep Bernice and Wally down at her place if need be?"

"She did that last night. But you and Wilson are gonna be together forever, right? So these cats have to get used to each other, right?"

I scowled at my beau, who was now standing at the closet admiring his small but alarming collection of Hawaiian shirts.

"Maybe," I said quietly.

"So what's the son like, Jess? He ready for a new mom?"

"He likes me about as much as Snowflake likes Bernice."

"Oh boy."

I got back to the topic at hand and mentioned how Snowflake and Bernice both enjoy snuggling and cuddling. "Maybe if one of you slept at my place, the cats would all end up on the bed together. Maybe even happily."

"I'll run downstairs and get my jammies after we hang up."

Dear Karen. I thanked her for her efforts, apologized for the inconvenience, and told her where to find fresh sheets. "It could backfire," I warned. "They could keep you up all night."

"We'll be fine," she insisted. "But Snowflake sure misses you."

I pictured my feline muse and smiled. "What's she doing?"

"When she's not hissing at the fat cat, she sits on your desk and stares at your empty chair."

"Tell her *My South Pacific Paramour* is coming along quite nicely."

"Huh?"

"Tell Snowflake not to fret—Urquit Snodgrass will not get the better of Delta Touchette."

"Huh?"

"Snowflake," I repeated. "Tell her not to let Bernice get the better of her."

"And vice-versa," Wilson mumbled.

***

"Don't tell me. Let me guess. You want pink drinks." The person manning the tiki bar looked up from the tattered index card he was studying and frowned. "And you have no idea how Davy made them, and you have no idea why he died in your mother's bungalow. Am I right?"

More or less. Wilson and I ignored the frown, flinched only slightly as the new bartender slammed his notes onto the bar, and plopped ourselves onto two barstools.

It seemed unnecessary, but we introduced ourselves anyway, and Wilson held out his hand. "You must be Buster's brother?"

"Ki Okolo. You guys want some Pele's Melees or not?"

We nodded, and Mr. Congeniality grinned ominously. "Guinea pigs," he said and started pouring ingredients willy-nilly into the blender. "Those are all the instructions my damn brother could find in the damn files." He jerked his head at the card, and I noticed the list of ingredients—no measurements whatsoever.

I watched dubiously as a generous portion of vodka got dumped into the mix. "I understand Davy was quite secretive about his recipe," I said. "Did you know him well?"

"Duh."

"For how long?" Wilson asked.

Ki reached for the rum. "Since I was in high school. Everyone knew Davy."

"High school?" Wilson squinted. "Didn't you and Buster just buy this place?"

"Inherited."

"From your parents?"

"Duh. From my grandfather Pono."

"Pono-Pono, Pono-Pono." Bee Bee swooped in and landed at the edge of the bar.

Ki snarled. "We inherited him, too. Stupid bird's gonna outlive us all." He flipped the "On" switch. Bee Bee squawked in surprise, but recovered quickly, and proceeded to imitate the blender.

It was a surprisingly entertaining racket. When Ki realized he wasn't annoying us nearly as much as he might have hoped, he turned off the machine. Bee Bee shut up also and waddled over to the index card.

"Don't you dare!" Ki yanked the card from under the bird's beak and jammed it into the pocket of his Hawaiian shirt. Then he poured out two glasses of pinkish stuff, shoved the glasses in our direction, and waited until we hazarded tentative sips.

I coughed hardly at all, wiped the tears from under my eyes, and waved a hand at the surrounding gardens. "This is quite an inheritance," I said once I had sufficiently recovered my voice. "It's lovely."

"It's a pain in the butt." Ki brandished the bitters bottle and dumped some in the blender. "I wanted to sell the place, but my stupid brother's convinced he's some great entrepreneur. 'Owning the Wakilulani Gardens will be perfect,' he says to me. 'I'll do all the work,' he says to me. 'You can be the silent partner. Stay with Carmen and rake in the cash.'" Ki stopped and glared. "You can see how well that worked."

"Who's Carmen?" Wilson beat me to the question.

"My girlfriend," Ki answered. "Where I'd be right now if I wasn't enjoying your company so much." He pointed to our beverages. "You guys aren't drinking."

Wilson frowned at his glass. "It's," he hesitated, "interesting."

Ki looked at me.

"Umm," I said. "I don't think you got the proportions exactly right."

He slammed his palms on the bar. "Well, gee thanks, lady. I'll be sure to put pink drinks on my list of problems to solve, shall I? Right before Derrick Crowe and right after people getting killed." He grabbed the rum bottle and was about to splash more into his blender, but Wilson leaned over the bar and stopped him.

"People?" he asked. "Who else got killed?" Apparently my beau the cop had forgotten all about our plan to leave things to Vega.

Ki told Wilson not to get excited. "We only have one murder on our hands. You happy now, Sherlock?" He added the extra rum and turned the blender back on.

I leaned over and switched it off.

"Do you, or do you not, want me to get this right, lady?"

"Who's Derrick Crowe?" I asked.

"Duh! Like, maybe the chef?" Ki shook his head at my obtuseness. "He's disappeared off the face of the earth." He resumed blending, much to Bee Bee's delight. "Luckily I found Bethany," he shouted over the noise.

"Bethany?" I asked as the noise subsided. "Did she replace Mr. Crowe?"

"Nooo." Ki continued shaking his head in disgust.

"Makaila Isiano's the new chef," Wilson, who never forgets a name, reminded me. "Bethany was our waitress last night."

Ki topped off our glasses. "Bethany found us Makaila. The girl's a gem."

"Girl's a gem, girl's a gem, girl's a g—"

"As is your new chef," I interrupted Bee Bee. "Our first dinner here was terrific."

Ki smirked. "Gee thanks. I'll sleep better just knowing you're satisfied."

Why was I even trying to be pleasant to this obnoxious jerk? I leaned forward, gearing up to tell Ki exactly what I thought of him and his supposed Pele's Melees, but Wilson stopped me.

He laid a gentle but firm hand on my knee. "Speaking of sleep," he said to Ki. "Where were you last night?"

"What? Are you a cop now?"

"Yep."

"A little out of your jurisdiction, aren't you, Sherlock?"

"Yep. Where were you?"

Ki blinked at Bee Bee, but the bird failed to produce an answer.

"I live with Carmen on the other side of the island," Ki finally informed us. "You know? Over in Nettles Corner? Where no damn tourist dares to tread?"

"You were there all night?

Ki poured himself a drink and took a gulp. "God, this is awful," he said.

"Yep," Wilson agreed. "And your alibi?"

Ki took another swig. "I was with Carmen, like I told the real cops when they came banging on our door at five a.m. And even if I didn't have a solid alibi, why would I kill Davy? He and his stupid drinks were the main attraction of this place. Without him, look who's stuck being the bartender."

"Cheer up," I said. "Maybe Buster will hire a replacement for Davy." I blinked at my pinkish beverage. "Soon," I added.

"What? So we can get another Rachel Tate?"

"Who's she?" Wilson asked.

"No one," Ki snapped. "We're not going there. You get it, Sherlock?"

That time it was Wilson who was gearing up to give the obnoxious jerk a piece of his mind, and it was me doing the hand on the knee thing.

"It doesn't sound like you're happy with how Buster's running things," I observed casually.

"My brother can barely tie his own shoes, much less run a business."

"At least Buster seems eager to please," I said.

"Yeah? What exactly has he done to please you? Enlighten me."

"Enlighten me," Bee Bee repeated and waddled over in my direction for a pat on the head.

I stroked the bird and tried to think.

"He built the beds," Wilson suggested with a wink in my direction.

"That's right," I agreed. "And he made us a very nice lunch today, and he promised us pancakes tomorrow morning."

Ki threw his hands up. "So now he's serving breakfast and lunch? Like we have the staff for this?"

"Come on, Ki," I said. "Buster is trying very hard. He put up that beautiful Christmas tree, for instance."

Ki harrumphed.

"He did that to please you," I said.

"Lady, my baby brother has no idea what pleases me."

"What pleases you?" Wilson asked.

"Buckets of pink drinks!" Louise called out.

"Pink drinks!" Bee Bee cried. He waddled over to the other end of the bar and did a bowing-wobbling thing as Louise and my mother approached.

"Buckets of pink drinks," Mother mused. "Doesn't that sound lovely, though?"

"Pink being the magic word," Wilson mumbled and got up to find her a seat.

Chapter 9

"These still aren't quite the correct color, are they?" Mother was assessing the contents of her glass, but my attention had landed further afield—on the dining room stage, where the Hoochie Coochie Brothers had just taken up residence.

"Off-key," I said.

"Off-color," Louise corrected me. "And what about the little gold umbrellas? What's an off-color Pele's Melee without a gold umbrella? I adore the umbrellas! Adore, adore, adore!"

"Me, too!" Mother and I got into the spirit as Buster walked by our table.

He stopped short and hovered over the pupu platter—a variety of Hawaiian delicacies—we were sharing. "What's wrong?" he asked.

"The food's great," Wilson was quick to reply. "But the ladies miss the umbrellas." He pointed to my woefully ungarnished glass, and Buster scurried off.

Lo and behold, a few moments later Ki emerged from behind the dining room bar holding a box of what we soon surmised were little gold umbrellas. He weaved his way around the tables, slamming down a handful on each. Eventually he made it to us.

"Here!" he said. He dropped the umbrellas and stormed off.

"Don't mind Ki." Bethany had come up from behind him and waited until he was more or less out of earshot. "He's forever grumpy." She helped Wilson distribute the umbrellas around the table. "Where's your son tonight?"

"With Emi. He got sick of hanging around with his old man all day."

"Lucky Emi." She collected our appetizer plates and wandered away.

I caught my mother's eye. "People always confide in you," I told her, as if this were news. "So when Bethany comes back, quiz her about Ki."

"Okay, Honeybunch."

"And his girlfriend—Carmen Someone," Wilson said. "And someone named Rachel Tate."

"Maybe Bethany knows about Derrick Crowe, too," I said. "He's the former chef, who's supposedly dropped off the face of the earth. Can you remember all that, Mother?"

Louise pointed a parasol at me. "What are you up to, Jessica Hewitt?"

"She's sleuthing, of course." Mother looked back and forth between Wilson and me. "You're trying to solve Davy's murder, aren't you?"

"Are we?" I asked.

Wilson cleared his throat. "Let's just say, we're curious."

"So the mystery man wants to know everyone else's deep dark secrets?" Louise asked.

"I'm just curious," he tried again.

"Deep, dark, or indifferent, we need to learn a few things," I insisted. "We need the history of this place. We need the details. We need—"

"Louise and I already know the history, Honeybunch."

I sat up straight. "Oh?"

Mother reminded me that she and Louise had talked to Davy quite a bit the previous day. "He was very cordial—somewhat of a gossip, even." She nodded to Louise. "And we were regular barflies, weren't we?"

"Back in the good old days when the pink drinks were all they were meant to be," Louise agreed.

"It's too bad Davy didn't tell us his secret recipe," Mother said. "But he did discuss the Okolo brothers. Buster and Ki inherited the Wakilulani Gardens from Pono. He passed away recently."

"The grandfather?" Wilson asked, and I could tell he was as disappointed as I. Unfortunately, Tessie didn't know anything more than we did.

Or did she? She was talking again—something about an accident. "The accident," as she put it.

Louise interrupted something about the "tragedy" and cut to the chase. "Buster and Ki's parents were killed in a car crash when the boys were still in school. Buster was eleven. Ki was seventeen."

I contemplated this stunning information. Tessie was right, of course. It was tragic.

"That's when they came to live here," Louise continued. "Buster's been here ever since. But according to Davy, Ki left the minute he had the chance. He went off to college and he's seldom returned since. He hates it here."

We glanced toward the bar, where Ki was talking with his brother. Make that, to his brother. They were struggling, tug-of-war fashion, with a dinner menu.

"He doesn't seem like the friendliest fellow, does he?" Mother asked.

"But he has a lady friend," Wilson said. "Davy mention anything about that?"

"Carmen Dupree!" Louise said. "I adore that name, Jessica! You should put a Carmen in your next book!"

"Oooo!" Mother exclaimed. "Perhaps with a Latin-type theme?"

Louise pursed her lips and twirled her little parasol. "I'm picturing Carmen," she told the umbrella. "She wears red dresses. Tight red dresses to match the flower she always puts behind one ear. Maybe like those hibiscus Buster has planted all over the garde—"

"Ki lives with her, right?" Wilson interrupted. "The real Carmen, I mean."

Louise sighed and gave up on outlining my next masterpiece. "Yes, Wilson. They live on the other side of the island. According to Davy, the place is absolutely, totally, and completely dreary. Personally, I do not see how that is even remotely possible. This is Hawaii, after all. I cannot imagine one single, unfantastical spot!"

"There are a few." Bethany had returned with our entrees and placed Mother's coconut curried chicken before her.

"Doesn't this look lovely?" Mother gestured toward her dinner. "And to think the chef is brand new. Isn't that what you told us last night, dear?"

"Makaila's fantastical." Bethany winked at Louise and worked on arranging the rest of our plates.

"But I wonder whatever happened to the previous chef?" my mother mused.

Bethany stood up empty-handed. "He's gone."

"Well now, that's what we heard. Evidently he's disappeared off the face of the earth?"

"Poof!" I said and threw my hands into the air for emphasis.

Bethany squinted at me. "Why are you guys so interested in Derrick?" She kept squinting. "You think he had something to do with last night?"

"Do you?" Wilson asked.

She stared at Wilson and considered her answer. "I think he owed Davy some money," she said eventually. "Derrick owed lots of people money. It's why he disappeared."

"Intriguing!" Louise exclaimed, but Bethany was still watching Wilson.

"You're a cop, right?"

"How'd you know that?"

"Word gets around. Halo Beach is a small place."

"Small but intriguing," Louise repeated.

Bethany shrugged. "It's just rumors. But supposedly Derrick and Davy hated each other."

"And Davy still loaned him money?" Wilson sounded skeptical.

"No, sir. They hated each other because Davy loaned him money."

Annoying but necessary—she wandered off to take care of the diners at the next table. Annoying but unnecessary—the Hoochie Coochie Brothers. I ate my mahimahi and wondered if the reggae set they were stuck in would ever end.

Louise must have read my mind. "Don't you need dreadlocks for that one?" she asked with a gesture toward the stage.

"Dreadlocks?" Mother was also distracted by the performance on stage. "Are those like accordions?"

Poor Wilson tried getting us back on topic. "Ask Bethany about Rachel Tate," he suggested to Tessie. "I think this Rachel character also worked here. Ki and Chris both mentioned her."

"Chris?" I asked, and Wilson reminded me that the woman who had rented Chris our surfboards had mentioned a "Rachel Somebody."

I shook my head. "You've been paying awfully close attention, Captain Rye. I mean, for someone's who's just curious."

"Who are you curious about now?" Bethany had returned with our desserts.

"Rachel Tate," my mother answered, and the woman almost dropped her dessert tray.

"Intriguing!" Louise exclaimed, and poor Bethany had to steady her tray again.

Mother waited patiently until all the desserts were safely served. "Bethany, honey," she said. "What can you tell us about Rachel?"

"Nothing good. Buster hired her, and Ki fired her. Buster's still upset about it."

With a bit more coaxing, we learned that Rachel Tate had been a "disaster." Apparently, Buster's choice for a desk clerk had never booked a single bungalow, and had even managed to cancel any on-line reservations that potential guests might have made for themselves.

"When people called to re-book she'd hang up on them," Bethany said. "Never mind Ki's fancy software system, Rachel couldn't even answer the phone right."

Wilson asked how we had managed to get reservations and tilted his head toward the stage. "Or those two?"

She explained that Hal and Cal Coochie had a standing reservation for Christmas week every year. "I guess they've been coming here ever since the first ukulele contest."

"Ten years, then," Mother said.

"What about us?" Wilson asked Bethany. "How did we get in?"

"You guys booked really late, right?"

"Correct," I said and reminded everyone that Wilson hadn't known his exact vacation schedule until Thanksgiving weekend. "The Wakilulani Gardens was the only resort in all of Hawaii with a vacancy for this week. And with the garden looking so beautiful on the website? I was very happy to find it."

Bethany explained why we had been so lucky. "Other than you, no one even tried booking that late for Christmas week. And Rachel was gone by then. When Ki was here at Thanksgiving, he fired her and took over the computer himself."

"I do hope the poor girl has found herself another job?" my mother said.

"Rachel's pretty good at landing jobs, Mrs. Hewitt. It's keeping them that's her problem. Last I heard she's working at Kamakakoa's. It's the big sports bar down near Shynomore, where I assume you got that thing." She pointed to Wilson's ridiculous shirt, and we were all distracted by the brilliance of his bicycles.

Mother reached out and tapped the pink specimen on his sleeve. "Wilson, honey," she said. "I do believe that's the color our Pele's Melees are supposed to be."

Chapter 10

"I can't believe we're doing this," Wilson said as we wended our way down Halo Beach a bit later.

"Nor can I," I agreed. "But you keep insisting you need more of these stupid things." I tugged on his shirtsleeve.

"Not the shopping, Jessie. I'm talking about the Kamikaze bar. What's our plan? What are we gonna say? Who are we gonna talk to?"

"It's Kamakakoa's, and hopefully Rachel Tate, correct?" I stopped short. "Are you feeling well?" I asked. "Because you're seeking my advice. It's altogether uncharacteristic."

"This investigation is altogether uncharacteristic." He pointed to the neon sign for Kamakakoa's Sports Bar, beckoning to us from just off the beach. "Normally, I would march in there, flash my badge, and start asking questions. No problem."

"But you're out of your jurisdiction."

"Yep."

"It's just a bar, Wilson. Act friendly instead of authoritative and you'll do fine."

He put his hands on his hips and frowned at the bar. "Friendly, huh?"

I rolled my eyes. "On second thought, leave the talking to me. This is exactly the kind of thing we amateur sleuths live for."

I started moving again, and he hastened to catch up. "You have a plan, Jessie?"

Heck, no.

***

Despite that pesky detail, I marched into the crowded bar exuding an air of confidence.

Enormous TVs and loud shouts of encouragement or hostility directed toward the various figures running around with various balls on the various screens greeted me. I checked to see if Duke were playing basketball on any of the screens. No, but that was just as well. If I got involved rooting for my alma mater I might forget my main purpose.

And far better than any basketball game, I spotted two pool tables near the back of the expansive room. I grinned and wiggled two fingers at Wilson.

He reached out for my fingertips. "How long has it been since your last game, Little Miss Cue-It?"

"Three days."

"You ever gone that long without holding a cue stick?"

I glanced at my right hand, now enclosed in his, and considered the question. "Not since I was four."

"You're a little scary. You know that?"

I told him to make himself useful and buy me some champagne. Then I headed toward the tables. I kept my eye out for Rachel Tate along the way, but all of the bartenders at both of the bars were male. I did notice one harried waitress racing between the tables. She might have been Rachel. But I had no idea what Rachel looked like, so I decided to get settled in before seeking my prey.

I stepped up to the nearest pool table and announced my mission. Well, not quite. But I did interrupt the two young men playing at table one. And when I asked if I might shoot a game with the winner, the action stopped at both tables.

Dare I say, this was not unexpected? Generating interest around a barroom pool table has always been one of my better talents. I scanned the ten or so pairs of eyes assessing me. Okay, make that my best talent. Indeed, in my younger days, when I was shooting pool to cover my tuition, I caused many a minor incursion just by batting my eyelashes and asking if anyone were willing to teach me. Ah, the good old days.

But that was then, and this is now. And nowadays people aren't so much intrigued by my beauty and naïveté, but by the fact that an old bat like me still shoots pool. If I do say so myself, folks get even more intrigued when they realize the old bat is pretty good. Okay, make that very good. I smiled to myself. Downright brilliant, even.

The tallest of the players stepped forward from the group of young men gawking at me. "You willing to wager on your game?" he asked.

I shrugged casually and was about to agree to a humble five-dollar bet when Wilson came up from behind us. "Watch it," he said.

I'm not sure whether he was addressing me or the tall guy, but we both bristled a bit. And prepared to be suitably indignant, I turned around. But bless his grumpy heart—Wilson held two champagne glasses in one hand, a bottle of Korbel in the other, and was busy pouring.

As I reached out and took a glass, I mouthed a stern "friendly" at him.

Wilson glanced around. "Trust me, guys." He smiled, all friendly-like. "You need to be careful. My lady friend is not what she seems."

"Oh?" several people, including myself, asked.

"She may drink champagne of all things, and she may be old enough to be your mother, but she's a damn good player." He addressed Tall Guy, "Sorry, buddy, but you're about to lose."

Another man might have bristled some more, but evidently Tall Guy was a big man in more ways than one. He looked to me for verification of Wilson's outlandish claims.

"He's right," I admitted. "But how about this? You guys let me play a game or two, and my boyfriend here will buy a few pitchers, whoever ends up winning. Deal?"

Apparently so, since several of the guys at both pool tables were already beckoning to the waitress and arguing about which brand of beer to order.

That issue was finally settled, but then other complications arose. First of all, the waitress ended up being a Sylvia, not a Rachel. Darn, darn, and double-darn. And after seeing my first victory against Tall Guy, everyone decided I should play at both tables at once.

It happens. But I pretended to be flattered by the challenge and agreed to give it a try. After all, while I kept track of two games at once, Wilson could do the chit-chat thing and work on learning about Rachel Tate, the Wakilulani Gardens, and anything else of use.

Yeah, right.

I was aiming at the eight ball of my fourth or fifth game when I realized Wilson the investigative professional stunk at amateur sleuthing. He was chit-chatting alright, but he seemed to have forgotten all about our mission and was instead interrogating the gang about hiking opportunities on The Big Island.

The eight ball disappeared at table one, I finished up at table two, and announced that I needed a break. I pointed to my glass resting forlornly on a nearby table. "My champagne's getting warm."

I stepped off to the side and elbowed my way between Wilson and the short bald guy he was talking to. At least they had gotten the conversation back to our island and were discussing the flora and fauna likely to be experienced by any "lucky" hiker on Kekipi Crater.

"Speaking of gardens," I said, dismissing the fact that no one was speaking of gardens. "The resort where we ate dinner tonight was beautiful. Wasn't it, Honey?"

It took Wilson an inordinate amount of time to realize he was my honey, but he caught on eventually. "Umm, beautiful," he mumbled.

"The Wakilulani Gardens?" I said and glanced around at several stunned faces. "The gardens and the restaurant were absolutely fantastic."

"Fantastic," Wilson agreed.

"Have y'all ever eaten at the Wakilulani?" I fluttered my eyelashes as if I were twenty-one again, and a few men muttered something about leaving the place to tourists and the cops."

"Cops?" Wilson repeated. He was beginning to remind me of Bee Bee.

Tall Guy shook his head. "Figures you guys wouldn't know about the murder."

"I'm afraid we haven't been keeping up with the news," I said, and the whole gang laughed. "What's so funny?"

Tall Guy patted me on the shoulder and explained why we would never hear about a murder on Halo Beach from the media. "The newspaper's too busy reporting on crap like the ukulele contest, and the local TV station refuses to broadcast anything that might scare away the tourists. Crime's off limits. We have to get that information from each other."

I gasped. "You mean there was a murder at the Wakilulani—the very place we ate dinner tonight? And no one even bothered to tell us?"

"Looks like it," said the blond guy who had taken over at table two.

I appealed to Tall Guy, and he once again enlightened me, explaining the basics of Davy's murder while I acted shocked and dismayed. He told me not to worry too much. "The cops will arrest the tourist who did it within a couple days. They always do."

I took a moment to digest that disconcerting little tidbit and watched Blond Guy sink the eight ball. "The Wakilulani is jinxed," he said as he stood up.

"Jinxed," Wilson repeated.

"Oh, yeah," the skinny guy at table one agreed. "The great Davy Atwell is dead."

"Dead," Wilson said, and I bit my lip.

Blond Guy nodded. "And don't forget about Derrick Crowe."

Oh, honey, I wouldn't dream of it. "Was this Derrick person killed, too?" I asked.

"That's one theory," Tall Guy said. "He was their chef. But now the guy's fallen off the face of the earth."

I tapped my chin, deep in thought. "Well then, maybe it's for the best Rachel doesn't work there anymore," I said. I pretended not to notice an immediate wave of tension in the air and continued, "The Wakilulani Gardens sounds a bit dangerous, doesn't it?"

"Did you just say, Rachel?" Tall Guy squeaked.

"Rachel Tate," I said loudly and watched his face drop. "She's an old friend. Well no, that's not quite it," I corrected myself. "Rachel's auntie is an old friend of mine. Cicely and I go way back."

"Way, way, back," Wilson agreed.

"Cicely was so excited to hear we were staying at Halo Beach on our vacation," I kept lying. "She made me promise to look up Rachel when we got here. She told me all about the Wakilulani Gardens."

Bald Guy asked if I didn't want to get back to the pool game. While the gang murmured agreement with that idea, I jabbed Wilson in the ribs, and he re-filled my glass.

"Maybe in a minute." I held up my now-full glass and returned to the subject at hand. "Of course we made a special point of eating at the Wakilulani to see Rachel, but the folks down there told us she works here now. So here we are!"

"Here we are!" You guessed it—Wilson.

I asked the gang about Rachel's next shift. "She does work here, no?"

"No." The waitress Sylvia had joined us with two fresh pitchers.

"No?" Wilson asked.

"She got fired." Sylvia groaned out loud, as did a few of my pool-playing buddies. "I'm sorry, lady, but your friend was a disaster. She couldn't, or wouldn't, keep up the pace." Sylvia took a credit card from Wilson and left to close out our tab.

I sighed for effect. "I feel like I'm on a wild goose chase." Sigh, sigh. "I don't suppose anyone can tell me where I might find Rachel now?"

"At the Primrose Tower," Tall Guy told me. "It's that fancy high-rise hotel at the north end of the beach. Rachel's their new night clerk."

"Good luck Primrose Tower," Blond Guy muttered under his breath.

***

Two more pool games and three Hawaiian shirts later, Wilson and I stood outside Shynomore Shirt Shop, debating whether or not we possessed the energy to venture further down the beach to Rachel Tate's newest place of employment.

"Not," we agreed and began our trek back toward home base.

We walked in silence. Perhaps Wilson was enjoying the lovely moon and the sounds of the waves crashing on the shore, but I was deep in thought about the Wakilulani—its history, its owners, its staff, its missing staff. Davy Atwell.

Louise Urko might say the place was intriguing, but I was more inclined to agree with the blond guy at pool table two. The Wakilulani wasn't just intriguing—it was jinxed.

Eventually we found our spot from the previous night, and as we plopped down in the sand, Wilson got right to the point. "Who's the killer?" he asked.

I reminded him he's the expert. "Who do you think killed Davy?"

"The only one I'm ruling out is Bee Bee."

I might have snorted.

"What's so funny?"

"You are." I pointed in the direction of Kamakokoa's. "Sorry, Captain Rye, but you sounded just like Bee Bee down there."

"Bee Bee?"

"At the bar, Wilson. You kept repeating everything everyone said."

"Everythi—" He caught himself and mumbled something about just trying to be friendly.

I patted his knee. "If it wasn't Bee Bee, who was it?

"Could be almost anyone. Right now, I'm thinking Bethany."

"The waitress? Why, for Lord's sake?"

"I'm betting all the turnover in staff is significant. For a brand new employee, Bethany seemed pretty involved in that."

"She found the terrific new chef," I agreed.

"And she was more than happy to tell us the rumors about the old chef."

"You did ask her, Wilson."

He shrugged. "She tried to hide it, but she has strong opinions about these people."

I remembered how my kiwi sorbet had almost landed in my lap when the subject of Rachel Tate came up. "Bethany certainly didn't like Rachel," I conceded. "But considering the reaction we just got at the sports bar, no one does."

"You were right about her, though."

I shook my head. "About who?"

"Rachel Tate. Back at Kamakaze's you said we were on a wild goose chase. I bet Bethany sent us down there to get us sidetracked."

"Oh, come on. She didn't order us to go sleuthing."

"Power of suggestion." He turned to me. "Okay, Miss Amateur Sleuth. If not Bethany, who?"

I thought about my own prime suspect. "It didn't necessarily have to be someone staying or working at the resort that night," I suggested. "I mean, anyone could have driven in, taken the knife, and then hidden in the parking lot to wait for Davy."

"Anyone like Ki Okolo?"

I jumped. "He's my prime suspect! How did you know?"

"That annoying Hewitt intuition must be rubbing off. Why Ki?"

"No reason, other than he's a misogynist jerk." I thought a second. "But then again, Ki seems to hate everyone—female, male, human, avian."

"Not his girlfriend."

"Carmen Dupree?"

Wilson leaned over and nudged his shoulder into mine. "What say we take a road trip to Nettles Corner tomorrow? Check out the other side of the island."

It took me a moment, but eventually I recollected where I had heard about Nettles Corner. Ki had told us that's where his girlfriend lives.

I cleared my throat. "Far be it for me to remind you of this, but aren't we supposed to be leaving these things to Captain Vega?"

"I changed my mind, Jessie. Vega isn't doing squat. The guy hasn't even been back to Wacky Gardens since last night."

"That's weird, isn't it?"

"It's wrong. I always make myself a nuisance at the scene of the crime. It's the crux of almost any investigation." Wilson caught my eye. "You remember how often I was at your place after Stanley Sweetzer died?"

I smirked. "That's because you thought I was cute."

"Or the murderer," he clarified. "I kept bugging you, because I wanted to get the details before jumping to conclusions. But Vega?"

"Is jumping to conclusions."

"You heard the guys at Kamakaze's—Vega's about to pin this on a tourist. Which means one of us."

"But there's no motive, remember?"

"Maybe, but Vega's used to blaming tourists, and it's two days before Christmas. I'd bet money he's gonna take the easy way out on this."

"Easy for whom?" I asked indignantly.

Chapter 11

Monster indeed! Delta Touchette sheathed her machete and nodded in self-satisfaction. For the Monster of Ebony Island was, of course, no monster at all. Just an ordinary man. But perhaps, not so ordinary. Delta took a cautious step forward to get a closer look at the person she was spying in the clearing ahead. Oh, he was most unpleasant. Filthy he was, with long, snarled, and disheveled hair, and an even worse beard.

And that beard was becoming more unsightly every moment. For the man was gnawing on some such bones he was pulling from the fire in front of him, seeming to care not at all what dropped or dripped onto his whiskers. His fingernails were long and yellow—the same color as his skin. Occasionally, he looked up from his unwholesome repast to flash a set of crooked yellow teeth at the crates, boxes, and chests that surrounded him in his den. Ill-gotten gains, no doubt.

Delta pursed her lips and furrowed her brow. Why, of course! She was looking at none other than the Pirate of Diamond Island. The Monster of Ebony Island was, in fact, the Pirate of Diamond Island! Wouldn't Skylar Staggs be interested to learn that!

Skylar Staggs. Delta closed her eyes and indulged in a brief yet exhilarating memory of the sheriff of Port Mekipii Hui. The only man on Diamond Island brave enough to escort her to Ebony Island. The only man Delta had ever—

A grunt from beyond pulled her out of her reverie. Delta opened her eyes as the creature before her yanked another grisly bone from the fire. She wrinkled her nose and backed away into the jungle from whence she came.

As she blinked at the gathering gloom, the urgency of her situation dawned on her. She was hopelessly lost. Her stomach growled, reminding her she was also hopelessly hungry. The dinner Auntie Eleanor had mentioned hours earlier had long ago come and gone.

Delta raised her sapphire eyes skyward, past the trees that towered overhead, and glimpsed the emerging stars. A wave of panic seized her when she realized she would have to spend the night in the jungle, for it would be impossible to find her way back to her Auntie's estate at this hour. Whatever that hour might be, exactly.

Reminding herself she was a brave and daring adventuress, afraid of nothing, and willing to endure any hardship or discomfort, Delta set off in search of a safe place to sleep. Why, in a jungle as lush as this, surely she could find a suitable spot? Preferably surrounded by fruit trees. Some running water would also be most welcome. A brook of some sort, from which she might refill her empty canteen.

A twig snapped in the distance, and Urquit Snodgrass snapped to attention. He looked up from the remains of his supper, and his beady yellow eyes darted back and forth into the brush behind his treasure trove. That was no monkey, he said to himself, and stood up to investigate.

***

Mother tut-tutted at the computer screen as she read my morning's work over her morning coffee. "Oh dear," she said. "I do believe Delta's in more danger than even a daring adventuress such as she is prepared for."

"Completely and totally!" Louise agreed. She looked up from reading over Tessie's shoulder and informed me I am brilliant. "I'm loving it, Babe! Delta is in serious peril, isn't she? Urquit Snodgrass is about to nab her!"

"Not quite yet." I reluctantly tore my eyes from my pancakes with coconut syrup to enlighten my audience that the loathsome Mr. Snodgrass would not actually kidnap Delta until the following day.

I blinked at the garden fountain gurgling near the edge of the patio. "Delta will happen upon a most idyllic and refreshing pool of clear blue waters the morning following her arduous night in the jungle. Of course, she'll strip down naked to bathe and revive herself and—"

"And let me guess." Wilson looked up from his own pancakes. "Just as this Snotgrass guy is about to grab her, some stupid hunk with a huge—"

I kicked him under the table and tilted my head toward my mother. He cleared his throat and tried again. "Just as Snotgrass is about to nab her, the hero guy will rescue her, right?"

"No, Wilson," Mother corrected. "First of all, his name is Snodgrass, not Snotgrass. And the nasty villain must first succeed in kidnapping Delta. Otherwise, our hero Skylar Staggs can't very well rescue her from serious distress. Isn't that right, Jessie?"

I was about to agree, but got distracted by some serious distress of my own—The Hoochie Coochie Brothers had begun tuning their ukuleles over in Song of the Sea bungalow, perfectly disturbing the serenity of our morning meal. I glanced across the garden and whimpered only slightly as the pajama-clad duo stepped out onto their porch, ukuleles in hand. They smiled and waved, and sat down to serenade us.

Mother clapped in glee. "They have a gig tonight," she informed us. "Is that the word? Gig?"

"You mean, someone is actually going to pay them to play?" I asked.

"Mm-hmm. For Holiday Hula at Halo. Evidently an act called the Smiley Sisters was scheduled for the luau, but they had to cancel. So Hal and Cal were asked to fill in."

"A luau?" Louise squealed. "That sounds beyond fantastical! Where is it? Let's go!"

Mother waved a hand. "Don't worry," she said as I began to worry. "It's just down the beach, and I promised the Coochie boys we would all be there." She smiled brightly. "I've never been to a luau before!"

"Me neither!" Louise said. "Not a real one in Hawaii anyway. Won't this be fantastically fun?" She turned to me for confirmation, and I enquired as to whether she had been tippling on a batch of early-morning pink drinks.

"Poor Hal and Cal were upset to learn that one of the Smiley Sisters has taken so ill," Mother explained. "But the show must go on."

"Must, must, must!" Louise agreed.

"The Holiday Hula could well be their big break," Tessie continued relentlessly. "I imagine they'll be practicing all day. They'll want to do their very best, won't they?"

I might have whimpered, but Wilson reminded me we'd be gone much of the day. "We're renting a car and exploring the island," he told the luau enthusiasts. "You ladies care to join us?"

Mother and Louise blinked at each other. "No, thank you," they said in unison, and Louise mumbled something about having some work to catch up on.

"Edits," she said. "Roslynn Mayweather sent me her latest manuscript right before I left New York. The Sultan's Secret—isn't that a fantastical title?" She pointed toward the swimming pool pavilion. "I'll be reading by the pool most of the day. What about you, Tessie?"

Mother yawned dramatically. "I think I'll take a nice long nap on my porch this morning. Surfing yesterday just about tuckered me out. And I'll want to be well-rested for today's lesson, won't I?

"Three o'clock sharp," Chris called from the edge of the patio. "You geezers are gonna catch some waves if it kills me." He pulled up a chair and sat down between my mother and his father. "Nice shirt, Dad."

While the rest of us frowned at Wilson's latest purchase, this one boasting an assortment of poodles in strange yet eye-opening colors, Chris hailed the waitress and ordered three eggs over easy and half a dozen pancakes with coconut syrup.

Faye, the morning waitress who was considerably older than anyone else on the staff, shook her head at me. "I have a son about his age, too. And just as thin. The kid eats like a horse."

Chris was quick to point out he is not my son. "Oh, and can I have a few strips of bacon with that, Faye?"

"Baby, you can have anything you want," she said as she watched him finish what was left in his father's coffee cup.

"Why's the coffee so good here?" he asked her.

"Kona," several of us answered. Faye promised to bring back a fresh pot and left for the kitchen.

"The coconut syrup is rad stuff, too," Chris informed us. "I can't believe you guys missed Buster's pancakes yesterday."

Personally, I couldn't believe Chris had actually managed to eat breakfast the day before. But apparently he had bonded with Faye over a plate of pancakes while we geezers had been sleeping in and recovering from our harrowing night of murder and mayhem.

"What's the plan for today?" he asked and immediately delved on into his own itinerary. "I'm renting some snorkeling equipment from Folly Rentals first thing. After that I think I'll try windsurfing. A guy down the beach said he'd show me how. Then I need to teach you guys to surf." He turned to his father. "And afterwards we can hike up Maka Koa Trail and find that cave we missed yesterday. You game?"

While my mother, Louise, and I muttered something about our own rather sedate plans, Wilson studied his son. "You're avoiding Vega," he said, and Chris almost fell off his chair.

Wilson waited patiently for his son to get re-settled. In the meantime, Faye returned with fresh coffee and refilled our cups. He continued to wait patiently until she was out of earshot.

"Vega," he repeated in case anyone had lost their train of thought. "He talked to you yesterday, without my knowing. Am I right?"

"Maybe." Chris stirred his coffee, even though he took his black, like his father.

"When, where, and about what?" Wilson persisted.

Chris dropped the spoon. "He tracked me down last night at Cabana Bananas. It's where Emi works. I was keeping her company, okay?"

"And Vega just happened to show up?"

"It was no big deal."

Wilson raised an eyebrow. "You're not that stupid."

"No, he isn't," my mother agreed. "Chris, honey, you should tell your father what Captain Vega said. You know, what we discussed last night?"

"Mother!" I exclaimed. "Do not tell me you two were in bed together again?"

"It wasn't like that!" the culprits said in unison.

Chris went back to stirring his coffee. "Vega says I had a motive to kill Davy," he mumbled.

"What!?" several of us asked.

"Because Emi dated him,"

"What!?" we said.

"But it was a long time ago, okay? Last summer, even." He turned to his father. "Emi has no idea how he found out, but Vega knew all about it. The guy's delusional, Dad. He kept insisting I'm jealous or something."

Wilson tried some deep breathing exercises as his son continued, "I kept saying I only just met Emi. And Emi kept saying she never even liked Davy. He was too old. She only went out with him twice. She was trying to get his Pele's Melees recipe. Her boss promised her a bonus if she could get the recipe."

"Did she?" I asked.

"Did she what?"

"Get the recipe," Louise said. "Because if she did, Ki needs it. Desperately!"

"That's Buster's brother, right?" Chris asked. "Vega kept lecturing me about how hard he works around here."

I rolled my eyes. "The only thing Ki Okolo works hard at is insulting the guests."

"I know what I heard, Jessie. Believe it or not, Captain Vega had my full attention."

Louise let out an exasperated sigh. "Sooo? Did Emi get the pink drink recipe, or did she not?"

"Not. Davy wouldn't give it to her, since she wouldn't give him—" Chris looked at my mother—"something else." He turned to his father. "But there's no way I was jealous of the guy. I hardly knew him, right?"

"Vega agree with your assessment?" Wilson asked.

Chris blinked twice. "No," he said quietly, and Wilson groaned.

"Come on, Dad." Rye Junior tried looking cheerful. "Vega won't really arrest me. I didn't do it. Cops don't put innocent people in prison for murder, right? Only the guilty, right? I mean think about—" He stopped short, and for some reason his gaze fell on me. "Think about it," he repeated, and his father groaned again.

***

I do believe we were all thinking about it, searching the depths of our coffee cups, when Faye returned. "You folks worried about Vega?" she asked, and all heads snapped upward.

She seemed not to notice, however, since she was too busy juggling the various components of Chris's breakfast. "I had Buster crisp up the bacon just like you asked yesterday," she said as she put down a large plate overflowing with food. "And here's some extra coconut syrup for those pancakes." She set down a small pitcher, a bowl of butter patties, and lastly, an empty coffee cup.

Her hands free, she placed them on her hips and looked at each of us in turn. "Well?" she said.

Wilson was the first to catch on. He jumped up to offer her a chair, and by the time she sat down, the rest of us had figured it out also. I poured coffee into the empty cup, and after asking Faye about the specifics, Louise added cream and sugar.

Chris glanced up from his eggs. "What's going on?"

"You're eating your breakfast, and I'm talking to your papa." Faye took a sip of her coffee and turned to Wilson. "Well?" she said.

He tilted his head toward Chris. "Vega's after him."

"I know that. Everyone knows that. We also know you're an ex-cop."

"Off-duty cop," Wilson corrected.

"But I imagine you're interested in the outcome here?"

He nodded, and they both looked at Chris, who had just remembered about the extra syrup. Wilson rolled his eyes and returned to Faye. "I take it you knew Davy?"

"Baby, everyone on Halo Beach knew Davy Atwell. His Pele's Melees were legendary. And he was a ladies' man. And he was an Atwell."

"That significant?" Wilson asked, and Faye rubbed her index finger and thumb together.

"Davy Atwell was the sole beneficiary of the Atwell family fortune," she informed us.

Louise sat forward. "How about you?"

"Do I look an heiress to you?"

"I think Louise meant, did you date Davy?" I said. "You say he was a ladies' man?"

Faye scowled. "Do I look like Davy's type? He was little young for me, don't you think?"

"Never stopped Jessie," Chris managed between bites.

"Can we get back to the murder?" Wilson asked.

A fine idea, but a particularly sour chord at the Song of the Sea distracted our attention. The Hoochie Coochies were attempting a rather unusual interpretation of "The Little Drummer Boy."

"Don't you need a drum for that one?" Faye asked.

"Davy," Wilson reminded her.

"Liked the ladies and vice versa. Word is he wooed many a girl with those pink drinks."

Chris actually looked up from his pancakes. "What girls."

"Tourists mostly."

"What about his co-workers?" Wilson asked. "Rachel Tate?"

Faye hesitated before answering. "That's what Rachel was hoping, but I'm not sure." She shrugged. "But I imagine Davy had no problem mixing business with pleasure."

"What about Bethany?" Wilson asked. "Anything there?"

"Between her and Davy?" Faye shook her head. "Bethany's way too smart. And she's way too busy for that kind of thing."

"She does seem to work hard," I suggested.

"Baby, you don't know the half of it. That girl's the reason this place is still in business. She helped the Okolo brothers hire a whole new staff after everyone quit."

"They quit when the grandfather died, right?" Wilson asked.

"Everyone but Davy did. That's when Buster hired Rachel, and Ki hired Bethany. And Bethany hired everyone else—the cook, the maids, me." Faye smiled. "She's one smart cookie."

I asked why everyone had quit when Buster and Ki took over, but Faye claimed not to know. "I'm one of the new people, remember."

"Take a wild guess," Wilson tried.

"Well," she said and gazed at the gurgling fountain. "Pono Okolo was a great guy by all accounts. But just look at his grandsons. Ki's a grouch. And Buster?" She shifted focus toward The Big House and lowered her voice. "He's nice enough, but maybe not so bright."

Wilson thanked Faye and turned to his son. "Give Bethany a call and ask her to join you today," he told him.

Chris finally put his fork down. "Why?" he said. "To, like, question her?"

"You know your old man."

"My old man's supposed to be on vacation. How do you even know I have her number?"

"Maybe because she's cute and under thirty."

Chris seemed about to protest, but my mother interjected. "What a clever idea, Wilson. Bethany was so helpful last night at dinner, wasn't she?" Tessie smiled demurely at Chris. "And a charming fellow like you could learn far more than the rest of us put together."

"No girl in her right mind would refuse you anything," Faye said, and Geez Louise began ranting some nonsense about how all the women simply "adored" Chris.

"Bethany won't be able to resist!" she exclaimed. "Get her to tell you all the deep dark secrets of the Wakilulani."

Chris seemed skeptical. "Why would Bethany know any secrets?"

"A smart cookie," we reminded him.

"I don't sleuth," he argued. "That's Jessie's job."

I pursed my lips. "We are not sleuthing. We're just curious. Ask your father."

He turned to his father.

"Nothing wrong with being curious," Wilson said.

Chris held up his hands in defeat. "Okay, okay. I'll call Bethany."

"That's the spirit." Faye patted his shoulder and stood up to clear the dishes. But she stopped short, syrup pitcher in mid-air, and stared down at the remaining pancake on Chris's plate. "What the—"

"Sorry, Faye," he said. "I guess I wasn't as hungry as yesterday."

Faye looked up from the dishes and slowly scanned the outskirts of the patio. "Where's the bird?"

"Bee Bee?" Louise stood up also and started peering into the shrubbery. "I haven't seen him this morning."

"But he's always out here at breakfast time." Faye tilted her head at Chris's leftovers. "Bee Bee never lets this happen. The stupid bird loves pancakes."

I looked up into the trees, suddenly cognizant of the void. Where was Bee Bee?

Chapter 12

"You're the navigator," I reminded Wilson as I donned my sunglasses and hopped into the driver's seat. We had splurged and rented ourselves a sporty little convertible in a royal blue color that clashed magnificently with his shirt.

"I feel like Nancy Drew's boyfriend," he said as he took the passenger seat.

"Nancy did drive a roadster something like this." I tapped the steering wheel affectionately. "Where to Ned?"

Wilson closed the phone book we had pilfered from Paradise bungalow. "Thistle Street, Nettles Corner." He told me to take a right out of the parking lot and began punching our destination into the GPS system.

I made the turns as directed by the GPS lady, and soon we were heading westward and upward, along hilly, winding roads, passing waterfalls, cliffs, and valleys in shades of green like I had never seen before.

"This is just the type of terrain Delta Touchette has found herself in," I said at some point. "Well, found isn't exactly the right word. Poor Delta is lost, of course. She could use a GPS system."

I glanced at my passenger for an appropriate sarcastic response, but clearly Delta Touchette's plight was the least of his concerns. He clutched the phone book to his chest in a most uncharacteristic way, deep in thought.

"You're worried about Chris," I said unnecessarily and downshifted to tackle one of the steeper hills. Wilson still didn't answer, so I tried again. "What do you think we'll find on Thistle Street?" I asked.

Finally, he released the poor phone book and tossed it at his feet. "Carmen Dupree's the goal."

"Maybe we should have asked Faye about her?"

"There's always tomorrow. Faye wants to help, and she likes to talk."

"An amateur sleuth's dream come true," I agreed. "But can we trust her?"

"She's not the murderer."

"What? How can you know that?"

"Size. Faye isn't much bigger than your mother. She couldn't stab anyone to death." He pointed to the turn the GPS lady was directing me toward. "Unlike my stupid kid."

I told him that his stupid kid surprised me as I veered off to the right. "He's way too trusting, and he seems way too confident in Captain Vega doing the right thing. It's naïve."

"He scares me."

"Vega or Chris?" I asked.

"Both. Vega's looking for an easy answer, and you got it, Jessie—Chris is naïve. He can't imagine the cops arresting an innocent person."

"That's because his daddy is so good."

"And his granddaddy. And even his grandmother—my mother was a dispatcher, remember. Chris thinks the police are always the good guys."

I cringed but insisted we would solve the murder ourselves, whether or not Chris thought we needed to. I cringed some more at the dramatic change in our surroundings. We had left the scenic stuff behind and were meandering our way downhill through an incredibly ugly housing subdivision. Indeed, it got drearier and drearier as we closed the distance to Thistle Street. Carmen Dupree's neighborhood might well have been the least scenic spot in all of Hawaii.

"Ki must really love this woman," I said as I made the final turn. "Can you believe he'd rather live here than at the Wakilulani Gardens?"

I slowed down and checked out the front yards we were passing. I recognized some of the same types of shrubs and trees as in the garden outside of Paradise, but no one in their right mind would call Nettles Corner paradise. Along with the exotic plants, almost all the yards were littered with debris. The houses were small bungalows but again lacked the charm of Paradise. Most needed a coat of paint, several needed new doors and windows, and almost every household looked in need of a newer car.

I was observing that cars equipped with tires are usually a bit more useful than those on cinder blocks, when the GPS lady announced we had reached our destination.

Wilson switched her off and told me to keep going. He pointed ahead. "Turn around at the corner and park behind those garbage cans."

I curled my lip, but he insisted the trash cans would hide us. "We should have thought harder before renting such a flashy car."

Thus I killed the engine next to the odiferous garbage cans, and we scooted down in our seats to stare at Carmen's house.

"So this is a stakeout?" I asked after what seemed a very long time, but in reality was probably about ten minutes. "It's not nearly as exciting as one would hope, Wilson. And it's a lot grosser." I waved a hand in front of my nose, attempting to dissipate the stench.

"We won't stay long—we're too obvious."

I swatted at a fly. "Remind me again what exactly we're trying to accomplish?"

"Damned if I know," he said and complained for the umpteenth time that he was out of his jurisdiction.

I sighed dramatically. "Alas, no waltzing up to Carmen's house and flashing your badge. Now you see what we amateur sleuths are up against. No badge, no authority, no earthly idea what we're doing."

He shrugged, and we resumed our altogether fruitless stakeout.

Fruitless, but not fruit fly-less. Trying to distract myself from a world-class case of the heebie jeebies, I broached a topic bound to take my mind away from the bugs. "Chris and Tessie sure are hitting it off," I said casually.

"Yep."

I took off my sunglasses and offered a meaningful look. "Chris has been confiding in her. He's been telling her all about his love life, your love life…" I stopped and let that last part linger while Wilson concentrated on staring straight ahead.

"Your deep dark secrets," I prompted again, and he threw up his hands.

"Okay, here we go," he said. "What's he told her, Jessie? What is it you know?"

"You mean about Dianne Calloway? Not nearly enough, I assure you."

"I'm gonna kill that kid."

"Fine with me, but at least wait until he's finished spilling his guts to my mother. Since I can't get the story from you, I intend to wrestle it out of Tessie."

Silence. Except for the buzzing of some very large flies who had decided to join the party.

Exhibiting unparalleled willpower, I ignored the ranks of the heebie-jeebie brigade and persisted. "Personally, I'd rather hear about the mysterious Ms. Calloway from you," I said. "The horse's mouth and all that."

Still silence.

"Come on, Wilson." I slapped at something on my forearm and got a red welt for my efforts. "Whatever your relationship was, it can't possibly be more embarrassing than my marriage to Ian. And you know all about that."

"Will you stop worrying about my past? It's ancient history."

I might have folded my arms and glared, but I was far too busy flinching and swatting at the stupid, stupid bugs.

At some point he took pity on me. "Tell you what," he said. "When we get back home, I'll tell you about Dianne. How's that?"

"Why not now?"

"Because we're supposed to be on vacation. Aren't we having enough fun trying to keep my kid out of jail?"

Okay, so maybe it was my turn for some empathy. I made sure to point out my exemplary patience and conceded temporary defeat.

"Temporary," I repeated when he seemed a bit too relieved. "We will have this conversation the very first night we get home." I took a swing at some obnoxious orange thing. "While you make me dinner." Swat, swat. "Spaghetti and meatballs."

Wilson grinned and attempted to catch my less frantic hand. "Deal," he agreed.

He gave up on my hand and pointed to Carmen's front door. "Unless she's planning on coming out of her own accord to tell us Ki Okolo's deep dark secrets, this is useless. Let's get out of here."

"Amen." I donned my sunglasses and started the engine. "As if the heebie jeebies from hell aren't bad enough, my entire left leg has fallen asleep."

"Nancy Drew, eat your heart out."

***

We escaped the bugs, and had turned the corner to escape Carmen Dupree's street, when a bright red sedan almost ran straight into us. I yanked the steering wheel to the right and slammed on the brakes just in time to catch a glimpse of my mother as she zoomed past.

My mother?

I would have shouted an obscenity, but Wilson beat me to it. And by the time I thought to check in my rear view mirror, Tessie Hewitt the lead-footed wonder had disappeared from sight.

I pulled over and took some deep breaths until my heart rate returned to normal. Then I hazarded a glance at Wilson.

"That was Tessie," he said.

"She was driving way too fast," I said.

"No shit."

"What was she doing on my side of the road?" I asked.

"What was she doing period? And Louise?"

"What!?"

"Oh yeah, Jessie. Geez Louise was in the passenger seat. She didn't look so good."

"Mother's passengers never do."

***

The good news? By the time we turned around to follow her, my mother was no longer driving.

The bad news? Louise was.

I took off my sunglasses to be sure I wasn't seeing things and watched as my agent ran over a curb—make that two curbs—on Thistle Street.

"She doesn't know how to drive," I said.

"No shit."

I pulled over yet again and watched in horrified fascination as Louise finally managed to bring her car to a halt behind those friendly neighborhood trash cans. I was busy blinking at her from behind my steering wheel, and she was busy blinking at me from behind hers, when Wilson gasped.

I do not believe I had ever heard the man gasp before. I turned to see what else could have startled him, and only then did my mother's whereabouts register—she was making her way up the uneven steps to Carmen's house.

Her flip flops were gone. In fact, she looked downright business-like in one of her old-lady skirt suits, replete with matching pumps. This one must have been her lightest-weight option, short-sleeved and cream-colored. Speaking of business-like, she was clutching a clipboard, which I failed to notice until she reached the door and began knocking.

I emitted a four-letter word, Wilson repeated it with a bit more gusto, and together we stared aghast as Tessie disappeared inside.

I would have closed my eyes and prayed for strength, but the action at Carmen's residence was far too riveting. The same door that had sucked in my mother spewed out three small and screaming children. They commenced running willy-nilly amongst the debris littering the front yard, and I ascertained that some of the debris must have been their toys.

"What the hell?" Wilson whispered in a hoarse voice.

I remembered Louise and waved at her until she looked up from the scene at Carmen's.

"What the hell?" I mouthed.

She lifted both palms from the steering wheel in a gesture of dismay.

"Call her," Wilson said. He fished my cell phone out of my purse and handed it over.

"What the hell?" I offered her by way of greeting.

She waved at me from across the short distance. "Jessica!" she spoke into her own cell phone. "Fancy meeting you here! I love that car! Love, love, love it!"

I glared emphatically, but Geez Louise never notices such subtleties.

"Tessie and I decided to rent a car today, too," she said.

"You don't drive, Louise."

"Of course not! But it was only for this block so I could drop your mother off."

"Whatever happened to reading The Sultan's Secret? And if I recall correctly, my mother was going to take a nap on her porch. Remember?"

"We changed our minds."

"Ask her what they're doing here," Wilson demanded. "Ask her what Tessie's up to."

I did so, and Louise informed me they were sleuthing. "We were curious," she said. "Just like you and that hunky heartthrob of yours, Jessica. You two look adorable by the way! Just like Nancy Drew and Ned Nickerson. Perhaps a tiny tad older than Nancy and Ned. But, Babe! That royal blue roadster really suits you. It matches Wilson's eyes. I can tell from way over here!"

I took a moment to groan, and was well into an extensive rant about my mother's safety and well-being, when she emerged from Carmen's. Still oblivious as to Wilson's and my presence, she spent several minutes discussing who knows what with the children, and then toddled on over to Louise. She smiled brightly and held up her clipboard in what I can only describe as a gesture of triumph.

The good news? Louise scooted over and gave the driver's seat back to Tessie.

The bad news? Louise scooted over and gave the driver's seat back to Tessie.

Chapter 13

Communicating through cell phones and wild gestures, we convinced Tessie the lead-footed wonder to follow us out of the neighborhood. At a moderate speed and without trying to pass me. Miracles do happen.

"I think I saw a restaurant not too far from here," Wilson said as we retraced our route. "It looked okay."

I remembered the place he was referring to. The outdoor bistro wouldn't be quite as pleasant as the breakfast patio at the Wakilulani, but at least it was a giant step up from the spot next to the trash cans on Thistle Street. I glanced at the rear-view mirror, made sure my mother saw what I was doing, and pulled into the parking lot. Tessie parked in the adjacent space without hitting me. Miracle number two.

"Oh, Honeybunch!" she exclaimed as she propelled herself from the driver's seat. "I didn't even see you at Carmen's house until Louise told me. Wasn't that fun?" She clutched her clipboard in one arm, took Wilson's elbow with the other, and they led the way toward the table the hostess was indicating. "I just love sleuthing," she told him. "I could do this all the time."

I glared at Louise, and she offered a semi-guilty shrug. "It's way more fun than surfing," she tried.

"And you got to drive," Mother added over her shoulder. She leaned into Wilson. "Louise has never driven a car before."

"I noticed," he mumbled.

***

"Let me get this straight." Wilson set down his iced tea and glanced back and forth between the two lunatics. "You guys rented a car this morning—right after us—and then drove to Carmen Dupree's house. So Tessie here could interrogate her?"

"Absolutely!" Louise said. "Tessie had the most fantastical plan."

"Always think ahead," Mother said brightly. "That's my motto!"

I gave up on trying to find an Advil in my purse. "Excuse me?"

"Thinking ahead," she repeated and began searching for something in her own purse. "I decided I would conduct a survey in Carmen's neighborhood. All pretend, of course." She looked up, a bottle of Advil in hand, and set it before me. "Jessie, honey," she said, "you should share those with Wilson."

I was divvying up the pills when the waitress arrived to take our lunch order. Once she disappeared, Louise continued, "I volunteered to be the one to actually approach Carmen, but Tessie insisted she should do it."

I frowned at my mother. "And why, pray tell, was that?"

"Because Louise is far too young, and pretty, and memorable. But me?" She waved a dismissive hand. "Bless her heart, Carmen won't ever remember me. I look like every other old lady in the world."

"So Tessie conducted the survey, and I stayed in the getaway car," Louise said.

Wilson reached for another pill while I tried simple logic. "Louise can't drive, Mother. Why would you put her behind the wheel of the getaway car?"

"Silly Jessie! We knew we wouldn't have to skedaddle away that quickly. We weren't robbing a bank, were we?" She tapped her clipboard. "We were just conducting a little survey is all."

Wilson groaned, or maybe whimpered, while my mother explained her pseudo-survey. "I planned on discussing a new senior citizens center for the neighborhood," she began. "But when Carmen answered the door with those children in tow, I quick put on my thinking cap and changed the senior center to a playground."

"Your mother's a genius!" Louise told me, and I wondered when the Advil would kick in.

"Carmen loved the idea of a playground," Mother mused. "And it was a good way to learn about her children."

"Genius, genius, genius!" Louise repeated, but before we could learn more about my mother's genius, the waitress brought our lunch. Tessie spent the next few minutes enjoying her avocado salad, admiring what the rest of us were eating, and making sure we were all happy with our meals.

After assuring her his grilled ahi was the best tuna he ever tasted, Wilson braced himself and asked about Carmen's children. Mother looked down at her notes and read off four names.

Okay, so math has never been my strong suit, but I can count to four. "There were only three children," I argued.

"The youngest isn't walking yet. But Carmen let me take a peek at him. He was having his morning nap."

"That's a small house for a woman with four children." I said.

"And Ki stays there, too, doesn't he? The poor things are very cramped, but I don't believe Carmen can afford a bigger place."

"She mentioned Ki?" Wilson asked.

"Mm-hmm. He's the baby's father."

"She actually told you that?" I asked.

"I keep telling you, Jessica! Your mother is a genius!"

"No," Mother corrected Louise. "But people do confide in old ladies, and Carmen was happy to talk about her children. We were discussing that playground, you see."

The waitress came back to clear our plates and ask about dessert. Everyone declined except my mother. We waited patiently while she discussed her options with the waitress and finally chose the mango custard. She giggled as the waitress left us and confessed that sleuthing must have built up her appetite.

Wilson took a deep breath. "Who's the father of Carmen's other children?"

"Well now, that's where things got interesting," Mother said. "I'm afraid I didn't get a last name, and I didn't learn the name of the little girl's father at all. She's the oldest. But a David-person is the father of the middle two boys."

I sat up straight. "David as in Davy?"

"It is a possibility, isn't it? Look here, Wilson." She tapped her clipboard. "Carmen used to work for Pono Okolo."

"No!" Louise and I said in unison.

Wilson scowled at Tessie's notes. "You actually found out the woman's employment history?"

"It was part of my survey, wasn't it?" She looked up as the waitress came back with the whipped cream-covered dessert. And while the rest of us marveled at her ingenuity and appetite, Tessie continued, "Carmen used to be a waitress at the Wakilulani Gardens. She complained the tips were bad, but I imagine that's how she met Ki."

"Soooo." Louise wiggled an index finger at me. "Carmen would have known Davy."

"And Faye told us Davy was a ladies' man," I mused.

"So Davy could be the father of those boys!" Louise continued.

"And Ki could have stolen Carmen away from Davy." My turn.

"And Davy would have been jealous," Louise added. "I'm seeing a love triangle! Carmen, Davy, and Ki." She used her index finger to draw a triangle in the air.

I squinted at the imaginary triangle and contemplated the chronology. "But then Davy would have killed Ki," I said. "Not the other way around."

"Are you done yet?" Wilson interrupted.

I abandoned Louise's triangle and shrugged. "So, umm, maybe we are getting a bit carried away."

"Maybe?" He looked at my mother. "Why did Carmen leave the Wacky Gardens? She tell you that?"

Mother tapped her trusty clipboard. "Ki asked her to quit once he and Buster inherited the place."

Louise jumped. "So maybe this does work, Wilson! Maybe Ki was jealous. He didn't like Carmen being around her old boyfriend Davy, so he made her quit. But then, maybe he was still jealous, so he killed Davy anyway!"

And maybe Wilson would have given this theory some thought, but my mother interrupted. "No," she said. "According to Carmen, Ki was only thinking of the other staff when he asked her to quit. He didn't want things to look unfair with the two of them so involved—him being the new owner and such."

"Because Ki's so fair-minded?" I said sarcastically.

"Mm-hmm. Carmen says he's a very level-headed fellow."

"Ki Okolo?"

Wilson squeezed my knee and suggested we move on. "Where's Carmen work now?" He pointed to the clipboard. "Did you get that?"

Mother flipped through her notes and pointed to something on the third page. "I'm afraid the poor girl still isn't making a decent living. She drives one of those Beyond the Beach tourist busses."

"The big green busses?" Louise asked. "We saw a few of those this morning!"

"That's right." Mother nodded. "In fact, I caught Carmen just as she was getting ready for work."

I turned to Wilson. "We could go this afternoon."

"What about the surfing lesson?" he asked.

What about it?

I argued that a bus tour with Carmen Dupree was much more important.

"Why?" he asked. "It's not like she's gonna lecture us on the details of her love life. She'll be talking about the volcano."

I was about to argue some more, but Mother reminded me how "disappointed" Chris would be if I stood him up. "He so wants to help you hang ten, Jessie."

Much to my chagrin, even Louise agreed with this faulty reasoning. She suggested we wait until the following day for our Beyond the Beach tour and asked if she might tag along. "I'd love, love, love to see more of this island!" She hazarded a glimpse at my mother. "Tessie drove by things pretty quickly today."

"Oh?" I glared at my mother, and trust me, Tessie Hewitt the mind-reader knew my exact meaning. But she pretended otherwise.

She held up her hands and declined the non-invitation. "No thank you, Honeybunch. Even if I am just another old lady, Carmen would likely recognize me if I climbed onto her bus."

"But how will the rest of us recognize Carmen?" Louise asked. "Did anyone but Tessie get a good look at her?"

Wilson and I shook our heads while my mother again rummaged around in her purse. This time she held up her cell phone.

"Tessie Hewitt, you are a genius!" Louise exclaimed as she reached out. "Genius, genius, genius!"

Wilson looked at me. "She didn't?"

I pointed to the phone Louise was now holding. "Apparently she did."

Louise tossed the phone to Wilson, and I leaned over to get a glimpse of Carmen Dupree, a very attractive brunette.

He looked up at Tessie. "I cannot believe she let you take her picture."

"It was part of my survey, wasn't it?"

He glanced back at the phone. "Genius," he mumbled.

Louise folded her arms and smirked. "Told you so."

Chapter 14

Wilson swatted at my computer. "Where's Russell Densmore when you need him?" he asked.

"Probably enjoying a week without his irritable boss." I leaned back in my chair and pointed to the bougainvillea vines surrounding our porch at Paradise. "I wonder if I could grow those in Clarence."

"Too cold," Wilson said without looking up.

"But they would get lots of sun." I pictured my rooftop garden back home. "I could bring them inside in the winter."

"Yeah, and who's gonna lug the things up and down that stupid stairwell for you?"

"Well, you."

"Good thing they have thorns," he said and banged a bit harder on the keyboard.

I glanced over at the poor innocent machine and suggested we go get Ki. "He's the computer expert, no?"

"That would be great. We could ask him to help us Google his girlfriend."

"Is that what you're doing?" I pretended to glare and leaned over to rescue my computer from further abuse. I might suck at the internet searching thing, but no one could be worse at it than Wilson. I set the machine on the coffee table, cleared the screen, and asked what I was looking for.

"Anything," he said and spouted off an array of topics I might try, including Carmen Dupree, Ki, Buster, and Pono Okolo, Rachel Tate, Bethany Iverson, and the Wacky Gardens in general. "And try Derrick Crowe, too."

Ah, yes. The guy who fell off the face of the earth. Where was Lieutenant Denmore when you needed him? No doubt the computer whiz extraordinaire of the Clarence PD and Wilson's right-hand man would have no problem finding useful and informative clues on the internet. All with one or two deft and efficient clicks of the mouse. But Wilson's extensive list could easily keep the far less skillful me busy for hours, if not days.

I whimpered only slightly and began tapping away while Wilson stood up to pace the porch and complain. "Research!" he said impatiently and spun around at my left. "That's what Densmore's for."

I lifted my eyes and watched him do another lap. "Even Russell Densmore wouldn't be able to concentrate with you jumping around like that," I said. "Make yourself useful and go get me a Pele's Melee."

"We're due for a surfing lesson in half an hour, Jessie."

Alas, no pink drinks. But at least Wilson did sit down, and at least I located the local paper's website. We found Davy Atwell's obituary, informing us the memorial service was postponed until after the holidays.

"Why is there nothing about the family?" I asked, exasperated. "And absolutely no mention of those children? Why, why, why?"

"Jessie," Wilson scolded. "We have no proof any of Carmen's kids are Davy's."

I shrugged and moved on to find the report on the murder. That article was downright miniscule, but it still managed to include a disconcerting quote from Captain Vega, wherein he assured the public that the tourist who committed this terrible crime would be apprehended shortly.

While Wilson muttered a few four-letter words, I continued onward. Or rather, backward. I found Pono Okolo's obituary and a mention of the transfer of the property to Ki and Buster. I even found a few advertisements for the refurbished, remodeled, and renovated Wakilulani Garden Resort. The ads included photos of the newly redecorated bungalows, the new koa tree beds, new kitchen, new dining room, new you name it.

"Altogether uninteresting," I concluded.

"But I bet the history of this place is important." Wilson stood up to resume pacing. "Find out more about the dead grandfather."

I saluted and resumed my efforts as the Hoochie Coochie brothers resumed yet another rehearsal over on the Song of the Sea porch. Despite myself, I just had to listen. What was that?

"Oh, my Lord," I said as it finally hit me. "Is that the "Chattanooga Choo Choo?""

Wilson stopped and perked up his ears. "Don't you need a horn section for that?" he asked and unwittingly began pacing to the beat.

I was repeating my observation that a pink drink would be nice when I actually found something that seemed promising. I gestured to Wilson, and he sat down to read as I clicked on an article from one of the Los Angeles papers. It was over a decade old, but it was an extensive travel piece on the Wakilulani Gardens, and even included a picture of Pono Okolo, his bird, and his chef.

I smiled at the screen. "Look at Bee Bee."

"You found him?" Buster called out as he and Louise raced toward Paradise. Wilson nudged me, and I closed my laptop.

I noticed the binoculars dangling from my agent's neck. "Is he still missing?"

Buster whined and raced off, calling Bee Bee's name.

"We'll take that as a yes?" Wilson asked Louise.

She waved her arms and acted frantic, even by Geez Louise standards. "Faye was right to be concerned this morning! Bee Bee is gone! Vanished! Poof!"

She flung her hands about, making poof-gestures, and managed to bop Buster in the nose as he emerged from a thicket of ferns.

"He's been lost all day," he informed us once he let go of his nose.

We asked for the details of the disappearance and got a lesson on the parrot's routine. Apparently Pono had established the rules decades earlier, and Buster had continued to follow them. As such, Bee Bee was always safely tucked away in his cage every night before the evening dinner rush.

"His cage gets covered up," Louise explained. "Birds need a dark, quiet place like that to sleep. Buster's been teaching me. But the cover was off this morning, and Bee Bee was gone! Poof!" she added, and Buster jumped back a step.

Wilson checked his watch. "And you're only now starting to look?"

"Well yes." Buster hung his head and wrung his hands. "Some mornings Bee Bee gets impatient and lets himself out. He can open the cage door. And he likes to drag the night cover around the balcony."

"So maybe his disappearance isn't that unusual?" I asked.

"But not for this long, Jessica!" Louise flapped her arms, and Buster jumped back yet again. "He's run away! Flown the coop!" With that, she was off and running, scurrying around the perimeter of our porch, her binoculars poised at every tree, shrub, and flower.

Meanwhile Buster became engrossed with something at his feet. He bent down to pluck a few tiny weeds between the stepping stones.

"Bee Bee, Buster!" Louise shouted as she rounded the porch.

He jumped to attention, dropped the weeds, and hastened off toward the ukulele players, all the while calling his bird's name.

Louise caught my eye. "Poof!" she said and disappeared in the opposite direction.

***

"Heebie jeebies," Wilson said firmly when he saw the look I gave him. He pointed past the manicured garden, and I wrinkled my nose at the jungle beyond Paradise.

"I suppose we would have to go off the beaten path if we helped out?"

"They don't need us anyway." He leaned over and opened my computer. "Sounds like Bee Bee's done this before. He'll find his way home."

I remained concerned, but Wilson tapped at the mouse pad until the screen came back on, and I was reminded of another missing creature—Derrick Crowe—who was "talented and edgy" according to that article from the LA newspaper.

"Chef Crowe has the high-strung personality so important to any great artist," we read. "He insists on only fresh, local ingredients."

"He was localvore before the word even existed," I said.

"Davy was cutting-edge, too." Wilson pointed to the passage about the bartender, and we read about the Pele's Melees.

"Containing six fresh fruit juices and untold quantities of vodka and rum, these cocktails are not to be missed. Be sure to admire the little gold umbrellas, and Davy might refill your glass on the house."

I looked up from the screen. "It sounds like this reporter was charmed by all the Wakilulani guys—Bee Bee, Pono, Davy, Derrick."

"Derrick, like in the old chef?" A bathing trunk-clad Chris Rye appeared at the edge of our porch. "Bethany says he disappeared off the face of the earth after Ki fired him"

"Old news," I mumbled under my breath as Chris sat down next to his father.

I closed the computer and asked what else Bethany had said, but Chris was already distracted. He picked up the clipboard on the coffee table and started shuffling through the pages. "This is your mother's?" he asked. "She told me what you guys did today."

Wilson pointed to the notes Tessie had loaned him and explained what she had learned, but Chris was only half-listening. I couldn't blame the kid—he had discovered my mother's drawings tucked away beneath her notes.

"I didn't know Miss Tessie's an artist," he said, and I had to smile. My mother is far too humble to ever claim such status, but she does draw. And as Louise would say, her pictures are fantastical.

"She complains her hand's becoming too unsteady," I said. "But she's still pretty good at pen and ink."

"Really good." Wilson leaned over to once more admire the drawings he had found after our lunch at The Nettles Corner Bistro.

I stood up and hovered behind the two Ryes, and we chuckled at Mother's rendition of Louise's first solo swim.

Chris was also most amused by Tessie's drawing of me fighting the waves and/or my surfboard. And all three of us were charmed by her drawing of Bee Bee playing with the fake daisy on my flip flop.

"He's missing," Wilson said, but Chris had already been informed. He assured us he was on the lookout.

I was busy feeling forlorn about poor Bee Bee when Chris flipped to the next page, and we admired a most forlorn Buster. Mother had certainly captured the man's essence. The younger Okolo brother was wringing his hands and looking altogether anxious about who knows what. No picture of Ki yet, but she had managed a sketch of the Hoochie Coochies and their ukuleles. We listened to a few bars of "String of Pearls" as Chris flipped to the next page.

"There's Dad hanging ten." He pointed. "But he hasn't done that yet."

"Yet," Wilson repeated.

"Mother does most of her drawings from up here," I explained and tapped my temple. "From her memory or imagination."

"And here's me." Chris flipped to the last page.

Wilson groaned. "You need to stop hanging out in bed with old ladies."

"You're one to talk."

I resisted the urge to smack the kid upside the head, and took another gander at my mother's portrayal of Christopher Rye, bare-chested and lounging on her bed, a tall Pele's Melee in hand.

"At least you're wearing shorts," I mumbled.

"Of course I am. You're the Hewitt in charge of pornography."

"Adelé Nightingale is not a pornographer," I said indignantly. "I write romance fiction."

"Yeah, right," father and son said in unison, and Chris dropped the clipboard onto the coffee table.

"Surf's up!" he informed us and bounded down the porch stairs.

I sighed dramatically, reminded Wilson I would require a very large pink drink when the torture was over, and went inside to change into my swimsuit. But Wilson did not follow. In fact, he was still studying Tessie's clipboard when I stepped back onto the porch.

"Aren't you coming?" I asked.

"Go ahead," he said distractedly, his eyes still on the clipboard. "I'll be there in a minute."

Testimony to how much I wanted the lesson to be over and the pink drinks to be flowing, I didn't argue and flip-flopped my unwilling body down to beach.

***

Pink drinks, pink drinks, pink drinks, I thought to myself over and over as Chris kept drilling me to "Paddle, paddle, paddle already!"

He had gotten Mother and me into the water, and we were furiously paddle, paddle, paddling to catch a wave when Louise arrived.

"Bee Bee?" I shouted over the waves and she shook her head no.

No?

Another wave slammed into me. Or more accurately, slammed into my board, which in turn, slammed into my head. Wilson showed up just in time to watch me almost drown. He gave me a thumbs up when I reemerged from the watery depths, and commenced demonstrating how handy upper body strength can be. The show-off barely had to paddle at all before catching a wave. And then another. He wasn't standing up, but he was clearly his son's star pupil.

I was deciding how jealous I should feel when yet another wave slammed my surfboard into the side of my head, and I went under again. Was this fun or what?

I remerged to see Wilson standing up. Up!

"He's up!" I shouted and pointed. "He's hanging ten!"

"Fantastical!" Louise shouted back, and my mother slapped her surfboard in glee as Chris joined Wilson for a father-son surfing-duo moment.

Dare I say, it really was a moment? I gave both of the Ryes my most joyful smile, and they both returned my effort. Both of them.

We decided to quit while we were ahead. Chris helped my mother, Louise and I managed to get ourselves in to shore, and Wilson came in riding another wave and grinning from ear to ear.

We women were too exhausted to congratulate the guy properly, however. More or less in unison, we staggered up the beach, rid ourselves of the stupid surfboards, and dropped, knees first, into the sand. It took us about three seconds to realize kneeling wasn't going to cut it. Again in unison, we twirled ourselves around and got horizontal. The sand in our hair be damned.

I reached out blindly and found my mother's hand. "Are you okay?" I asked.

"Fine," she said in a rather small voice. "But I do believe I'll sleep well tonight."

I reached out my other hand to Louise. "How about you?" I asked.

"Pink drinks," she mumbled. "An enormous vat of them."

"Pink drinks!" Chris said enthusiastically from above us, and I heard his young feet racing off, hopefully toward the tiki bar, as Wilson plopped down somewhere near my feet. I tapped one of his knees with my right foot. "Congratulations, Captain Rye."

He tickled a few of my toes and insisted I would soon be hanging ten myself.

Me hanging ten was about as likely as Delta Touchette sailing off into the sunset with Urquit Snodgrass, but I was too weak to argue.

***

We had managed to sit up, and were even offering my triumphant beau a few super slow-motion high fives, when Chris returned with a drink-laden tray.

Mother offered an enthusiastic thanks as he handed her the first plastic glass of Pele's Melee. "And look at the color, girls. They're pink again."

Louise and I stared at our decidedly pink drinks as Tessie took her first sip. "Oh! Taste them, too," she said. "Ki got the recipe right this time."

Sure enough, the drinks were perfect—Davy Atwell perfect.

"Bethany saw how unhappy you guys were with the drinks last night," Chris explained. "She's up there right now, teaching Ki what to do before the evening rush starts. She says it's getting the guava juice just right. It's what makes them pink."

Wilson lowered his glass. "Bethany Iverson knows how to make a decent pink drink?"

"Decent?" Louise wiggled her Pele's Melee. "Earth to Wilson! Clearly the woman knows a lot more than that. These are perfect!"

No one argued, and as the rest of us enjoyed our beverages, sipping gratefully and emitting the occasional squeak, Chris regaled us with the events of his busy day. Bethany had been thrilled to spend some time with him and had talked non-stop—kind of like Chris himself was doing. He described the coral reef surrounding Halo Beach, which apparently was teeming with sea life.

"I've got to get you geezers snorkeling," he said and turned to his father. "The butterfly fish make those shirts you keep wearing look dull."

Wilson defended his wardrobe only briefly and reminded his son of his main purpose with Bethany. "What did she have to say about the Wacky Gardens" He pointed toward the bungalows and Chris glanced over at Misty Breezes.

"She complained a lot about her boss."

"Who can blame her?" I said. "Ki is impossible."

"No, Jessie. It's Buster that bugs her. Bethany says he makes stupid mistakes."

"Such as?" Wilson asked.

"Well, like he's always wasting time in the garden and not really doing anything. And he hired that Rachel Tate woman Faye was telling us about. Bethany really didn't like Rachel. And here's the dirt." Chris turned to me. "Because I know you live for dirt."

I rolled my eyes and quietly sipped my Pele's Melee.

"The dirt?" Louise reminded him.

"Rachel definitely dated Davy. Remember what Faye said this morning? Well, Bethany definitely knows for sure."

"Intriguing!" Louise said. "Since we now know Carmen Dupree also dated him."

"We're not sure about that," Wilson reminded her, but Louise wasn't listening.

"I'm seeing a love triangle," she said. She passed her glass to my mother and used both hands to draw another of her imaginary triangles in the air.

I thought about this new triangle. "Rachel, Carmen, and Davy?" I asked.

"Exactly, Jessica! Nothing but trouble, I tell you. Nothing, nothing, nothi—"

"What about Bethany?" Wilson interrupted. He held up his Pele's Melee, and we all blinked at the perfectly pink beverage. "Bethany and Davy," he elaborated. "Think about it, people."

Chapter 15

"Bee Bee's a clue." I leaned over Buster Okolo's brand new pool table, took aim, and broke. "I can feel it in my bones," I said as the four ball disappeared. "I'm calling solids, by the way."

Wilson turned around from the game room window in time to see the six ball sink. "Bethany's still up there talking to Ki." He jerked a thumb in the direction of the tiki bar. "Maybe we should be there, too."

I argued that one happy hour spent with Ki Okolo had been plenty for me. "Besides, Wilson, you promised me a game. You know I need to think."

"Jessie always does her best thinking at a pool table." Mother had tiptoed into the room. "Who's winning?" she asked as she closed the door behind her. "And who killed poor Davy Atwell?"

Wilson frowned at the yellow ball as it disappeared and asked Tessie how she knew where to find us.

"Intuition," she answered. "I was about to lie down for a few minutes after my shower. But I just knew Jessie would be in here thinking. You don't mind if I join you?"

We assured her three heads were better than two, and while Wilson took a turn at the table, I stepped over to the window to take a turn at spying on the tiki bar. Sure enough, Bethany was still talking to Ki—showing him something about the blender.

"I'm surprised Louise isn't up there," I said. "But perhaps she's back to Bee Bee hunting."

"Maybe so," Mother said. "She drove off someplace with Buster."

Wilson missed the fourteen ball. "She's driving again?" he asked, and I grabbed the cue stick he had let go of before it fell to the floor.

"Silly Wilson. Buster was driving." Mother clapped as I made the five ball. "They were in his jeep. Now then, who killed Davy?"

"I'm not sure," Wilson said. "But your daughter says Bee Bee."

"That is not what I said." I appealed to my mother. "But I do think his disappearance is significant."

"Oh, absolutely," she agreed. She studied the table and pointed me toward the two ball before sitting down. "Poor Bee Bee witnessed something important the other night."

"The bird?" Wilson remained unconvinced. "But the murder happened out in the parking lot, and Bee Bee was inside, in his cage, covered up." He shook his head in dismay. "And I cannot believe I'm standing here discussing the possibility of a parrot being a viable witness."

"The killer could have spoken to Davy before they moved outside," Mother argued. "Bee Bee could have been listening, even if his cage were covered up. Bless his little heart, he does pick up on things, doesn't he?"

"Exactly." I hit the seven ball off the back bumper and into the side pocket. "Bee Bee might have heard the killer's voice. He might have started repeating something the killer said."

Wilson gave it some thought. "So you're saying the bird needed shutting up. So the murderer killed him."

Mother and I gasped in unison.

"Can't we just say he's been kidnapped?" I asked.

"That's right, Jessie. Let's just say kidnapped." Mother pursed her lips. "I do not believe Bee Bee's dead."

"So we think Bee Bee was kidnapped." Finally, Wilson was catching on. "But why didn't this happen yesterday? Bee Bee had all day to inform on the killer. If," he emphasized the if, "the bird is that smart."

"Maybe the killer didn't realize Bee Bee was a witness until later," Mother suggested. "It is a rather far-fetched notion, isn't it?"

"Or maybe the killer had a hard time catching him," I said and sunk the three ball. "Bee Bee flies, remember."

I called the eight ball and was about to take aim when Wilson asked if I planned on giving him any chance whatsoever. I took a haphazard shot, told him to have at it, and went to sit with Tessie. It was only then that I noticed the background music. The Hoochie Coochies, but of course.

I watched several balls disappear and wracked my brains to identify the tune wafting toward us from Song of the Sea.

"Highland Cathedral," Mother answered my unasked question.

I groaned out loud. "Don't you need bagpipes for that one?"

"They have a fascinating repertoire, don't they?" she said as Wilson took aim at the twelve. "I can't wait until the luau tonight."

I stifled another groan and asked if she thought the Coochie brothers might be involved in the murder.

"No, I don't think so. They're such nice boys."

"They're close to my age, Mother."

"And you're such a nice girl," she said defiantly and patted my knee.

Wilson asked her about Bethany as he took aim at the ten. He missed the shot and looked up. "Is she a nice girl?"

"She's a smart cookie," Mother answered. "And isn't she clever to teach Ki how to mix Davy's Pele's Melees?

Wilson took my seat as I stood up to finish the game. "I don't want to scandalize you," he told my mother. "But I get the impression there was only one way for a woman to get that recipe out of Davy."

"You mean sex?" she asked as an ear-piercing scream interrupted my shot at the eight ball.

Before I could even drop the cue stick, Wilson was out the door.

Mother and I followed. We had made it to the lobby and were rounding the Christmas tree when a young woman in a chef's uniform emerged from the dining room.

She stopped short when she saw us. "Call the police!" she shrieked and fainted into Wilson's arms.

***

"Call the police!" Wilson ordered me as if I needed reminding.

He knelt down to place the woman—Makaila Isiano, presumably—onto the lobby floor. He checked for a pulse, and headed toward the dining room.

Mother ran to the woman, I ran to the phone behind the counter, and Ki and Bethany ran in from outside.

"Makaila!" Bethany screamed and leapt across the room.

I dialed 911.

While I listened impatiently to the ring tone on the other end, I caught a glimpse of Ki. Unlike the rest of us, he stood stock still. He slowly turned his head toward me, and for some reason I felt compelled to tell him it wasn't our fault.

"What isn't your fault?" the dispatcher asked.

"Makaila Isiano," I said into the phone. "She's fainted!" I added and explained the situation as best I could.

My best wasn't very good, however, since I really didn't know the situation, even after Wilson emerged from the dining room, and even after Makaila came to. Wilson held his hands, palms up, and announced he couldn't see what the problem was, either in the dining room or in the kitchen behind it.

We looked at Makaila, who had her head in my mother's lap, and her hand in Bethany's. Speechless and shaking, evidently she wasn't capable of enlightening us either.

Meanwhile the dispatcher continued giving me a hard time. "You want us to send the cops out because someone fainted?" she asked and became even more belligerent when I mentioned that Makaila had woken up. "What's the problem then? You need an ambulance?"

I didn't think so. I tried reasoning that Makaila was clearly upset by something, and had told us to call the police.

"Is this a crank call?"

"No, this is not a crank call! The chef wants the police. And considering the recent murder on the Wakilulani premises, it seems only fit—"

Wilson took the phone from me. "Tell Vega to get his ass over here," he ordered and hung up without further ado.

***

"Where's your son?" Ki asked Wilson.

"Where's your brother?" Wilson asked Ki.

"That's the million dollar question, Sherlock." Ki pointed to Makaila. "The dinner rush is about to begin, my stupid chef's sprawled out under the stupid Christmas tree, and my stupid brother's gone AWOL."

"Makaila is not stupid," Bethany argued as she and Tessie got the poor woman into a chair.

Makaila was beginning to focus again. Everyone watched as she reached out, took her chef's toque from my mother's hands, and carefully adjusted it back onto her head. With her headgear only slightly askew, she looked up at our expectant faces. "The knife is back," she said quietly.

"What!?" we said loudly.

"The butcher knife," she elaborated and pointed a shaky finger in the direction of the kitchen. "It's in there. It's back in its slot in the butcher block and everything."

Ki muttered a four-letter word and started toward the dining room, but Wilson reached out and grabbed him. "No one goes in the kitchen until Vega gets here."

"Oh? And what about you, Sherlock? Weren't you just in there?"

Chapter 16

Captain Vega slammed the bagged and tagged butcher knife onto the patio table and sat down. "Where's your son?" he demanded.

Wilson stared at the murder weapon. "I don't know," he said.

"What do you mean, you don't—"

"I know." Mother raised her hand to interrupt. "He's at Emi Ulii's place. She's such a lovely girl, isn't she? Chris is taking her to the luau tonight." Tessie smiled serenely. Indeed, she seemed completely unconcerned that, along with Wilson and me, she, too, had been ordered to have a seat to discuss the knife incident with Captain Vega.

But Ki, Bethany, and Makaila? Vega had seen fit to dismiss those three after ten whole seconds of questioning. Apparently the needs of the Wakilulani Gardens dinner crowd were deemed far more urgent than some silly old murder investigation. The Hoochie Coochie Brothers were also off the hook. They claimed their presence was needed down at the luau, and Vega had shooed them away, too.

Vega directed his frown at me. "And where's your friend? The loud-mouthed redhead?"

I folded my arms and glared. "I understand Louise went off somewhere with Buster. You know, Captain Vega? Buster Okolo, the co-owner of this place? He's missing also." I pointed to The Big House, and the four of us watched the early bird diners stream in.

"You sure you want people traipsing in and out of there right now?" Wilson asked Vega.

"Shut up, Sherlock," he snapped and delved into a bitter diatribe, scolding Wilson for daring to enter the kitchen himself. "How much of my investigation do you plan to screw up?

Wilson stared at the stupid cop until he saw a slight squirm. "You want me to shut up, or tell you what happened?"

"Talk!"

Wilson did so. Valiantly ignoring Vega's many and assorted grunts of disapproval, he explained the basics of Makaila Isiano's rather dramatic reaction to finding the murder weapon.

"And you took it upon yourself to run into the kitchen and take care of things. Is that it?"

Wilson raised an eyebrow. "That was the plan. I assumed someone was hurt. I'm trained to help in emergencies."

"You're trained to do nothing on this island, you hear me." Vega leaned forward and pointed an index finger in Wilson's face.

Wilson slapped it away. "Point that at me one more time, and I'll twist it off."

"You wiped it clean, didn't you?"

"Excuse me?"

"The murder weapon," Vega clarified. "You told your son to return it where it belongs and get the hell out of here."

"You're an idiot, you know that? Anyone and his brother has had access to that kitchen. On the night of the murder, and ever since."

Ignoring simple logic, Vega continued his fantasy. "But you didn't trust Christopher to do it right, did you? So when the cook gets all upset about finding it, you take the first opportunity to run into her kitchen and cover your kid's tracks."

While the two men snarled at each other, I turned to my mother. "If only Adelé Nightingale had as much imagination as this guy." I tilted my head toward Vega, and Mother giggled.

Vega redirected his snarl at me. "Adelé Nightingale," he said. "You of all people should understand what's happened here."

"Oh?"

"Oh yeah, lady. I've been looking into you. This is just like those books you write."

"It is?" Evidently Wilson was as confused as I.

Vega shook his head at our obtuseness. "The knight in shining armor crap? Christopher Rye wanted to protect his new girlfriend's honor, so he killed Davy Atwell. He was trying to prove himself to Emi Ulii."

"Silly Captain Vega." Mother was also shaking her head. "Adelé Nightingale's heroes don't murder people. Haven't you read her books?"

Vega failed to respond, which Mother took as a no.

"Well then, let me recommend A Deluge of Desire," she said. "Men tend to enjoy that one the best, you see. But of course my favorite is Temptation at Twili—"

"You can cut the senile old lady act," Vega interrupted.

A very long moment of stunned silence ensued until Wilson finally spoke. "You want to apologize." It was not a question.

Vega frowned at my mother. "I'm sorry," he said. "You're not senile, but you're not all that innocent, either."

"I beg your pardon?"

"Leon Cue-It Hewitt," he announced proudly, perhaps under the impression that the rest of us needed reminding about who my mother's husband, and my father, had been.

"Dear Leon." Mother sighed at some distant memory. "Now there was a knight in shining armor."

"He was a pool shark, lady."

"That was one of his talents, yes."

Wilson cleared his throat. "What's your point, Vega?"

"My point is—the whole Hewitt family is a bunch of criminals. Pool sharks and pornographers." He curled his lip and pointed that index finger at my face. "Some of them are both."

Wilson reached over to help me out, but my mother beat him to it. She slapped Vega's hand away. "My daughter is not a pornographer," she said indignantly. "She writes romance fiction. Jessie can't help it if she's just better at it than everyone else."

Vega might have intended to argue, but my most loyal fan was on a roll. "You really should read A Deluge of Desire," she continued. "It would do you a world of good."

I bit my lip to keep from laughing out loud, but Wilson wasn't quite so diplomatic.

Vega considered his response, but must have decided he was no match for Tessie. He turned to Wilson instead. "I've been looking into to your history also," he said.

"Oh goody." Wilson stopped laughing. "What do you got?"

"I got all your dirty little secrets. And you've got a history of protecting the people you care about."

"Damn straight."

"Darling, darling, darling," Mother interjected with a fond smile aimed at my beau.

I was once again biting my lip when Vega reached out and actually poked me in the bicep. "He protected you from a murder rap."

I straightened my face and stared at the finger until Vega reeled it in.

"You know about Dianne Calloway?" he asked.

I blinked twice, and an "Umm" was my less than brilliant answer.

"Ask your boyfriend about her," Vega ordered. "He protected her, too. But that didn't quite work out. He—"

"What does any of this have to do with Davy Atwell's murder?" Wilson interrupted.

"Hello, Sherlock. This time it's not a woman you're protecting. It's your son."

"You're an idiot, you know that?" Wilson didn't wait for an answer. "First of all, if I was protecting Chris, why the hell did I get you over here tonight? Your stupid dispatcher was all set to ignore us."

Vega grunted.

"And have you even bothered asking yourself why the murder weapon was put back in the kitchen? Don't you think that's a little odd?"

Vega glanced at the murder weapon, but still had no response.

Wilson sat back. "In case you haven't noticed, Vega, the murderer's gone off the deep end. We're looking for a lunatic."

"We?"

Luckily, Wilson could pretend not to hear that because his cell phone rang. He took it out of his pocket, and I caught a glimpse of a very slight grin as he checked the number.

"Who's that?" Vega eyed the phone. "Your son? Answer it."

Wilson put the phone back in his pocket and waited for it to stop ringing. "I don't take orders from you."

Vega turned his attention back to me. "And what about you?" he asked.

"I'm afraid Jessie doesn't take orders very well either," Mother answered for me.

Vega closed his eyes, perhaps praying for strength. "I meant," he said as he opened them again, "why did you tell my dispatcher it wasn't your fault?"

"Excuse me?"

"Your 911 call. You point blank said 'It's not our fault.'" Vega made air quotes. "Who were you trying to protect?"

I looked out into the gathering gloom of the evening and considered my answer. "I wasn't trying to protect anyone. I was simply stating a fact." I gestured to Wilson and my mother. "Here we were, trying to help poor Makaila. And what was Ki Okolo doing? Making ugly faces and acting like it was all our fault." I shrugged. "My comment was directed at him, not your dispatcher."

Vega studied me with unadulterated disdain. "You people might think there's strength in numbers," he said eventually. "But I'm warning you, I will get to the bottom of this. And when I do, why do I know your precious Christopher Rye will be there?"

"Because you're an idiot," Wilson answered, and Vega practically levitated out of his seat.

Once again my mother tried to diffuse the tension. "Jessie has a theory that may help catch the real killer," she interjected.

"Mother!" I cringed.

"Jessie thinks there was a witness," she continued. "Go ahead, Honeybunch." She gave me a nudge. "Tell Captain Vega your idea."

I took a deep breath, ignored Vega's less than encouraging snarl, and suggested Bee Bee might have heard something important that night. I waved at my mother. "We think it may explain why he's disappeared. We think the killer's kidnapped him."

"Let me get this straight," Vega said. "Davy Atwell's dead, and you're worrying about the bird?"

"You bet your boots we're worried about the bird!" That was Louise.

We looked up to see her and Buster rushing over from the direction of the parking lot.

"Where have you been?" I asked, but Louise wasn't paying any attention to me.

She grabbed a stack of papers out of Buster's arms and handed them to a rather startled Captain Vega.

"I am so glad you're here!" she told him. "So, so, soooo glad!" She pointed down to the fliers she had given him, and I caught a glimpse of a full-color photograph of Bee Bee with the caption "Missing Parrot! Reward! Reward! Reward!" printed beneath.

"You need to get your people on this right away," Louise was instructing Vega. "We need those fliers put up everywhere. Bee's Bee is lost!"

Vega stood up and shoved the fliers back at Louise. "Find your own damn bird. I'm looking for Christopher Rye."

He flashed Wilson one last snarl, grabbed the bag with the knife, and probably had every intention of making a dramatic exit. But instead he tripped over Buster's kneeling form and fell flat onto the patio.

Buster the ever-vigilant was down there weeding. He looked over from his handful of leaves and shoots and caught sight of the knife Vega had dropped. "You found it?" he asked.

Wilson's phone rang again, and this time he answered it. He stood up, stepped over Buster and Vega, and started up the hill towards Paradise. "You found it?" he asked.

***

"Found what?" I asked as I tried catching up with him. "Who are you talking to?"

Wilson made it to our porch before turning around. He told whoever was on the line to hang on a minute and glanced past me down the hill, presumably to check if we were out of earshot. "Why don't you walk your mother over to the luau?" he suggested.

"Why don't you tell me what you're up to?"

"I will." He tapped at his phone. "But first I need to find out, myself."

I squinted at the phone as he assured me he'd meet me at the luau in a jiffy.

"A jiffy? Those shirts you're wearing are starting to affect your brain, Captain Rye." I pointed to the altogether ridiculous specimen he had chosen for the evening—this one boasting some sort of insect theme in purples, greens, and golds.

He twirled his free index finger as if to turn me around. I mumbled something about my ever-cooperative nature, turned, and called out to my mother and Louise to wait up.

Indeed, everyone was dispersing from the patio as I retraced my steps. Buster dropped his handful of weeds, reminded Vega about the Wakilulani dinner crowd, and scurried toward The Big House. Vega grabbed the murder-weapon baggie and also stood up. He glanced after Buster for the briefest of moments, warned us he'd be back—Arnold-Schwarzenegger style—and headed toward the parking lot.

I glanced at my mother and Louise.

"Luau bound!" Mother squealed and wiggled her hips in a hula-esque fashion.

Chapter 17

"Buster and I were getting nowhere!" Louise informed us as we wended our way toward the Holiday Hula. "And you know how impatient I can be, Jessica. But!" She stopped and pointed to the Pacific. "Our latest surfing fiasco must have joggled my brain."

"You put your thinking cap on?" Mother asked.

"I did! I told Buster we need help. And he asked me who, or how, or what, and it came to me in a flash." Louise held up her stack of fliers to show us Bee Bee's picture. "This flier! Buster found the photo in Pono's old files, and then we drove down to the copier place and put these together."

She lifted her stack of fliers aloft, and the winds on Halo Beach almost grabbed them away from her. She twirled around to keep control and noticed some other people roaming down the beach. Off she ran, shouting something about the missing bird, and waving one of her fliers.

"I hope she has some luck," I said to my mother as Louise made yet another detour toward another group of startled beachcombers. "She'll be heartbroken if, well, you know."

"Bee Bee is not dead," Mother said firmly. She stepped forward as Louise returned to us. "Louise, honey," she said brightly. "Where did you and Buster put your posters?"

"We drove all over, Tessie. Here, there, and everywhere! This island is beyond fantastical. Oh!" Louise stopped again. "Speaking of fantastical—we drove past Davy Atwell's house."

"No!" Mother and I said in unison.

"Yes!" she insisted. "Buster made sure to point it out to me. The place is a mansion. Faye was absolutely right this morning. Davy Atwell was rich, rich, rich!"

"And yet he bartended at the Wakilulani Gardens?" I asked. "It doesn't make sense."

"But I think he enjoyed his job, Honeybunch. Davy was a sociable fellow, wasn't he?"

"Sociable with women." I looked at Louise. "You didn't by any chance ask Buster about Carmen Dupree and Davy?"

Louise's face dropped. "We were so busy talking about Bee Bee, I forgot all about our other mystery."

Well, darn.

"But!" Louise perked up. "Maybe I did learn something after all! Buster told me Davy's house is a stop on the Beyond the Beach tour. Supposedly they talk about the architecture of the place. And there's a lot of architecture to talk about."

"Oh dear," Mother said. "Poor Carmen has to give tourists lessons about her old beau's home?"

"I guess so."

"Okay, so think, Louise." I related the murder weapon incident she had missed and emphasized how Captain Vega was becoming more and more convinced of Christopher Rye's guilt. "Did Buster tell you anything else that might help us?"

Louise pursed her lips, deep in thought, and we actually walked for a few minutes in complete silence.

"Buster and I discussed the new Pele's Melees," she finally offered. "I mentioned how pleased we are with Ki's latest version, and Buster said he hopes he can get his brother to stick around the Wakilulani for a while."

She sighed dramatically, clearly exasperated with herself. "I'm sorry, Jessica. I simply am not the fantastical sleuth that you are."

"No one compares with my Jessie," Mother agreed.

"Thank God." You guessed it—the ever-charming Christopher Rye had caught up with us.

I waved a greeting to Emi and asked Chris if he had seen Captain Vega recently. "Did he tell you about the knife?"

Emi tilted her head toward her escort. "Why do you think he's in such a good mood?"

***

"Nice shirt, Dad," Chris continued the sarcastic flow as Wilson joined us in the Holiday Hula queue.

"This is my favorite so far." Rye Senior smiled proudly and tapped at one of the colorful bugs on his chest as Louise shoved a flier into his other hand.

"I already know what Bee Bee looks like," he reminded her. "You should give these to the people who don't."

She swept the flier out of Wilson's hand and ran off to accost some other would-be luau attendees.

Mother turned to Emi. "I've never been to a luau before."

Emi patted her shoulder. "We'll have fun, Mrs. Hewitt. I think you'll like it."

"I'm sure I will," Mother agreed. "I'm sure we all will. Oh, and that reminds me." She reached into her purse and pulled out her credit card. "This is my treat," she announced as Louise re-joined us. "It's my Christmas present. Let's have a marvelous time, shall we? We'll listen to the Coochie Brothers and let our cares just slip away. Don't they sound good, though?"

Masochist that I am, I perked up my ears to better hear the uninspired strumming of the Hoochie Coochies as they sang "Camptown Races." Some people in line behind us already seemed to be having the marvelous time Mother mentioned, doo-da-ing along at the appropriate intervals.

I whimpered only slightly and thanked her for her generosity before whispering to Wilson, "What are we going to do for Christmas gifts? Louise told me the other day, she's taking the gang on a whale-watching tour Christmas day, Mother's doing the luau, Chris the surfboards." I cringed. "What about us?"

"What about us? You mean you don't have a plan?"

"You mean you do?"

He grinned and told me he'd fill me in later.

"Who was on the phone?" I asked, but before he could answer we were distracted by the woman selling Holiday Hula tickets to my mother. She was wearing a grass skirt and—I swear to God—a bra made from coconut shells.

"Candy Poppe should try selling those at Tate's," Wilson said.

"Candy!" I exclaimed, recollecting my neighbor the bra-saleswoman and her temporary charges. "We need to call Candy and find out how the cats are doing."

Wilson reminded me of the time difference, and I agreed to wait until morning as the luau-lady adorned us with leis. We women also were given flower garland crowns to wear for the evening, and thus we entered the fray.

***

Always one who thrives on the fray, Louise began mingling immediately, distributing her Bee Bee fliers throughout the crowd while the rest of us took a moment to get acclimated.

The scene was everything my mother could have hoped for and more. A section of the beach had been cordoned off with tiki torches and an array of hanging paper lanterns, but no one could miss where the action was—the enormous stage. Some drummers and a guy playing a string instrument I am not familiar with had joined the Hoochie Coochie Brothers. And a group of about twenty young hula-outfitted women took to the stage and started dancing to a tropical-sounding tune.

Wilson found my mother a chair, and she sat down to watch the show as a bare-chested young man literally bounced onto the stage in front of the dancers. He, too, wore a grass skirt, and—what was startling indeed—he carried four huge torches. Apparently unconcerned about the fire hazard, he commenced juggling the torches to the complete delight of my mother.

Dare I say, it really was a mesmerizing spectacle? After emitting a few gasps of my own, I made sure to thank Tessie again for her early Christmas gift. I glanced around at the vast crowd. "It looks like the entire island is here tonight."

"Everyone comes out for the Holiday Hula at Halo," Emi said and turned to Chris. "It's fun being a spectator for a change. I'm usually one of them." She gestured toward the stage, and Chris's mouth dropped open.

"Don't tell me you're a hula dancer?" he asked and took an appreciative gander at Emi's figure. Delta Touchette, eat your heart out.

"Pretty much all girls around here learn a little hula," Emi explained. "I was in Hula Club in high school. Kind of nerdy, huh?"

"No!" Mother objected. "You must be very talented to put on a show like this." She lifted both arms to the stage, where the women had been joined by a group of men, and all were in the midst of demonstrating the proper technique of a Limbo dance.

"You can do that?" Chris asked, clearly intrigued by all the writhing going on. One by one, the dancers sashayed their way across the stage and beneath the Limbo pole while the juggler did the fire-juggling thing above them.

"Yeah, I can do that." Emi sighed. "I probably shouldn't tell you this, seeing how you spent the whole day with her, but so can Bethany Iverson. And Makaila. They were in Hula Club, too."

Okay, now this was intriguing, but Wilson beat me to the questioning. "You girls went to school together, right?" he asked.

"They were two years ahead of me."

"You're all friends then?" I asked, wracking my brains as to how a high school hula club connection could have any bearing on Davy's murder.

"To be honest, I never really liked Makaila," Emi said. "She's always been so melodramatic."

I thought about the fainting spell scene at The Big House. "She did seem quite upset today," I agreed.

"What about Bethany?" Wilson asked. "Were you friends with her?"

"Everyone liked Bethany. She's so smart. And she was president of just about everything—Student Body, Hula Club, Kekipi Club—"

"Kekipi?" Chris interrupted, and Emi explained it was the hiking club.

She pointed to Wilson. "But remember your father likes hiking, too. You don't need to be taking Bethany up the mountain."

Chris grinned and announced he was starving. He grabbed Emi's hand, and they set off to join the line for the buffet table. But Emi thought of something and came back to us. "Can we bring you a plate?" she asked my mother.

Mother said that would be lovely, but insisted she was in no hurry to eat, and resumed watching the show.

Most disconcertingly, it had gotten to that inevitable part where the dancers were swarming down the stage steps and enlisting hapless audience members to join them onstage. Of course my mother jumped up to volunteer. And I ask you, what performer could resist the adorable, enthusiastic, and far too-energetic-for-her-age Tessie Hewitt?

"I've never done the hula dance before!" she told the handsome Hawaiian who swept her away toward the stage. Before I knew it, Wilson was whisked off by an equally attractive hula girl. Oh, good Lord, and then one of the dancers zeroed in on yours truly.

I closed my eyes and prayed for strength, but that only meant that I was being dragged blindly onto the stage. I decided I'd better open my eyes and warned my young partner the only dancing I'm any good at is rocking to The Beatles. But apparently my hula tutor didn't know who The Beatles were. He smiled broadly and assured me I would "do fine."

Yeah, right.

***

Luckily the stage was incredibly crowded. I was elbowing my way to the back of the assembled amateurs when the Hoochie Coochie Brothers spotted me. By the excited looks on their faces I deduced that I was about to be embarrassed.

Needless to say, I was correct. Hal, or maybe it was Cal, stopped the music.

"What a treat!" he exclaimed into the microphone. "Our neighbors from the Wakilulani Gardens have joined us." He pointed us out—Tessie, Wilson and me—and the crowd cheered. Clearly these people had never seen me dance.

Encouraged by the Hoochie Coochie Brothers, the pros on stage worked on parting the rest of the amateurs so that the three of us were up front and center. The music resumed, and before you could say aloha, we were hula-ing.

Some of us were hula-ing better than others, of course. Wilson, for instance, seemed a master at the skill. Perhaps that ludicrous shirt he was wearing inspired him. And my mother? Cute as hell, let me tell you. At one more or less frenzied point Tessie performed a rather remarkable hula-pirouette thingy, and my beau the ham executed some sort of Hawaiian-looking jig around her. The crowd went wild.

As for my performance? About the best I can say is at least I wasn't wearing a coconut bra.

And eventually I was released from the embarrassment. Louise was there to catch me as I staggered off the stage. "You were fantastical," she insisted, but I noticed the complete lack of exclamation point at the end of that sentence.

While I gathered the remains of my dignity, Wilson took a triumphant bow and hopped off the stage to join us. Emi and Chris came back with dinner for my mother, who somehow managed to pull away from an adoring throng of fans to reclaim her seat.

"You did great," Emi told Tessie as she set the plate before her. "It's like you belonged in Hula Club your whole life."

"But you're worse at dancing than you are at surfing," Chris the ever-charming was quick to inform me.

Wilson tapped me on the shoulder. "Mai Tai?" he suggested.

I nodded curtly and headed toward the bar. Pink or otherwise, I needed a drink.

***

Pink or otherwise, those first Mai Tais disappeared rather quickly. Wilson had left in search of refills when a woman about my age approached me. "Jessie, right?" she asked. "You're one of the people Chris Rye is teaching to surf?"

"One of the geezers," I clarified and held out my hand. "Jessie Hewitt."

"Gail Fazio," she said, and we shook hands. "I own Folly Rentals. Chris pointed you out to me when you were up there." She tilted her head towards the stage, where things had settled down considerably. The Hoochie Coochie Brothers had the entire expanse to themselves and were regaling the crowd with a medley of what I assumed were luau classics.

I turned back to Ms. Fazio and thanked her for renting us such nice surfboards. "Although I'm afraid I'm not much better at surfing than I am at hula-ing," I added.

"But you are a good sport."

"Did Chris say that?" I asked doubtfully.

She again gestured toward the stage. "I could see that for myself."

I told Gail I wasn't too concerned about hula-ing ever again. "But unfortunately Chris isn't going to give up on me so easily." I grimaced. "He actually expects me to hang ten."

Gail patted my hand and was giving me a few tips for the surfing-challenged older woman when Wilson returned. He handed me my drink, and I introduced him to my new friend.

"May I get you one?" he asked and held up a Mai Tai.

"I better not. I have to work tomorrow. But I can understand why you guys need a few of those." She pointed to Wilson's drink.

"I take it you know about Davy Atwell?"

"Oh yes. And about Vega. And about your son's involvement. I'm sorry your vacation is turning out so bad."

"Chris didn't do it," Wilson said firmly.

"I know that. But you folks need to understand—Vega always goes after a tourist."

"Why is that?" I asked indignantly. "It seems like everyone around here hates tourists."

"Not everyone, Jessie. Some of us know who's buttering our bread. Which reminds me." She waved at the buffet table. "Have you guys eaten?"

We hadn't, so Gail guided us to the buffet line where the main attraction was the kalua pig—a pig baked underground, as she explained. "It's standard luau fare," she told us, but she suggested we try the other dishes also. Thus the three of us filled our plates with pork, grilled pineapple, mango salsa, tomato couscous, sweet and sour cabbage, roasted breadfruit, the works. Then we found seats as far from the stage and as separated from the crowd as possible.

Before sitting down, I scanned the luau for my mother. She and Louise were doing fine, talking to some strangers and missing me not at all. Chris and Emi were nowhere in sight.

I took my seat and tuned in to Gail and Wilson's conversation as they continued the discussion of tourists versus locals. Not too surprisingly, Ki Okolo's name came up.

"He really hates tourists," Gail said. "It all goes back to the accident. You guys know about that?"

Wilson summarized what we knew about how and why Ki and Buster had ended up living with their grandfather. "But what did tourists have to do with it?"

"A carload of them ran the Okolos off the road at Ka Pua Cliffs." Gail shook her head. "It's a really treacherous stretch of road." She speared a piece of mahi-mahi. "Ki was driving."

"What!?" Wilson and I shouted in unison, and the poor woman dropped her fork.

"It's awful, isn't it?" she asked.

"It explains why he hates the Wakilulani Gardens," I suggested.

"You got it, Jessie. Tourists killed the kid's parents, and then he and his brother had to move into a tourist trap. It didn't help that Ki had to change high schools his senior year, or that he had to leave cute little Iwatanii Town behind and move to a whole different island."

"I take it this Iwatanii place isn't a tourist trap?" Wilson asked.

"No," she said. "It's way off the beaten path. But it's a charming place if you ever get over to The Big Island."

"Iwatanii Town," I repeated. Where had I heard that name before?

But I would have to think about it some other time since Gail Fazio was still discussing the Okolos. Apparently Folly Rentals had been a fixture on Halo Beach almost as long as the Wakilulani Gardens, and Gail had been friends with Pono Okolo for decades. And she had known Ki and Buster ever since they came to live at Halo Beach.

"It sounds silly, but I'm beginning to think those guys are jinxed," she said. "Buster's never been the smartest coconut in the grove, but even so, no one deserves his bad luck."

We discussed the recent troubles at the Wakilulani, namely Davy Atwell's murder. But she didn't seem to know anything more than we did. We moved on to the Rachel Tate mystery, and Gail agreed we were probably on a wild goose chase.

"I understand Buster was rather smitten with Rachel," I said.

"Smitten?" Gail asked. "I guess so. He had a crush on her, and she had a crush on Davy. What a mess."

"And she and Davy were together, right?" Wilson said. "At least for a while?"

"It wouldn't surprise me. Whatever her work ethic, Rachel was darn cute."

"What do you know about Bethany Iverson?" he asked.

"A great work ethic there. The Okolo brothers did something right for a change by hiring her."

"You have any idea how she got hold of Davy Atwell's pink drink recipe?"

Gail's face dropped, and Wilson nodded.

"Yep," he said. "The Pele's Melees are once again flowing at the Wacky Gardens. Thanks to Bethany."

Gail considered this news. "She must have had sex with him." She shook her head. "But no," she argued with herself. "Bethany's way too smart for that." She sat back and scowled, perhaps pondering Bethany's intelligence.

"What about Derrick Crowe?" I asked. "He's also a mystery, correct?"

"You got it, Jessie. The guy's fallen off the face of the earth."

"Crowe's been located," Wilson said, and Gail and I both jumped.

"Wilson!" I scolded. "What have you been up to?"

He might have answered me, but the luau people had other plans. As the party began to wrap up, grass-skirted men and women got busy removing the dining tables. They literally took ours out from under us as a conga line started weaving around the luau arena.

With the Hoochie Coochies leading the way, people of various ages and levels of sobriety congaed past us. Some carried Mai Tais in their free hands, some carried tiki torches, and some carried each other. The word bacchanal came to mind, despite the fact that everyone was singing a vaguely Hawaiian version of Jingle Bells. Oh yes—and a few people carried sleigh bells.

Chris and Emi danced by without even noticing us, but Mother and Louise did see us. They waved us into formation, and someone handed Wilson a tiki torch. He brandished it aloft as I grabbed onto his hips.

Chapter 18

Everyone in their right mind went home after the Holiday Hula. But Wilson and I are not in our right minds. First of all, we were still on that wild goose chase to track down Rachel Tate. And lest anyone should forget, the Shynomore Shirt Shop is a twenty-four-hour operation.

Louise promised to get Tessie back to the Wakilulani Gardens safely, so we bid them goodnight and headed down the beach.

"What did Russell Densmore find out?" I yawned expansively and stumbled a bit.

Wilson reached out to steady me. "How do you do that?" he asked.

"Do what?"

"Know who I've been talking to. Intuition, right?"

Actually no. This time I had relied on something much more mundane—simple deductive reasoning. First of all, Wilson had been late to our surfing lesson that afternoon. Why? Because he was busy calling Lieutenant Densmore—giving his right-hand man orders from half-way around the world.

"He called you back while we were talking to Vega," I continued deducing. "And when you didn't answer, he called you again. Which can only mean Russell got something good." I stopped and turned. "He found Derrick Crowe, didn't he?"

"Yep. Crowe's working at a culinary school in northern California. Densmore called him."

"You need to give that man a raise, Wilson."

"Cops never get raises. But listen to this, Jessie—Crowe swore up, down, and sideways it was Buster who fired him. Not Ki, like Bethany told Chris."

"So she lied?" I asked.

"That, or she doesn't know the whole story. But whoever fired him, Crowe wasn't happy about it. Said he didn't deserve to be treated like that by an Okolo after all the years he worked for Pono."

"Did Russell ask about the money he owes people?"

"Crowe denied it. Claims that's why he left Hawaii—to get away from the rumors."

"Did Russell believe him?"

"No, but he let it slide. He didn't want to alienate the guy in case we need to talk to him again." Wilson stopped and caught my eye. "Which we may."

"Oh?"

"Derrick Crowe is the father of Carmen Dupree's oldest child."

"What!?"

"Densmore's identified the fathers of all her kids."

"What?" I said again, increasingly incredulous at the amazing Russell Densmore's remarkable research skills. "How did he do that?"

"Birth records, hospital records, who knows? Densmore's way better at the internet than you are."

"No kidding. But this had to be more than basic research. Did he hack into stuff illegally?"

"You want to hear this or not?"

I took the low road and said I did.

"Crowe's the father of Carmen's oldest, and you and Louise were right—Davy Atwell is the father of numbers two and three."

"And Ki Okolo is the baby's father." I looked up at Wilson. "This has got to be significant."

"I think so. And it gets worse."

"Do tell."

"Densmore looked into Carmen's child-support arrangements with these guys. She's supposed to get something from Crowe every month, but she doesn't anymore."

I frowned. "Because he's disappeared, correct? Carmen must be one of the people he owes money to."

"And then there's Davy Atwell."

"Crowe owed him money also."

"No, Jessie. I'm talking about Carmen's child support. Carmen and Davy duked it out in court about a year ago, haggling over the amount."

I shook my head. "So let me guess. Russell got into the court records?"

"Yep. Carmen wanted the payments to be based on Davy's net worth. But Davy and his lawyers argued—successfully—that her child-support should only be based on his current income."

"From his earnings as a bartender?" I thought about how unfortunate that was for Carmen. "So she was getting very little from him, even though he was rich. Louise saw his house today, by the way. It's a mansion worthy of a stop on the Beyond the Beach tours."

"Carmen must love that."

"We need to take that tour tomorrow," I insisted. "Whether or not it interferes with our surfing lesson."

Wilson nodded consent. "According to Densmore, Davy Atwell was worth at least three million. Not including the house."

"So Davy's death could mean quite a windfall for Carmen, correct? She, or at least two of her children, may stand to inherit a good bit of his wealth."

"Bingo."

Bingo—we had arrived at the Primrose Tower.

"Did Russell discover anything about Rachel Tate in all his research?" I asked as we stared at the monolith before us.

"Nope." Wilson tore his gaze from the Primrose and glanced at me. "Which can only mean that Rachel Tate—at least the Rachel Tate we're looking for—doesn't exist. Whoever this woman is, I'd bet money she's using a false identity."

"Wild goose chase," I reiterated as we approached the entrance to the Primrose Tower.

"You have a plan this time, Miss Amateur Sleuth?"

I reminded him that having a plan was not exactly my style and hopped into the revolving doorway.

***

The doorway ejected me into the Primrose Tower, and I stopped short to take in the awe-inspiring surroundings. The lobby was about the size of the entire acreage of the Wakilulani Gardens. Chrome, glass, and enormous mirrors dominated the décor, and with scads of white Christmas lights strung onto every conceivable object, the room literally sparkled.

"Use Plan A from last night," Wilson suggested as we hiked our way across the expanse of marble flooring.

As we closed in on the check-in counter, I concluded Rachel Tate, or whoever the heck she was, was not working that night. The clerk was male and even older than I.

"I hope you're not looking for a room," he said as we approached. A name tag informed us his name was Lloyd, and Lloyd informed us the Primrose Tower had no vacancies. "We're full through New Year's."

"No, no, no," I said with a wave of my hand. "But I do hope you can help us, Lloyd. We're looking for an old friend." I leaned on the counter. "Well no, that's not quite it," I corrected myself. "Rachel's auntie is an old friend of mine—"

"Cicely and Jessie go way back," Wilson finished for me.

"Way, way back." I said. Apparently I was to take the Bee Bee role this time.

"Cicely was so excited to hear we were staying at Halo Beach on our vacation," Wilson continued. "She told us to be sure to look up Rachel while we're here. Gosh, this island is glorious."

I blinked twice. Did Wilson Rye just say gosh? And glorious?

He was waiting for me. "Umm, glorious," I mumbled, and he continued raving about this, that, and the other "glorious" thing we were enjoying about Hawaii.

"The beach!" he exclaimed. I kid you not—exclaimed. "And that volcano? We are having such a wonderful time!"

I managed a hoarse "Wonderful."

Lloyd frowned and turned to Wilson. "What is it you're looking for, sir?"

"Who," Wilson corrected him. "Who."

"Who," I repeated dutifully.

"Rachel Tate," Wilson clarified, and poor Lloyd winced accordingly.

Wilson pretended not to notice. "You see, Lloyd, Cicely told us Rachel worked at the Wakilulani Gardens, so we went there for dinner last night."

"Dinner," I Bee-Beed.

"But lo and behold, the folks there told us she works at the Kamikaze Sports Bar."

"Kamakokoa," Lloyd and I both corrected.

Wilson continued, "So we popped over there last night, too, didn't we, Jessie?"

"Popped."

"But lo and behold, those folks told us she works here now. They said she's your new night clerk. So here we are!"

"Here we are!" Enthusiasm personified, I elbowed my way in front of Wilson. "I can't wait to see her! If you could tell me when her next shift is, I'd be forever grateful. Rachel does work here, doesn't she?"

"She did work here," Lloyd said. "But she got fi—." He cleared his throat. "She quit last night."

Why was I not surprised? I sighed dramatically and asked Lloyd where we might find her. Of course he had no idea. And of course he refused to give us her phone number or forwarding address.

Wilson muttered something under his breath about how handy a badge could be, and would have wandered off had I not reached out and grabbed his shirttail. I maneuvered him back into place and once again turned my attention to Lloyd.

"We had a very nice dinner at the Wakilulani Gardens," I said. "If any of your guests are looking for a good restaurant, I would highly recommend it."

"I hear the new chef's great," Lloyd agreed.

I pretended to admire the chandelier above his head. "But to be honest, we were a bit disappointed with the drinks. Cicely told me to be sure to order a Pele's Melee at the Wakilulani, but dare I say, they were nothing to write home about?"

Lloyd shook his head at my ignorance. "That's because their bartender just died. He kept that drink recipe a deep dark secret—probably took it to the grave with him." He shook his head again. "Great chef or not, that place is jinxed."

"Oh?" I used my most beseeching look, and Lloyd gave us a brief account of Davy's murder. We acted shocked and dismayed, but he told us nothing we did not already know.

I was feeling rather disappointed in our lack of progress when he pursed his lips. "If you ever do track down Rachel, you should probably know she was engaged to the dead guy."

"What!?" we practically shouted, and the poor guy backed up a step.

"That was her latest excuse for slacking off anyway," he said. "She was in mourning." He did the air-quote thing, clearly not convinced of the woman's grief. "I'm sorry, madam, but your friend wasn't a very good employee to begin with. And then when Davy Atwell got himself killed?"

Lloyd stopped and let us think about it.

"She was worse than ever?" Wilson asked.

"Something like that."

***

"We're looking for a lunatic," Wilson said. He had lost the silly amateur-sleuth persona and was back to his normal self.

"I thought we were looking for Rachel Tate," I argued as we found our favorite spot in the sand and sat down. I gazed out at the Pacific. "Do you think we'll ever find her?"

"Nope. But Densmore will. I told him to figure out who she really is, come hell or high water."

"And who else is the talented Lieutenant still investigating? Bethany, I assume?"

"Nope. I changed my mind about Bethany."

I turned from the sea to face Wilson. "Why's that?"

"I've been too hard on her. At the luau tonight Emi confirmed what Densmore told me earlier about all three of those girls."

I cringed. "You didn't actually have Densmore look into Emi Ulii?"

"You bet I did. As you would say, Chris is smitten with her. So Densmore checked her out."

"You don't trust anyone, do you?"

"Nope. Densmore found the high school connection—Emi, Makaila, and Bethany—but there's nothing there."

"Alas, no sinister Hula Club connection?"

He chuckled. "All three of them were good kids in high school and ever since."

"But Bethany lied to Chris about who fired Derrick Crowe," I argued. "And she knew how to make a Pele's Melee." I nodded meaningfully. "She was sleeping with Davy, correct?"

"Maybe, but you heard what Gail told us—Bethany's smart. She probably watched Davy make so many pink drinks, she caught on by osmosis."

"But if Bethany was sleeping with Davy," I persisted, "and now we know that Rachel was engaged to him?"

"We don't know either of those things for a fact."

Ah, the pesky fact factor. My beau the cop is such a stickler in that regard.

"I can't believe you're dismissing your prime suspect at this critical juncture, Wilson." I drew a love triangle in the sand to illustrate my argument and pointed to each corner. "Bethany, Rachel, and Davy," I insisted.

Wilson pointed to each corner. "Carmen, Ki and Davy," he said and reminded me that just the previous night Ki had been my prime suspect. "And with what Densmore learned about Carmen's kids? Think about it, Jessie."

I conceded that Carmen had good cause to be a bit angry at Davy. "And a possible inheritance from his estate would be a powerful motive."

"For Carmen and for Ki. And then there's the Ki-Vega connection."

"Excuse me?"

"I'm not sure, but Denmore's checking into it. Why is Vega refusing to even look at the owners or the staff at the Wacky Gardens?" Wilson didn't wait for an answer. "Vega said something earlier that bugged me."

"Vega says a lot of things that bug you."

"He called me Sherlock."

My face dropped. "Ki calls you Sherlock."

"Bingo." Wilson offered one of his meaningful cop-like looks. "It's a common enough expression. But."

"So you think Vega and Ki are friends, maybe?" I did the deductive reasoning thing. "So Vega may be protecting Ki? Like some sort of conspiracy?"

"It's possible. But let's see what Densmore finds out before jumping to conclusions." He patted my knee. "And in the meantime, let's check out Davy Atwell's place."

I nodded eagerly. "We'll take the Beyond the Beach tour tomorrow."

"Maybe, but let's do our Nancy Drew and Ned imitation first. We'll get directions from Louise and you can drive me over to the mansion."

I squinted. "What are you up to, Captain Rye?"

"I need to get into that house, Jessie. See what I can find."

"Oh, my Lord," I hissed. "Are you actually thinking of breaking in?"

He grinned. "Didn't Nancy Drew ever break into a house?"

I looked up at the almost full moon and laughed out loud. "Let me guess—you know all about how to pick a lock, disconnect burglar alarms, et cetera, et cetera."

He shrugged modestly, and it occurred to me, yet again, that there was a lot about this man I did not know. "Did Dianne Calloway teach you how to be a criminal?" I asked.

Wilson lost the grin. "What?"

"I don't know what, Wilson. But Vega mentioned something about you protecting her. So I'm thinking maybe she was a criminal of some sort."

Wilson glared at me until I again reminded him I did not know what I was talking about. Then he poked his head into his Shynomore sack and pulled out one of the shirts he had purchased on our way home from the Primrose Tower.

He held it up to the moonlight. "I like this one the best."

I took stock of the assortment of Dr. Seuss characters. "You're trying to change the subject."

"Yep."

Chapter 19

"Urquit Snodgrass truly is evil, isn't he?" Mother asked.

"Downright dastardly." I looked up from my breakfast and winked at Louise. "You'll be happy to know he's finally kidnapped her."

Louise gasped. "Delta Touchette? What? When? Where? How? Tell me, tell me, tell me!"

"At the Goochie Leoia Gorge," Mother told her and then repeated herself. "Goochie Lee-O-I-A. Did I say it right?" I nodded as she continued scrolling down my computer screen and explaining, "Just like Jessie mentioned yesterday. He kidnapped Delta while she was taking her morning bath."

Wilson put down his fork. "Snotgrass actually nabbed her naked?"

"Snodgrass," Mother corrected him.

"And of course not," I said. "Delta might be a daring adventuress, but she is still quite modest. She wasn't likely to let the evil villain see her naked for very long."

Mother giggled as she read further. "Very clever, Jessie." She stopped reading to enlighten Wilson. "Despite her harrowing night all alone in the jungle, Delta Touchette has kept her wits about her."

"And bathing in the clear blue waters of the Goochie Leoia Gorge has revived her considerably," I added. "So she's very alert."

"There now, you see?" Mother reached a fork over to nab a bite of my pancakes.

Wilson shook his head. "I can't believe I'm asking this—but see what?"

"Delta, of course," Tessie said after swallowing. "She could just feel Urquit Snodgrass's eyes upon her when she was attending her morning toilette, so she ever so quickly hopped out of the pool on the farther bank and wrapped herself in a leaf."

Wilson blinked twice. "Did you just say, leaf?"

"A big huge tropical leaf," I elaborated. I pointed to a few examples in the garden surrounding the breakfast patio, and then at some sort of vine-twine stuff hanging from the nearest tree. "And then she used a vine like that one and fashioned a belt to hold the thing on." I tapped my chin and pictured Delta. "She looks quite fetching, actually."

"I am sure she looks fantastical!" Louise interjected. "Very, very, very sexy!"

Wilson groaned and went back to his pancakes as Tessie summarized the actual kidnapping scene for Louise's edification.

Duly intrigued, my agent fretted about Skylar Staggs. "He must arrive to save Delta soon, Jessica! That leaf, no matter how large, isn't going to deter Urquit Snodgrass for very long!"

I looked up from the last of my pancakes. "Louise," I scolded. "Exactly how many of my books have you read by now? Do you really think Adelé Nightingale would ever allow any of her heroines to be violated by the bad guy?"

She sat back and considered. "Good point," she said. "And I do apologize for doubting you." She wiped her brow in a motion reminiscent of the distressed Delta Touchette herself. "I'm just so worried about poor Bee Bee, I can't think straight. Where oh where can he be?"

I exchanged a meaningful look with Wilson, and then with my mother. They both nodded encouragement.

I took a deep breath. "Umm, Louise," I began as Tessie reached over to take her hand. "We have a theory about Bee Bee's disappearance that, umm, maybe you should know about." I cringed, and Louise's face dropped. In fact, she looked like she was about to cry.

"You think he's dead, don't you?"

"No, no, no, no," I hastened to reassure her and explained the basic kidnapping idea while Mother patted her hand and mumbled a few "There-theres."

Louise swallowed a sob. "So you think the killer kidnapped Bee Bee?"

"Bee Bee heard something important that night," Mother said. "The killer needs to keep him quiet, doesn't he?"

"This guy—this person—has gone wacko," Wilson added. "Think about it, Louise. They returned the knife to the kitchen for no good reason. And they're hiding the stupid bird."

Louise sipped her coffee and thought about it. "But Bee Bee isn't stupid," she said in a surprisingly calm voice. "That's why they're hiding him." She put down her cup and sat forward. "But!" she said loudly, and we all jumped.

"But what?" we asked.

"But where are they hiding him? Where, where, where!? Bee Bee would make far too much noise anywhere inside. Sooo." Her eyes darted back and forth around the patio. "So the killer must have hidden him out there!" She pointed toward the volcano and turned to me. "We need to go out there and find him, Jessica!"

"We?" I squeaked. "Out there?" I cringed. "In, like, the wilderness?"

"Yes, we! Yes, out there!" Louise waved her hands around the breakfast table. "All of us need to go, except maybe Tessie. There must be all kinds of places to search." She again indicated the big, bad, bug-infested wilderness. "Caves, caverns, nooks, crannies!"

I appealed to Wilson to save me. "Umm, we have some other plans for the day. Don't we, Wilson?"

"Our plans can wait." He spoke to me, but he was watching Louise, who looked like she might start crying again. "But we'll get a lot further without Jessie," he added, and I breathed a sigh of relief. "We don't want her with us, slowing us down and screaming bloody murder at every bug and cobweb."

"Jessie gets the heebie jeebies," Mother explained. "I'm afraid she wouldn't be helpful at all."

"She'd be useless," Wilson added.

"Useless," Mother agreed.

"Useless?" Louise repeated in case someone hadn't yet caught on.

I rolled my eyes. "I'm not that bad."

"Yes you are," my mother and my beau said in unison.

"We'll bring Chris," Wilson announced, summarily dismissing my would-be contributions to the effort. "The kid's got better eyesight and hearing than the rest of us put together. If Bee Bee's out there, Chris will find him."

Mother shook her head. "No, Wilson honey. Chris has plans to go free-boarding with Emi today."

"Free-boarding?" I asked. "What is that, even?"

"It's suicidal, is what it is." Faye approached our table with a fresh pot of coffee. "They hook their surfboards up to a boat like waterskiing. My kids swear it's not as dangerous as it looks, but I can't watch." She topped off a few cups and turned to Wilson. "And your son was out late at the Holiday Hula last night, right? I hope he's resting up."

"He is," Mother assured us. "He got in very late last night after walking Emi home. He told me he'd sleep in this morning before his lesson. I understand Emi's quite accomplished at this free-boarding skill."

"Better your kid than mine," Faye said ominously as Wilson handed her his empty plate.

He glanced at Louise. "So it's just us and the Kekipi Crater."

I looked up at Faye and waved an index finger back and forth between Wilson and Louise. "Speaking of suicidal, these two are going off into the wilderness in search of Bee Bee."

"Buster will be glad to hear it. The poor guy's been worried sick." Faye gathered the rest of our plates and wandered off toward The Big House.

"Give me a minute to go get my hiking boots, and I'll meet you by the Christmas tree," Wilson told Louise. He stood up but remembered to bend down and kiss me. "And we'll take our little excursion later on?" he whispered in my ear.

I pretended to pout. "Maybe then I won't be so useless."

He reminded me I really did not want to go hiking. "But here's something you can do." He reached into his pocket and handed me his cell phone. "I'm expecting a phone call."

"Densmore?" I mouthed.

Wilson jerked a thumb volcano-ward. "There's no signal up there. You'll take a message?"

I assured him I would, and he wandered off in the direction of Paradise. Louise and Mother were staring at me when I turned back to the table.

"What are you two up to now?" Louise asked.

"Silly Louise," Mother said. "They're still sleuthing, aren't they?"

I reminded Louise that she, too, was sleuthing. "If Bee Bee's a witness and you find him on this hike of yours, you'll be a hero."

Louise pursed her lips. "Do you think I should have mentioned to your paramour that I've never actually been hiking?" She tore her gaze from the volcano. "Hiking's kind of like swimming and driving for me."

"Oh, but look how well you're doing at both of those things," Mother said encouragingly and I rolled my eyes.

"I don't even own a pair of hiking boots," Louise confessed. "What should I wear, Jessica?"

I pointed to my useless self. "You're asking me?"

Apparently she was, so I told her to avoid anything she had gotten at one of her fancy Manhattan shoe stores.

"How about sneakers?" Mother suggested. "Didn't you bring anything with traction?"

"My running shoes." Louise stood up and faced the Kekipi Crater. "If Delta Touchette can face the sinister Urquit Snodgrass barefoot and wrapped in nothing but a leaf, surely I can go hiking in my Nikes!"

She ran off in search of her shoes, and I rolled my eyes yet again.

***

"To Bee Bee," Mother said and clanked her coffee cup against mine.

I pursed my lip and studied the old gal. "Did Christopher Rye visit your bed again last night, Mother?"

"It wasn't like that!"

"I know that. But I still don't understand what the two of you find to talk about night after night."

"I told you, Jessie. We talk about you and Wilson."

"And?" I asked. "Has Chris divulged his father's deep dark secrets?"

Mother sighed dramatically. "That poor, sweet, darling man."

"What?" I said. "Please tell me. Pleeeease?"

She shook her head. "Didn't we agree you should ask Wilson about this yourself?"

"I did ask him. And he agreed he would tell me everything. But not until our vacation is over." I sat back and slumped. "How annoying is that?"

Mother patted my hand and stood up. "Patience, Jessie." She wished me luck getting Delta out of her current predicament and tottered off toward Misty Breezes bungalow. "I'll be resting on my porch if you or Skylar Staggs need any advice," she called over her shoulder.

I frowned at the cluster of massive poinsettia bushes stationed at the edge of the patio. Yep, I thought, annoying about sums it up. Not only was my mother ignoring my plight, but Faye had also disappeared, and was completely neglecting my empty coffee cup. Wilson and Louise had forgotten about me, too. Deep in conversation about their impending Bee Bee-hunting expedition, neither of them gave me the slightest notice as they passed by the table.

"Buster will have some ideas of where we should start," Wilson was saying to Louise.

"Where, where, where?" she repeated and followed him into The Big House.

Chapter 20

Eleanor Touchette sat down and had herself a good cry.

Alarmed and stunned, Skylar Staggs stood before her, trying to understand what he had said to upset the lady so. He rocked from foot to foot until Eleanor finally looked up. She apologized for her unmannerly greeting, but when Skylar reached out and tentatively offered her his handkerchief, the woman sobbed even more.

Poor Skylar was again at a loss. For the lawman of Port Mekipii Hui was unaccustomed to provoking this kind of reaction from any woman, no matter her age. Hoping for the moment to pass, he stood silently and stared at the portrait of a young girl hanging over the mantle.

Eventually Eleanor Touchette did get hold of herself. She sat up straight and invited Mr. Staggs to join her on the settee. She even composed herself enough to enquire as to why he was back on Ebony Island so soon after escorting her niece over.

"The Pirate of Diamond Island," he answered. And at the risk of provoking another emotional outburst from the older woman, he reported that an unseemly and degenerate-looking man had been spotted lugging large canvas satchels of who knows what into the jungles of Ebony Island.

Actually, Skylar did have a theory about what was in those satchels. "Gold," he said. Gold and jewels—ill-gotten gains from a recent robbery back at Port Mekipii Hui.

Eleanor Touchette let out another sob and gazed up at the portrait of the beautiful little girl. Skylar looked also, and it finally dawned on him who the child was—Delta Touchette, of course! He asked how the younger Miss Touchette was enjoying her visit to the South Seas, only to have the older Miss Touchette resume wailing. Skylar braced himself and again wondered out loud what the trouble was.

"Delta!" Eleanor cried between many sighs and tears. And with much wringing of hands, she finally explained what was upsetting her so.

"You mean, she's out there!" Skylar jumped to his feet and hastened to the parlor window as Eleanor mumbled something about Delta's quest to find the ferocious jungle monster.

How ridiculous, he thought to himself. But even if the supposed Monster of Ebony Island didn't interest him, Delta Touchette certainly did. Skylar stared out the window and harkened back to sailing the seas with the lovely and rather forward young lady by his side. Oh, but she was a feisty one! And when that storm had almost destroyed his sailing vessel? The brave and daring damsel had taken it in her stride, and despite her lack of experience, had handled the rigs and ropes most proficiently. In fact, he never would have been able to right his ship without her assistance.

Skylar smiled to himself, remembering the scene after they were back on more friendly seas. The lady was friendly, too…

But Eleanor Touchette was tapping him on the shoulder. He recovered himself and remembered his purpose as she confessed how profoundly worried she was. Delta had failed to return for supper the previous evening, and had now been gone for well over twenty-four hours!

Eleanor wrung her hands. "Whatever could have become of her?" she entreated Mr. Staggs.

Skylar knew not. But he vowed to find out.

He did not wish to cause Miss Eleanor further alarm, but a most disturbing thought occurred to him as he took his leave of Emerald Estate. For Skylar Staggs was quite certain that wherever he found his passionate adventuress, he would also find the Pirate of Diamond Island.

***

Speaking of criminal behavior, the Coochie brothers were back at it. I looked up from my work as an utterly uninspired rendition of "Folsom Prison" wafted its way from the Song of the Sea up to the porch at Paradise. Apparently the brothers didn't realize they needed Johnny Cash for that one.

Prison. I closed my eyes and listened to the lyrics, and my overactive imagination pictured Christopher Rye behind bars. Okay, so he wasn't exactly my favorite person, but he was Wilson's son. And more importantly, he was innocent.

I opened my eyes and glared at Wilson's cell phone. What could be taking Russell Densmore so long to call back? After all, Wilson had only given the guy about ninety different assignments the previous evening. Surely the research whiz of the Clarence PD had ascertained most of the answers by now?

And what about me, for that matter? Why was I, a world-class amateur sleuth, lollygagging around letting everyone else do all the work? Lieutenant Densmore, Wilson, and even Geez Louise were all being far more productive than I. So maybe the conclusion we had reached at breakfast had been accurate. Maybe I was useless.

I stood up and started pacing to "A Boy Named Sue," and Sue was embroiled in a rather unpleasant showdown with his father by the time I remembered something I could do. I sat back down and grabbed my own cell phone.

"Oh, Jessie!" Candy cried the second she answered and commenced sobbing Eleanor Touchette-style.

I sat up straight. "What's wrong?"

"The ca—" she stuttered. "The ca—" A hiccup. "The ca—"

"The cats?" I said as my heart rate reached for the stratosphere. "Did they hurt each other? Is anyone dead? Oh my Lord, Candy! Is it Snowflake?"

"It's Wally!"

"Wally's dead!?" I screamed, and the Coochie brothers actually shut up as Candy screamed back a few thousand no's.

Hal, or Cal, or whoever called over to ask if everything were okay. I waved a distracted hand and told them to keep playing.

Then I interrupted Candy's incessant sobbing. "So Wally isn't dead?" I clarified in as calm a voice as I could muster.

"No, but he is hurt."

Wally? I scowled at the bougainvillea and reminded Candy everyone got along fine with Wally. It was Snowflake and Bernice who were having such a feline feud.

"Yeah, but —" Hiccup, sob, wail. "But—"

"Oh, for Lord's sake. But what?"

"But it wasn't a cat fight, Jessie. It was me!" she squealed and continued crying. "I'm the one who hurt Wally. I stepped on him. I feel so bad about it."

I bit down on my right fist and let out a sob of my own. I imagined Candy did feel bad, but probably not as bad as poor little Wally. My friend Candy Poppe is the queen of stiletto heels—four-inch, sharp, pointy stiletto heels.

"Which pair were you wearing?" I asked in a hoarse whisper.

"The gold ones. It was at breakfast-time this morning."

Okay, so I know what you're thinking. Gold stilettos at breakfast-time? Well, yes, actually. I could even picture the exact pair, adorned with gold glitter and silver satin bows. Candy is a rather flamboyant dresser. And it was the holiday season, after all.

"I was trying to keep Snowflake and Bernice from killing each other," she was saying.

"Snowflake doesn't like it when Bernice eats from her bowl."

"And Wally?" I asked.

"He was playing with Puddles. You know Puddles? My poodle?"

I took a deep breath and reminded Candy that of course I knew who Puddles was, since the little dog spends about half of his life in my condo.

"Yeah, well, Puddles and Wally were running around while I was feeding the other two, and I guess I wasn't watching what I was doing, and I stepped backwards."

I braced myself. "Where?"

"In your kitchen. Right next to Snowflake's food dish."

"Candy!"

"Oh," she said. "You meant where did I step on Wally, huh? His right front paw. He screamed so loud Bernice stopped eating. It was awful."

I cringed as I pictured the damage.

"Crunch," Candy added, and I cringed some more.

"You took him to the vet?" I asked.

"Karen did. I was too upset, so I stayed here with Snowflake, and Bernice, and Puddles."

"What did Dr. Smith do?" At the thought of Annie Smith, I allowed myself to feel at least slightly relieved. She's the best vet in Clarence, and she knows Snowflake, Puddles, and both of Wilson's cats. If anyone could heal Wally, it was Dr. Smith.

Sure enough, Candy reported that Wally was going to be okay. "Nothing's broken, just badly bruised," she elaborated. "He's got his paw all wrapped up for a few days. Dr. Smith promises he isn't in pain anymore, but I still feel so bad."

She threatened to begin crying again, so I tried to set her mind at ease, reminding her it was an accident, and how hard her job was, and reassuring her Wilson would actually be grateful she and Karen were taking such good care of his cats.

"The main thing is Wally is going to be okay," I added firmly.

"Dr. Smith says he'll be good as new. But no more chasing Puddles around. Not this week anyway."

***

"Wild goose chase," were the first words out of Lieutenant Russell Densmore's mouth.

Clearly under the impression he was speaking to his boss, he didn't wait for any sort of acknowledgement, but simply continued his report. "Her real name is Samantha Dimmery," he said as I reached for my mother's clipboard. "Dimmery has a history of moving from job to job, and island to island. She also has a history of petty crime. I'm guessing the woman has to resort to petty theft, since she can't seem to hold a job for more than a few days. Her gig at the Wakilulani Gardens was something of a record—six whole weeks. But now she's moved on to Honolulu, looking for her next job. You want me to keep track of her progress, Captain?"

I looked up from writing "petty crime" and "Honolulu" next to "Samatha Dimmery."

"We're talking about Rachel Tate?" I asked, and I do believe the Lieutenant dropped his phone. I jotted down "Rachel Tate" in parentheses next to the "Dimmery."

"Jessie?" Russell said eventually.

I verified, but somehow this did not set his mind at ease. "Where's Captain Rye?" he demanded. "And what about Captain Vega? And what about Chris? Don't tell me he's already been arrested? Where is my boss, Jessie? Why are you answering his pho—"

"Russell!" I scolded. I told him to take a deep breath and explained the latest developments.

"Let me get this straight," he said as I finished. "Captain Rye is off somewhere in the jungle searching for a bird?"

"Bee Bee is not just any bird. We think he's an important witness."

Dead silence.

"Bee Bee is a very smart parrot," I reiterated. "But let's move on, shall we? What else have you found? Some good dirt, I hope."

"Are you alone?"

I gazed out from the porch. The Coochies were within eyesight, but with the maid's vacuum cleaner running down in Louise's bungalow, I couldn't hear what they were playing over at the Song of the Sea. I assumed they could not hear me either, but just in case, I picked up the clipboard and went inside Paradise.

"All alone," I said and sprawled out on the bed.

"Are you sitting down?"

I sat up. "Yes."

"Here's the dirt—Captain Jason Vega and Ki Okolo are friends. They have been for years."

"No!"

"Yes. But don't get too excited. Ki Okolo has lots of friends."

I told Russell I found that hard to believe, even as I scribbled down Ki and Vega's names and drew a big thick arrow between them. "Ki is very abrasive," I said.

"Maybe. But he's also a computer genius. Practically everyone on that island has needed his help at some point.

The Halo Beach PD actually keeps him on retainer. I get the idea Vega's even worse at technology than my boss."

"Wilson's lucky to have you for all this techie stuff, Russell."

"Maybe. But the Halo Beach cops don't have me, they have Ki Okolo. They call him Sherlock."

"Everyone calls everyone Sherlock around here. Vega uses the expression, as does Ki."

"Like I said, they're friends."

"Sooo." I wrote Sherlock in parentheses under Ki's name. "If Ki's the murderer, it's in Vega's best interest to protect him. He needs to keep Ki out of prison and available for the next Halo Beach PD computer crisis."

"Don't get too excited, Jessie. We have no proof Ki's the killer."

"But Vega always lets the locals off the hook. Rumor has it he always blames a poor hapless tour—"

"Let's stick to the facts," Russell said firmly.

"You're just like your boss, you know? Facts this, facts that."

"So here's what we know for fact," he continued, dismissing my complaint. "Ki Okolo visits police headquarters at least once a week to work on something or other, and he and Vega usually take a long lunch afterwards."

I shook my head in dismay. "How did you learn all this stuff, Russell?"

"Practice," he said humbly and turned the subject to the other Okolo brother. "Big brother Ki might have clients all over the place, but Palakapola, a.k.a. Buster Okolo, has never worked anywhere except the Wakilulani Gardens. He moved in with his grandfather at age eleven and never left."

"Buster loves it here," I agreed. "His grandfather Pono trained him to take over the business."

"Good sleuthing, Jessie."

"More like simple observation." I scanned my notes. "So who else did you get the dirt on?"

"There's very little dirt," Russell said.

"But there has to be dirt," I insisted and explained a few of the intriguing love-triangle theories to prove my point.

Bless his heart, Russell gave each some consideration.

"I found nothing to suggest that Samantha Dimmery, a.k.a. Rachel Tate, was engaged to Davy Atwell," he said eventually. "And there's no evidence Bethany Iverson was involved with the guy either, even if she does know how to mix what the Captain tells me are some damn fine pink cocktails."

"But Russell," I whined. "We worked so hard to figure out those love triangles."

"Okay, how about this? I will agree that any triangle involving Carmen Dupree might have potential. She and those kids she had with Atwell could stand to inherit a fortune."

I wrote "Carmen Dupree" in big block letters on top of my notes. I almost confessed our plans to break into Davy Atwell's house later that day, but thought better of it and instead mentioned the Beyond the Beach tour.

"Carmen's a tour guide, so we're going this afternoon," I explained, and suddenly antsy to get going, I got up from the bed to pace the room. "Beyond the Beach actually makes a stop at Davy Atwell's mansion."

Russell told me to have fun. "Better yet, learn something useful. Break into the place. Captain Rye certainly knows how."

I stopped short and blinked twice.

"Try to find Atwell's will while you're in there," Russell suggested. "Computers might stump him, but Rye can crack a safe faster than anyone I know."

Excuse me? Not only was Wilson Rye adept at breaking and entering, but he could also crack a safe?

I was standing in front of the closet, and for some reason felt compelled to open it and take an inventory of Wilson's stunningly silly shirts. My beau—the clown, the cop, and the criminal. What's the saying? An enigma wrapped in a mystery? And wearing a fluorescent green shirt. The pink and orange spider-web specimen caught my attention, and I remembered another expression—something about tangled webs and deception.

"Jessie? Are you still there?"

I snapped out of it and closed the closet. Skeletons in the closet.

I snapped out of it again. "Umm, Russell," I ventured. "You don't by any chance happen to know anything about Wilson's past?"

Dead silence.

I soldiered on. "Something about a Dianne Calloway?"

I heard a loud clang and ascertained that the good Lieutenant had once again dropped his telephone.

Chapter 21

"Housekeeping. Knock, knock!"

I glanced through the open doorway to see the maid struggling up the stairs with a vacuum cleaner.

Mother's clipboard and Wilson's phone landed in the nearest dresser drawer, and I met the maid on the porch with a big smile on my face. Maybe I wasn't having such a useless morning after all. I mean, there before me stood a member of the Wakilulani staff who had not yet been interrogated. At least not by me.

Still smiling, I stepped forward and introduced myself.

The fifty—or maybe even sixty—something woman put down her vacuum with an exaggerated grunt and gave my hand a cursory shake. "Leslie Coochie," she said.

My mouth dropped open, but Ms. Coochie didn't even notice since she was already back to struggling with her machine.

I stepped in her way. "Coochie, as in Hoochie Coochie?" I fluttered a few fingers Song of the Sea-ward.

"Cousins," she mumbled. She got a firm grip on the vacuum cleaner and maneuvered it around me and into Paradise. "I'll be about a half hour if you want to wait down by the pool."

Yeah, right.

While she moved back and forth carrying loads of sheets and cleaning supplies from her cart to the bungalow, I hung around on the porch pretending to fiddle with something on my laptop. How had we failed to notice this woman in all our sleuthing?

Well, she must have cleaned our room while we were out spying on Carmen Dupree the day before. And the morning before that she would not have disturbed us. That had been the morning after Davy's murder, when we slept in. Also, maybe we had simply not given the cleaning staff much thought. I scolded myself for being such a snob and walked to the doorway.

Ms. Coochie had already stripped the bed and was arranging the clean sheets. She looked up at me. "Can I help you?"

"No, but I can help you." I hastened to the opposite side of the bed and gestured for her to throw me a corner of the sheet.

Instead, she clutched the sheet in both fists. "What are you doing?"

"Umm, I thought I'd help," I said weakly. "I don't mind."

She frowned and asked me to please get out of the way.

So much for being helpful. I stepped back to let her get on with it, and with a few more frowns in my direction, she made the bed. She was tucking in the last corner on Wilson's side when I gave up and resorted to honesty.

"My friends and I are curious about Davy Atwell's murder," I blurted out as she hustled her way into the bathroom.

"Tell me something I don't know," she called from the vicinity of the shower.

"Actually, I was kind of hoping you could tell me something I don't know." I smiled encouragingly as she emerged from the bathroom with an armload of dirty towels.

She dropped the towels onto the pile of dirty sheets. "Not likely." She gathered up all the laundry, and left me while she carried it outside to her cart.

I reminded myself an amateur sleuth's job is never easy and waited patiently for this annoyingly efficient maid to return. Sure enough, she came back with a stack of clean towels, but I stepped directly into her path to the bathroom.

She stopped. "Whaaat?" she said. "I don't know anything, okay? I just work here." She looked pointedly around me. "At least I'm trying to."

I reached out to her shoulders, backed her up toward the bed, and firmly pressed down until she was forced to sit.

She shook her head. "Ki warned me about you."

"Excellent!" I said and noticed the slightest hint of a smile.

I encouraged the effort and pulled up a chair to face her. Smiling or not, Ms. Coochie was still holding her stack of clean towels and was poised to spring towards the bathroom at the first opportunity. Therefore, I ignored my rather involved list of suspects and love triangles and got right to the point. I asked only about the Coochie cousins. When need be, I, too, can be efficient.

She shook her head again. "You're wasting your time and mine," she told me. "Hal and Cal did not kill the bartender."

"Oh, no, no, no," I hastened to agree. "But they were here that night. They had just checked in. And, well, I'm just curious is all. I love their music."

Ms. Coochie ever so slowly raised an eyebrow.

"Okay, so maybe not," I said to the eyebrow. "But I am curious about them. I understand they stay here every year." I pointed to her maid's uniform. "And you have to admit, it is an intriguing coincidence that you work here. Have you had this job long?"

Leslie—she relaxed enough to let me to call her Leslie—informed me she was new to the staff, and with a few persistent prods and pleas from me, offered a bit of her history. Apparently Hal and Cal were her second cousins, sons of a favorite cousin on her father's side. And Leslie was a retired school teacher trying to make a little extra income to supplement a not-so-great pension.

"After decades of dealing with kids, parents, principals, and anyone else who cared to blame teachers for every problem under the sun, I wanted a job where I can work all alone." She again raised an eyebrow. "Something where I don't have to talk to anyone. Where I'm ignored and left all alone."

She kept emphasizing the "all alone," but I refused to take the hint and tilted my head expectantly.

She sighed in resignation and told me Cal had found her current job for her. "He thought I'd like the Wakilulani. I mind my own business, work all alone, and I'm done by noon. Then I get to enjoy the beach the rest of the day." She shrugged. "It's touristy, but I like Halo Beach—I can be anonymous here. Not like in Iwatanii Town."

Iwatanii Town?

I sat up straight as a flood of information suddenly collided in my brain. Iwatanii Town was Buster and Ki's hometown, Leslie Coochie's place of origin, and—I remembered the last connection—the town listed on Hal Coochie's driver's license!

I worked to regain my amateur-sleuth poker face, but it was hard to keep from smiling.

"Whaaat?" Leslie asked.

"Iwatanii Town." I tapped my chin. "Isn't that where the Okolo brothers are from?"

Leslie actually set aside her stupid towels in order to fold her arms and glare at me. "Yes," she said emphatically. "And before you start jumping to conclusions, yes. We all know each other—the Okolos and the Coochies. Everyone from that stupid little town knows each other." She harrumphed. "For better or worse."

I leaned forward. "Did you know Buster and Ki's parents?" I asked. "They must have been about your age?"

"It figures you'd know about the accident."

I mumbled something about curiosity, and she continued, "Yes, I knew the parents. And if you must know, I taught both Ki and Buster when they passed through the fourth grade. But so what?" Leslie pointed to me. "From the look on your face, you're finding this far more interesting than it really is."

She stood up, awkwardly stepped around my chair, and reached for her vacuum cleaner. She had it plugged in and running before I could stop her.

I gave up and yelled a "Thank you," over the racket.

Leslie waved her duster attachment at me. Or maybe she was brandishing her duster attachment at me.

No matter. I had other fish to fry. Or at least other Coochies to annoy. I stepped back to the porch and gazed at the Song of the Sea.

***

But just my luck, just when I needed them most, the Coochie brothers had abandoned their porch.

No matter. I scavenged my flip flops from underneath my chair and moseyed down the garden path.

"Hello-o," I called out as I got closer to the Song of the Sea. "Knock, knock," I sang.

No answer. And no music.

I called out another greeting, climbed the porch steps, and knocked. Again, no answer.

I glanced backwards. Leslie had turned off her vacuum cleaner, but she was still in Paradise. I told myself she was busy cleaning the bathroom, and creature of habit that I am, I tried the Coochies' door. And creature of habit that I am, I assumed it would open.

Imagine my chagrin when it did not. Indeed, the stupid thing was locked. Of all the inconvenient—

"What the hell are you doing?"

I jumped ten feet in the air and almost fell off the porch. Erasing the cringe from my face, I forced myself to turn around. This time it wasn't Wilson's questions I would have to answer, it was Leslie Coochie's.

But for some reason I had lost my zeal for interrogations. I waved nonchalantly, and with as much dignity as I could muster, made my way down the porch steps and onto the pathway.

In a most disconcerting role reversal, Leslie stood her ground and blocked my progress, and I felt like a recalcitrant fourth grader. "Were you looking for something?" she asked.

"Oh, no, no, no," I said all breezy-like. "I just thought I'd say good morning to your cousins."

Leslie continued to stand her ground.

The only way around her was to venture off the garden path and into the surrounding brush. I cleared my throat and did so, and with nary a backward glance, beat a hasty and embarrassed retreat.

***

"Bee Bee."

I stopped short at my porch steps.

"Bee Bee."

I perked up my ears and heard it a third time. Off in the distance. Back behind Paradise. I looked toward the Song of the Sea to see if Leslie heard it also, but she had already disappeared inside.

"Bee Bee."

There it was again! Bee Bee had found his way home! Or at least close to it.

I quick ran inside and scanned the room for the binoculars, but then remembered Wilson had them. Muttering a four-letter word, I ran back outside and straight into the jungle behind our bungalow. In fact, I had taken several giant steps into the wilds before something tickled my toes and stopped me dead in my tracks.

I glanced down at my feet. What was I doing? And why in the world was I doing it in those stupid sandals?

While I frowned at my flip flops, something stung my shoulder. I swatted at it frantically and managed to stumble a few more steps backward into the wilderness before I could stop myself. I took a deep breath and planted my feet firmly in the—I looked down again—firmly in the whatever. That plant, which I swear was wrapping itself around my bare ankles, was not poison ivy, was it? Hawaii doesn't even have poison ivy, does it?

Oh, for Lord's sake! Who the heck knew! And who the heck knew how I had managed to get myself so far out into the jungle in shorts, a tank top, and those stupid, stupid flip flops. Making sure not to move any farther into said jungle, I looked up and located the backside of Paradise. So close, and yet so far...

"Eeeee—"

My head jerked to attention. What was that?

Okay, so it took me a moment to realize the high-pitched whining had been coming out of me.

I cleared my throat, and decided it was time for some deep breathing. I did so and again focused my attention on Paradise.

The bungalow wasn't that far away. Why, it was practically right there in front of me. I would simply take ten or twenty careful, cautious, and well-placed steps, and soon I would be back in civilization. It would be easy. I would start right awa—

"Bee Bee."

I put my foot back down and recollected what had gotten me into this predicament in the first place. Bee Bee was out there. Bee Bee needed me.

Courage, I told myself, and harkened back to something Louise had mentioned earlier. If Delta Touchette could face Urquit Snodgrass, barefoot and dressed in nothing but a leaf, surely I could hunt for Bee Bee dressed as I was? Especially if I kept Paradise within sight.

Feeling downright heroic, I held my position and scanned the treetops. I even managed to squeak out a few "Bee Bees."

Nothing.

I was turning to face the opposite direction when some movement near my right knee caught my eye. I glanced down at a mass of moss-covered, rotting, vegetative who-knows-what. The thing was swarming with ants.

Oh. My. God.

I screamed bloody murder and likely would have fainted of my own accord, but something hit me from behind and expedited the process.

My last conscious effort was to fall to my left—away from the ant hill from hell.

Chapter 22

"Wake up."

Huh?

"Wake up!" The voice behind me grew more impatient, and something—maybe an elbow—jabbed into my ribs.

"Huh?" I mumbled.

"Wake! Up!" This time he was really irritated, and the voice sounded familiar. Sort of.

"Wilson?" I whispered.

"Chris. Jessie?"

"Chris?" Okay, so maybe this wasn't the most compelling of conversations. But considering how my head felt, I think I was doing quite well, thank you.

With Chris—Christopher Rye?—encouraging me and harassing me, I finally did wake up. I lifted my head, and with much fluttering of eyelids, eventually managed to get my eyes open.

For what that was worth. Wherever I was, it was almost pitch black.

As I continued to return to consciousness, I took stock of my position. I was sitting in some sort of gravel, with my legs outstretched in front of me and my hands tied behind my back—tied to someone else's hands.

"Chris?" I asked again. "Where are we? Are we actually tied up together?"

"Like, duh. Would you wake up already?"

"Okay, okay." I tried to squirm into a more comfortable position. "I'm awake now, so answer me."

"Yes, we're tied up together," he answered. "And I don't know where we are, but I'm guessing this is Pele's Prison."

"The cave?" My voice cracked. "The one you and Wilson never found the other day?"

"We're in deep shit, Jessie. I think we've been kidnapped."

"By the murderer?" I squeaked.

"No, by Santa Claus."

I took a deep breath and attempted another perfectly reasonable question. "How did we get here?"

"I have no idea how you got here. Santa's sleigh?"

I rephrased the question. "Okay, how did you get here? Elves, reindeer, what?"

Chris backed down a bit and in a much less snippy tone assured me it probably hadn't been elves. "I was getting out of the shower this morning, when I heard that bird calling," he said. "I threw on some shorts and sneakers and ran outside to find him."

"And let me guess. He lured you farther and farther away from your bungalow."

"Yep."

"And into the wilderness."

"Yep."

"And then someone knocked you unconscious."

"You, too, Jessie?"

I recollected the ant hill and shuddered accordingly. "Something like that," I mumbled. "But it wasn't Bee Bee we were hearing, was it? It was the killer pretending to be Bee Bee."

"Bee Bee."

We both jerked forward in our separate directions, quite effectively tightening the ropes that held us together.

"Let's not do that again," Chris suggested wisely.

I blinked into the darkness, which was beginning to lighten to a dull grey as my eyes adjusted. "Bee Bee?" I called out.

"Bee Bee," Bee Bee answered.

"Bee Bee?" I repeated.

He responded again, and we went back in forth in yet another less than compelling exchange until Chris finally interrupted us. "I see him over here." He paused. "Oh, my God."

"Oh my God, what?" I asked.

"He's hobbling around, Jessie. I think he's hurt."

Okay, so I might have started crying.

"Do not start crying."

"I am not crying," I argued. "I'm just breathing a little funny."

"Yeah, right," Chris said, but I noticed he was breathing a little funny, too.

"That's just sick," he said eventually. "Hurting an animal like that."

"Let's keep talking to him." I swallowed hard and forced myself to speak up. "Bee Bee likes it when people talk to him. Don't you, Bee Bee?"

"Bee Bee," he answered, and I swear he did sound a bit perkier.

I continued reassuring the bird and explained in a highly upbeat voice that Louise and Wilson were out searching for him. "They'll find you, Bee Bee. And then they'll find us."

"But first they have to find Pele's Prison," Chris interjected.

"Prison," Bee Bee repeated.

I ignored the pessimism and continued, "And once we're all rescued, we'll take you to the vet—"

My voice caught at the mention of veterinarians—Bee Bee was injured, Wally was injured. I blinked back my tears and kept going, "We'll take you to the vet, and you'll be good as new. We'll all be good as new."

"Good as new," Bee Bee agreed bravely.

"Good as new," Chris chimed in, and the three of us repeated our new mantra several times.

Bee Bee hobbled over towards me, and dim light or no, I tried to see what ailed him. He was staggering, but his wings were perfectly aligned, and I saw no blood. "I don't think he's injured," I concluded. "I think he's just really disoriented."

"Aren't we all," Chris muttered.

I practiced some more deep breathing and asked Chris to tell me about Pele's Prison.

"You want the good news or the bad news?"

I considered my options. "How about both?"

"The bad news is this cave is really hard to find unless you know what you're looking for."

"And the good news?"

"We're not too far from the beaten path. Supposedly Pele's Prison is right off the main trail."

"Excellent!" I said. "So all we need to do is scream for help." Wasting no time, I began screaming for help.

Bless his heart, Bee Bee caught on and commenced screeching. This was going to work! Some hiker somewhere would surely hear the racket and rescue us at any moment.

I screamed away, "Help! Help!" until a very sharp jab in my ribs shut me up. It took a few more seconds to calm down Bee Bee.

"You guys didn't wait to hear the rest of the bad news," Chris said once everyone was quiet again. "Pele's Prison has this weird echo-chamber. All the trail guides mention it. Once inside, no one can hear you from the outside."

"Excuse me?"

"It's a natural phenomenon. Hawaii has lots of those."

"Excuse me?" I repeated. "That is the stupidest natural phenomenon I've ever hear of. Who comes up with this stuff anyway? It's like we're in La La Land."

"Maybe, but it's probably why Santa Claus didn't gag us."

"So screaming won't help?" I asked.

"La La Land," Chris said.

"La La Land," Bee Bee confirmed.

I rolled my eyes, and some amorphous specter to my upper left caught my attention. At least it can't be an ant hill, I told myself. And stupid me, I glanced up to get a clearer view.

And that's when I blacked out for the second time in one day.

Chapter 23

Chris and Bee Bee were still discussing the many-splendored natural phenomena of La La Land when I came to. I ignored them and hazarded another glance upward at my very own natural phenomenon. Yep, there really was a spider web up there. And, honey, I do mean spider.

I stared at it, mesmerized and aghast, and tried to convince myself it's the teeny-tiny spiders one had to be cautious of. But the big guys? The big, gold, glow-in-the-dark, hairy jobbies, like this one poised directly over my left breast? They were never, ever poisonous. Right?

But then again, what did I know? It was entirely possible that I was looking at the queen mother of all the poisonous spiders of the South Pacific. Nay, the queen mother of all the poisonous spiders in the world!

I shuddered like I have never shuddered before.

"What's wrong?" Chris asked.

"Spider," I squeaked, and that's when I noticed what Ms. Huge and Hairy had trapped in her extensive web.

A bug. Oh, but that's putting it mildly. This was a bug to beat all bugs. This guy was about the size of my fist, and boasted a rainbow of colors that rivaled the loudest of Wilson's Hawaiian shirts. Indeed, this bug was a veritable smorgasbord of purples, greens, yellows, and oranges. He was a living flashlight, for Lord's sake. And he was writhing in agony as Ms. Huge and Hairy crawled, or whatever it is that spiders do, over to eat him.

Needless to say, I shuddered again.

"It's just a spider," Chris said. "Do us all a favor and forget about the heebie jeebies, will you? And will you stop it with that annoying whine?"

Oops. Dare I say I was emitting that high-pitched "Eeeeee" sound again?

I swallowed the next stanza. "It's my heebie-jeebie hum," I said. "I don't even know I'm doing it."

"Fantastical," Chris muttered as Ms. Huge and Hairy took a few self-satisfied gulps of bug flesh.

"We are all going to die," I concluded.

"Thanks for the positive vibes, Jessie. Really helpful."

"Listen, I do not know what's happening on your side of this hell-hole," I argued. "But over here we have an apocalyptic scene of Biblical proportions going on. The largest spider on planet Earth is devouring the largest bug on planet Earth. And when Ms. Huge and Hairy is done with her current snack, one can only assume she'll set her sights on me!" I shut up in order to allow the cold sweat to start flowing.

"Oh, my God," Chris said. "There's one of those bugs over here, too. It looks like the shirt Dad was wearing yesterday."

"La La Land," Bee Bee added helpfully, and I let out a sob.

"Come on, Jessie." Chris tilted his head back in order to touch mine. "Try to get a grip, okay? Dad told me you're a gardener, right? And gardens have bugs, right?"

"No. Not right. Let me assure you I have never, ever, seen anything like what I'm witnessing right now in my rooftop garden in Clarence, North Carolina. My garden is not the big, bad, wild wilderness. There are no spiders, no bugs, no rats, n—"

"Rats!?" Chris screamed.

"Rats!?" Bee Bee screeched, and I hastened to say I had not actually seen a rat.

"Really?" Chris's voice was a bit unsteady.

"Really," I said firmly. "In fact, I think I read somewhere that there are no rats in Hawaii."

"What? Like how Ireland has no snakes?"

"Exactly." I did some quick thinking. "Somebody, umm, some Hawaiian god, drove all the rats out of Hawaii, just like Saint Patrick did with the snakes in Ireland."

"Really?"

"Oh, yes." I nodded enthusiastically even though Chris couldn't see me. "It was Maui, actually. Not the island, but the god. Maui was a helpful god, you see. He wanted to help mankind. So he got rid of the rats. He, umm, he gathered them up and herded them out to the Pacifi—"

"Jessie?"

"Yes?"

"You're making this up, aren't you?"

"Maybe."

"Maybe we should concentrate on the bugs."

Maybe. I went back to obsessing about the bugs and soon noticed something disconcertingly indiscernible scurrying along near my feet. Why oh why was I wearing those stupid, stupid flop flops? I almost started the heebie-jeebie hum again, but stopped myself in order to concentrate more fully on my imminent demise.

"Maybe the two of you are not going to die here," I said. "But I am quite certain I will perish."

"Yeah, right."

"No, really," I insisted. "So when you do get out of here, I want you to give your father and my mother an accurate report of what killed me."

"The heebie jeebies?" Chris asked.

"Heebie jeebies, heebie jeebies," Bee Bee added.

"Exactly," I said as whatever was near my toes turned around and scurried back in the opposite direction—no doubt sizing me up for its dinnertime repast.

"Maybe we should think about something other than rats or bugs," Chris suggested in an almost-kind tone of voice.

"Like what?"

"I don't know. What do you usually think about when you're trying to take your mind off your troubles?"

"Sex."

***

It took the stupid kid an inordinate amount of time to stop guffawing.

I waited patiently and then reminded him I write romance novels. "I'm almost always thinking about my stories and my characters," I said over one final guffaw. I tilted my head and grimaced at Ms. Huge and Hairy. "There is a bitter irony here, you know?"

"What's that?"

"Virtually all of Adelé Nightingale's heroines end up getting themselves kidnapped at some point or another. Some evil, vile, and altogether unsavory character holds them captive in some altogether nasty and uncomfortable location."

"But your stories always have a happy ending, right?"

"Of course."

"So think, Jessie." Chris sounded remarkably upbeat. "How do these women escape? How do they get away from the clutches of the evil bad guys?"

I pursed my lips and thought about the various and sundry predicaments Adelé Nightingale's heroines had found themselves in over the years. "First of all," I said, "none of my heroines has ever had to deal with bugs. Let alone Ms. Queen Mother Spider, Huge and Hai--"

"Yeah, but what do they do?"

I blinked at Ms. Huge and Hairy. "Umm, I think I've lost my train of thought."

"Concentrate!" Chris ordered, and I flinched. "How do your heroines escape from the bad guys?"

"Their paramours rescue them, okay? The handsome and dashing hero swash buckles his way down to the dungeon or up to the turret and saves the day, and the damsel, from certain ruin." I paused. "You didn't happen to bring a sword with you?"

"What else?" he persisted. "What would happen if the hero didn't show up with his sword?"

"Well," I said, "modern women like reading about other resourceful women. So more and more, I'm having my heroines find their own solutions."

"Such as?" Chris asked eagerly.

"Such as, in Temptation at Twilight. Alexis Wynsome solicited the help of a servant in the evil Lord Derwin Snipe's household. Alexis just happened to know Annabelle Goodloe from childhood. And so, with Annabelle's help, she discovered an escape route out of the dungeon. There was this handy-dandy tunnel that no one had ever noticed before—"

"Jessie?"

"Yes?"

"We gotta get out of here."

I sighed dramatically. "Yes, Chris. We do."

While Bee Bee regaled us with a sing-song "We-do, we-do, we-do," I asked Chris if he had ever been a Boy Scout.

"Yeah. Why?"

"It has been my experience that former Boy Scouts know their knots. I was a Girl Scout for a short time until they wanted me to go camping. But even women of my generation who were Girl Scouts for years and years never learned knots like the boys. Hopefully time has rectified this oversight, and girls today are learning their knots, but I myself could not tie a decent knot if you paid me."

"What the hell are you talking about?"

"Knots," I said. "Let's see if we can untie this thing behind us."

"If we work together maybe we can."

And so we worked together, blindly fiddling with the ropes that bound us. I dutifully followed Chris the former Boy Scout's instructions. Bee Bee helped also. But boy or not, Bee Bee had clearly never been a Boy Scout. And the pecking of his inch-long and remarkably sharp beak at our wrists was more than a bit distracting. Never mind that we also had to avoid crushing the poor thing in between us. Thus, with lots and lots and lots of patience, cooperation, and contorting of arms and wrists, we finally made things worse.

We stopped and regrouped, and the three of us had ourselves a little contest of who could sputter out the most four-letter words.

We tried again.

What's the saying? When there's a will, there's a way? And when Ms. Huge and Hairy got hungry again and started propelling herself downward, I had a pretty good incentive. I ignored Chris's complaining that I was hurting him and frantically tugged and pulled and pried.

And we did it!

"We did it!" Chris shouted and jumped to his feet.

My own fifty-two-year-old body was a bit slower to cooperate. But with Bee Bee's encouragement and Chris's assistance, I finally hobbled to a more or less upright position.

I stepped aside from the trajectory of Ms. Huge and Hairy, and that's when I noticed the only way out of the cave. A tunnel—no doubt a spider-infested tunnel.

Heebie jeebies, here I come.

***

Actually, it could have been worse. The tunnel looked relatively short, and it was bright and sunny. It had provided us with what little light we had, and now it was our path to freedom. That tunnel was my friend.

Chris and I would have been right on it, but Bee Bee was not so easily convinced. Who knows what was going through his bird brain, but the poor thing was clearly terrified of the tunnel.

"This is probably why he wasn't tied up like us," Chris said as he tried in vain to get the bird to cooperate. Bee Bee happily hopped onto Chris's wrist, but instantly flew off whenever Chris stepped toward our escape route.

I suggested we try to get him to walk, and sure enough, that worked. I took the lead, coaxing and encouraging him from ahead, and Chris took up the rear, corralling and scooting him forward. And thus, inch by slow inch, Bee Bee waddled his reluctant way out.

Proof that there is a God in heaven—we finally did reach the end. We staggered into the sunlight and waited for our eyes to adjust.

Not a big surprise, we now stood in a dense, and no doubt, bug-infested jungle. To make matters worse, it must have rained while we were in Pele's Prison. Everything—every leaf, bough, branch, and bug—glistened with raindrops, which in case you do not realize, only serves to exacerbate the heebie jeebies.

I reminded myself that at least I was out from under the clutches of Ms. Huge and Hairy and watched as Chris spent a few moments stretching and smiling at our newfound freedom. Bee Bee also seemed his old self. He fluttered his wings, and ruffled his feathers, and hopped around from bush to bush.

"Good as new!" he chirped.

"Good as new!" Chris repeated, and they both looked at me.

Oh, what the hell? "Good as new," I said and swatted at a mosquito.

Chapter 24

I scanned the immediate vicinity. "When Alexis Wynsome emerged from Derwin Snipe's tunnel, a handy-dandy white stallion was tied to the nearest tree to whisk her away to safety." I pointed to a few trees and appealed to Chris. "So, like, where's the horse?"

"Nice try, Jessie." He invited Bee Bee to hop onto his wrist, and this time the bird readily accepted the offer. "Let's roll," he said, and the two of them disappeared into a thicket of who knows what. I sighed dramatically and hastened to follow before I lost them completely.

With Chris in charge of leading the way, Bee Bee in charge of repeating our mantra whenever the mood struck, and me in charge of flailing frantically at the numerous and varied flying insects of Hawaii, we pushed forward, desperately seeking the trail that supposedly ran so very close to Pele's Prison.

Far be it for me to burst Bee Bee's bubble, but trust me, we were not good as new. And we were altogether unprepared for any sort of arduous hike. Chris was bare-chested, since he had just gotten out of the shower when he was abducted. But at least he was wearing running shoes. No socks. I myself was still clad in the ever so impractical tank top, shorts, and flip flops—an outfit about as useful as that leaf Delta Touchette was sporting.

Needless to say, we were slow-going. But Chris the wilderness expert insisted we just needed to keep moving.

Yeah, right. Even I, the wilderness wimp, knew we were hopelessly lost. Maybe the rain had camouflaged it, or maybe Chris had gotten almost as disoriented as Bee Bee while we were in the cave, but the Maka Koa Trail remained stubbornly elusive.

At some point Ranger Rye must have given up on finding it. He stopped saying it had to be right around the next grove of sandalwood trees or the next clump of oleander bushes, and started suggesting we would find an actual road.

"A road?" Skepticism veritably oozed out of my every bug-bitten pore.

"It's got to be right here," Chris hallucinated out loud. "Right past those trees up ahead." He waved toward the trees. "Think about it, Jessie. Whoever kidnapped us couldn't have carried us all the way from the Wakilulani. They had to have driven us up here, right?"

"Right," I said as I stumbled over a tree root.

He continued revising his theory, "If we keep heading downhill we're bound to find the road, right?"

"Right," I was forced to agree again.

I reminded myself that Christopher Rye had been a Boy Scout. Also, he and his father had likely been hiking in various woods and forests since the kid could walk. Chris would find the way out of La La Land. Please, God—Chris had to find the way out of La La Land.

***

About four thousand bug bites and an hour later, we were still roaming around La La Land. I was wondering if the situation could get any worse when Bee Bee flew away.

Well, that answered that question.

We cursed the Hawaiian gods and searched high and low for the bird. The good news? We finally did locate him. The bad news? We managed to get ourselves even more lost and confused in the process.

Altogether unconcerned with our plight, Bee Bee was perched in some sort of bush, munching contentedly on an abundance of large purple berries.

Chris plopped down on a nearby boulder, and testimony to my frazzled state, I accepted a seat beside him without even checking for bugs beforehand.

"I hope they're not poisonous," he said, and I sprang up.

He rolled his eyes and patted the boulder again. "There's nothing on this stupid rock, Jessie." He pointed to Bee Bee. "I'm talking about those berries."

"Bee Bee's smart," I said as I sat back down. "I'm sure he knows what he's doing."

"I wonder how long he was in Pele's Prison before we got there."

"Two days, I imagine. He needs to eat."

I studied the bird and tried not to think about Chris and my own dietary needs. If possible, we were even less equipped for our jungle adventure than Delta Touchette. At least she had possessed the foresight to bring along a canteen.

I tilted my head toward the stream we had just hopped across in our search for Bee Bee. "We should drink some water," I suggested.

"No way. You can get giardia from drinking out of the streams up here."

"Is it worse than the heebie jeebies?" I slapped an insect from Chris's right shoulder as he regaled me with all the unpleasant consequences of this giardia thing. I will spare you the details, but yes, apparently giardia is worse than the heebie jeebies.

"We'll find the road soon enough," he repeated for the umpteenth time. "Then we'll get rescued and get some water."

"Hopefully before we die," I mumbled and swatted at the bugs swarming overhead.

"Will you relax?" Chris grabbed my flailing hands and pushed them back into my lap. "Can't you try to enjoy this?"

"Excuse me?"

"That's right, Jessie. Enjoy. This place is amazing." He continued to hold my arms down and pointed outward with his free hand. "Take a look around."

I grumbled something about hating the wilderness and took a look around.

Okay, so maybe it was beautiful. First, there was the pleasant babbling of that brook off to my left. And then there was the lush jungle in all directions. The greens were out of this world. All the flowers were lovely, too. And the orchids. And the slow, steady, and refreshing breeze. The air smelled nice—sweet and fresh. Nothing like yours truly at that moment.

"La La Land," Chris said and flashed a Rye-grin.

I squeezed his hand and replaced it on his own lap. "So who did it?" I asked as Bee Bee moved to a bush bearing red berries. "Who's the killer, who kidnapped us, and why?"

"You're the sleuth. You tell me."

"Well then, I think we can rule out a woman," I said. "At one point your father suspected Bethany, but clearly she couldn't have gotten us into that cave." I nudged my companion. "You're a rather large specimen to lug around."

"And you're not exactly petite," Chris added. "But Makaila the cook could have helped her. Emi says the two of them are best friends. And Bethany loves hiking."

I recollected that Bethany had been president of her high school hiking club.

"She knows her way around Kekipi Crater," Chris was saying. "She showed me all kinds of cool places yesterday."

"But not Pele's Prison."

"Nope. We went out to Loraleii Rapids instead." He caught my eye. "You don't think she purposely kept me away from the cave, do you? You know, because she was hiding Bee Bee?"

I said it was a possibility. "But only a slim one. Russell found absolutely nothing untoward about Bethany, Makaila, or Em—"

Oops.

Chris narrowed his eyes. "Emi? Don't tell me Dad put Lieutenant Densmore on Googling detail?"

"Wouldn't you?"

"Maybe. But what's he doing checking out Emi?" he asked indignantly. "What's Dad have against my new girlfriend?"

While Chris huffed and puffed, I assured him Wilson had nothing against Emi. "She came out clean as a whistle, even under Russell Densmore's thorough scrutiny. She's not a suspect, okay?"

Chris let out one last huff. "Sometimes I hate being the son of a cop."

I patted his knee and told him I felt his pain. "How about the Hoochie Coochie Brothers?"

"They're painful, alright."

"No. I meant, I wonder if we should rule them out."

I told Chris about my rather enlightening morning, Leslie Coochie the maid, and the Coochie-Okolo-Iwatanii Town connection. But if I expected the kid to be impressed with my sleuthing skills, I was sorely disappointed. He informed me I was imparting old news—he had known who the maid was since the morning after Davy died.

"What? For Lord's sake, Chris. Why didn't you say something?"

He insisted it was no big deal. "I talked to her while you geezers slept in that day. I don't think the ukulele players had anything to do with any of this."

"They know this mountain from all those bird watching excursions," I argued. "And they're strong enough to get us up here. And this morning? They mysteriously disappeared from the Song of the Sea just moments before I was knocked out." I nodded meaningfully, but Chris was not convinced.

"So they had the strength to kidnap us," he said. "But why? This is all about the murder, right? Why would they kill Davy Atwell?"

I had no idea, but was not about to give up. "The light was on in their bungalow that night. It was after two a.m., mind you."

"So what? If staying up late makes you look guilty, we should add your mother to the list of suspects."

I folded my arms and pretended to glare. "Well then, what's your theory? Surely the offspring of Wilson Rye has an idea or two?"

Apparently Bee Bee was also interested in Rye Junior's theory. He hopped over from the berry bush and blinked at us. "Good as new!" he announced with a gleeful ruffle of feathers.

***

"Your theory," I reminded Chris as we started moving again.

"Emi and I think it was Buster," he said nonchalantly and disappeared around a huge tree. "That's an ohia tree," he changed the subject. "Aren't they great?"

With nary a glance upward, I hastened around the ohia tree and tried to catch up. "Buster!?" I called out. "No way. If it was one of the Okolo brothers, it was Ki. Or Ki working in cahoots with Carmen Dupree."

"Buster," Chris insisted over his bare shoulder.

"Ki." I extracted my right flip flop from a tangle of unidentified groundcover and frowned at its rather forlorn and bedraggled fake daisy. "Davy was the father of a couple of Carmen's children, and he was very wealthy. Carmen and Ki were looking for an inheritance." I slipped my flip flop back on and stumbled along. "Money is a powerful motive, no?"

Chris stopped and turned. "What about him?" He indicated Bee Bee. "What's Ki's motive for kidnapping this kooky bird?" As if on cue, Bee Bee pooped a big blob of purple stuff onto his running shoe.

"Good as new!" the bird informed us, and I bit my lip to keep from laughing.

"Next time it could be you," Chris warned ominously and pointed to my bare toes.

I cleared my throat and pretended to glare at Bee Bee. "He must have heard something that night—something Ki didn't want him to. What did you hear, Bee Bee?"

Bee Bee blinked slowly and repeated his name.

I turned back to Chris. "Russell told me Ki and Captain Vega are good friends. I think Vega's going out of his way to protect Ki."

"KiKiKiKiKiKi—"

"But using that logic," Chris spoke over Bee Bee, "couldn't Vega also be protecting Ki's brother?" He bent his arm so the bird faced him. "What about Buster?" he asked, and Bee Bee switched from Ki's name, to repeating Buster's name a few thousand times.

I sighed dramatically. "Okay, so Bee Bee's holding out on us. But I'm still sure he heard something useful."

"Why kidnap him? Why not just kill him?"

Bee Bee squawked at that notion, and Chris hastened to apologize. "Just saying, buddy."

I mentioned Wilson's theory that the killer had gone off the deep end. "He's stopped making any sort of rational sense."

"Well then, it's got to be Buster," Chris said and started moving again. "Think about it. He's so flakey and inept. And all this stuff that's been happening is pretty flakey and inept."

"Therefore, he wouldn't ever kill Davy," I argued. "Davy was good at his job. Buster needed him."

"How about those love triangles Geez Louise is so excited about?" Chris was getting farther and farther ahead of me. "How about a Buster, Davy, and Rachel Tate triangle?"

"Her real name is Samantha Dimmery."

"Say what?"

I explained Lieutenant Densmore's research into the Samantha-Rachel person, and then Chris explained the love triangle he was picturing.

"Buster had a crush on Rachel, or Samantha, or whoever she was, but she had a crush on Davy."

"So Buster was jealous of Davy?" I asked.

What a shocker, Chris was picking up the pace. I was tired of groaning, moaning, whimpering, and sighing, so I simply walked faster and pondered Buster Okolo's supposed motives. No offense to Chris and Emi, but the inheritance motive between Carmen and Ki still seemed far more compelling.

But yet, either of the Okolo brothers probably possessed the strength to transport Chris and me up to Pele's Prison.

"Why would Buster kidnap us?" I called out.

"To get away with murder," Chris said. "Buster needs to pin this on someone from our group. And our disappearance makes Dad look guilty, right?"

"Your father? But Captain Vega is after you, Chris."

"He's been harassing me, but the guy he really hates is Dad."

Oh, my Lord. I stopped short while a new brand of panic seized me.

Could Vega actually be blaming Wilson for our disappearance? At that very moment? Surely our disappearance must have been discovered by then. I glanced past the tree tops toward the sun and ascertained it was getting on for late afternoon. Was Wilson out searching for us? Or was he already under arrest?

Chris must have noticed I had stopped following him. He turned around and came back.

"I'm sorry," he told me. "But Vega will blame Dad when they realize we're missing. He'll say we found out Dad's the murderer, so he had to get rid of us. Vega always blames a tourist, right?"

I closed my eyes and prayed for strength, and conceded that Chris was indeed right. I mean, what other tourist could Vega possibly be blaming at that point? My mother?

Chris must have read my mind. "Miss Tessie thinks it was Buster. She told me last night she has a funny feeling about Buster."

I opened my eyes and blinked at Bee Bee. One ignores Tessie Hewitt's funny feelings at their own peril.

"Okay," I said. "We think it was Buster."

***

"Oh, my God." Something behind my left shoulder had caught Chris's eye.

I turned and saw the road. "The road!" I shouted. "The road! The road!"

"The road!" Bee Bee shouted. "The road! The road!"

"The road," Chris mumbled with far less enthusiasm and pointed to the stream that separated us from said road. What had been a babbling brook uphill a ways had morphed into a surging stream. It was a rather wide stream. A river, in fact.

"I bet it's been over there all along," Chris was saying. "We've been on the wrong side."

"Should we try to get over there?" I asked.

"Let's see." He handed Bee Bee to me and slipped off his sneakers, and Bee Bee and I watched as he plunged on in. It was deep, and at one point he had to swim a few yards to get to where he could stand up again. He waded some more and finally found solid ground on the other bank.

"Your turn, Jessie." He waved. "Toss me the shoes."

I pointed to Bee Bee. "What about him?"

"He flies."

"Here goes," I told the flying creature. I threw the cleaner sneaker across to Chris and then grimaced at its mate. Not that I was the epitome of cleanliness and hygiene at the moment, but I could still be grossed out. I wrinkled my nose and picked up the Bee Bee-soiled shoe, doing my dainty best to keep my hand away from the bird droppings.

I am happy to report that somehow that sneaker also made it clear across the river, although I wish I could say the same for my flip flops. One made it over. Its partner, however, was not so cooperative. The wind grabbed hold of it and it landed a few yards from Chris. In the water. Bless his heart, he did his best to try to save it, but apparently my flip flop was desperate to escape. The three of us watched in disbelief as it merrily bobbed its way downstream. The fake daisy disappeared from sight, I grumbled accordingly, and tiptoed into the water.

Chris waded in from his side and coaxed gently while I endeavored to shoo Bee Bee from my wrist. But Bee Bee had once again decided to be disoriented and confused. Chris and I proceeded to explain, as logically as possible, that he was going to have to fly the few yards while I swam it. The bird listened attentively but refused to let go of my wrist.

"Can you swim one-handed?" Chris asked me.

I didn't think so. But I could dog-paddle.

I frowned at Bee Bee. "Here goes, you stupid bird." I introduced him to the top of my head and for this treat he happily abandoned my wrist. Have I mentioned Bee Bee's claws?

Wasting no time I plunged on in and dog-paddled at record speed. My eyes were shut tight since Bee Bee was not too well-balanced up there. But Chris was laughing so hard I had a sense of the right direction at all times. And then Bee Bee pooped.

The good news? I couldn't see it. The bad news? I could definitely feel it. Have I mentioned all those berries he had eaten?

Despite the total gross-out factor I soldiered, or at least dog-paddled, on and made it across. I do believe it was Jessica Hewitt's most heroic moment.

I handed the stupid, stupid bird to Chris and plunged back into the water to rinse my hair. Then I staggered back to dry land, only to decide if I wanted to walk barefooted the rest of the way or with one flip flop.

Chris held up his shoes, but I declined the offer. "Very chivalrous of you, Mr. Rye, but I'd never be able to keep them on my feet."

"Well then, use the one flip flop, Jessie. A little protection on one foot is better than none at all."

I muttered various obscenities and donned my lone flip flop as Bee Bee tried to convince me I was "Good as new."

Chris also encouraged me to look on the bright side. He pointed at the road we were now standing on, and I frowned at what was in reality nothing more than a deeply rutted dirt path.

He glanced at my feet and then up at the top of my head. "At least you've stopped worrying about the heebie jeebies," he tried.

"Because now I'm worrying about your father." We started hobbling our way downhill. "Do you really think he's been arrested?"

"It wouldn't be the first time."

Chapter 25

We stopped short and stared each other.

"Oops," Chris squeaked.

You'd better believe, oops. I folded my arms and glared until Chris found his voice and actually told me I needed to ask Wilson for the details.

"Yeah, right," I said. "I do not need to ask Wilson for the details, because I am asking you for the details!" I stamped my lone flip flop. "I demand to know your father's deep dark secrets, and I demand to know them now, now, now!"

Silence from Chris, and a "Now, now, now!" from Bee Bee. I always did like that bird.

"Now!" I repeated and continued to stamp my foot, wave my arms, and shout vague threats. Throwing a temper tantrum might have been beneath my dignity, but a bird had just pooped on my head. Let's face it—I was running a little low on the dignity thing. In addition I was, right then, in imminent danger of dying from a lethal combination of dehydration and the heebie jeebies. I had suffered a very, very rough day, and I refused to die in a state of ignorance.

When I reminded my companions of all these compelling and relevant facts, they simply kept walking.

Walking!

I ran, or something akin to it, grabbed Chris's free elbow and yanked him to a full stop.

"Okay, I'm begging," I said. "Have pity on me?"

His eyes moved to the top of my head. "You are pitiful."

We negotiated, and with much ado and haggling, finally came to an agreement. Chris would tell me all about Wilson's deep dark past as long I kept walking. Deal, baby!

"How much do you know about Dianne Calloway?" he asked as we staggered downhill.

"Nothing except for her name. But why is this Dianne person Wilson's deep dark secret? Why did they break up? Why was he arrested? What was her connection? And when was all this?"

"If you shut up, I might tell you."

I shut up.

"Here goes." He took a deep breath. "They met in Raleigh. You know Dad used to live there?"

I did. Wilson had moved to Clarence only in the past few years. Raleigh was his hometown, where he grew up, and where he had raised his son.

"Dianne and Dad were together for about two years—my junior and senior years of high school," Chris continued. "Everyone expected they would get married after I started college."

"Were you okay with that?"

He shrugged. "I liked Dianne. She made Dad laugh. There were a few years after my mother died—" Chris stopped talking.

"When Wilson didn't laugh?" I asked gently.

He nodded.

"What happened?"

"Dad got arrested the night of my senior prom."

"What!?"

"It sucks, huh?"

"What for?"

"Murder."

"Murder, murder, murder," Bee Bee said gleefully.

I shook my head and tried to concentrate. "Let me get this straight. Dianne Calloway was murdered?"

"No, Jessie. Dianne's ex-husband got killed. They blamed it on Dad, but he had nothing to do with it."

"Of course he didn't."

"Dianne did it," Chris said. "But the guy was really beaten up. She killed him with a—" He took another deep breath. "Let's just say they decided Dianne had to be innocent because of her size. No one thought a woman could have done it."

I cringed. "Wilson, however."

"Could have done it," Chris said, and I cringed some more.

"I assume your father figured out the truth?" I asked.

"He said it wasn't that hard since he knew he was innocent. What was hard was convincing everyone else. He was on mandatory leave of absence from the police force so he didn't have access to much." Chris glanced over and actually grinned.

"What?"

"In case you haven't noticed, Dad stinks at amateur sleuthing. You're way better at it than he is, Jessie."

I shrugged humbly and asked how the truth had come to light.

"An old friend on the police force finally helped him out," Chris answered. "Dianne was arrested on my graduation day."

"Oh, my Lord. Wilson arrested her, didn't he? She's in prison now, isn't she?"

"Yep, and yep."

"Yep, yep, yep," Bee Bee verified.

Again, I tried to concentrate. "So, this is why you've been," I hesitated, "let's say, hesitant about me?"

"Dad did almost arrest you the night you guys met, right? For murder? And you've had lots of problems with your ex-husband, right?"

I frowned at Bee Bee. "Yep, yep. And yep."

"Dad keeps telling me you're not like Dianne," Chris said quietly.

"I'm not like Dianne," I agreed.

He scowled at my hair. "But you are a little scary."

***

Speaking of scary, we finally encountered some other hikers. You'd think this would have solved our most immediate problems. But our would-be rescuers, a middle-aged couple who clearly prided themselves on their hiking prowess and insane love of nature, took an instant and intense disliking to us.

We tried to explain our unusual appearance and arduous ordeal—the murder investigation, the kidnapping, our escape, et cetera, et cetera—but the Harveys, Wendy and Roger, remained unimpressed.

"You two were involved in the murder at the Wakilulani?" Wendy pursed her lips.

"We hear a couple of tourists did it." Roger was even better at pursing his lips than his wife. He looked us up and down while Chris and I squirmed.

"We didn't kill anyone," Chris said.

"Although we are staying at the Wakilulani," I added. "Did you happen to know Davy Atwell? I understand his Pele's Melees were something of a legend."

"We do not consume pink beverages, alcoholic or otherwise," Roger informed me with another prim pursing of lips. "My wife and I drink nothing but green tea, pomegranate juice, and spring water."

"Water!" Bee Bee exclaimed, and Chris and I nodded enthusiastically.

"We could really use some water if you guys have any extra." Chris gestured toward Roger's backpack. "Jessie and I are parched."

"Missing happy hour, are you?" Wendy asked.

I folded my arms and glared. Clearly the we-should-be-rescuing-these-poor-dehydrated-creatures theme that Chris, Bee Bee, and I were ourselves so clear about was somehow lost on the Harveys.

Mr. Harvey directed the next scolding at poor Bee Bee. "Pets are not allowed on Kekipi Crater," he said. "It is against trail rules."

"Oh, for Lord's sake!" I stopped glaring and stepped forward to once again explain our dire circumstances, but Roger was having far too much fun tut-tutting.

"Where's your shirt?" he asked Chris. "We are not surfing here, you know? Kekipi Crater is not an amusement park. I've been saying for years that proper hiking gear should be required before any tourist is even allowed on these trails."

He pointed smugly to his own outfit—a tee-shirt embossed with a save the planet logo, khaki cargo pants, a knapsack, no doubt filled with canteens, water bottles, and high-energy snacks, and last but not least, a pair of worn but sturdy-looking hiking boots.

I made the mistake of sighing forlornly at those boots, and the Harveys switched their attention back to me. Wendy kept her eyes planted firmly on my one bare foot while her husband produced my wayward flip flop from his backpack.

"Yours, I presume?"

I leapt for joy and lunged for my shoe. But Roger jumped back and, I swear to God, refused to hand it to me.

"Littering is a crime," Wendy informed me.

I blinked at the fake daisy dangling just out of my reach. "Excuse me?"

"Littering," Roger snapped. "I found this on the banks of this lovely river." He pointed to the lovely river with one hand and flapped my flip flop in front of my nose with the other. "How dare you deface these pristine waters."

Have I mentioned I was having a very rough day? I reminded the stupid Harveys of this fact and commenced wrestling Roger for my stupid shoe.

"Watch it," Chris said, and we both turned.

He jerked his head toward me. "Jessie is one very tough woman, Roger. I'd give her the shoe if I were you."

"Give her the shoe. If I were you." Bee Bee liked the little rhyme of that.

I pried the shoe out of Roger's stunned hand and slipped it on. Meanwhile Wendy reminded everyone that pets are not allowed on Kekipi Crater and poked her finger at our parrot. Chris stepped back, but bless his feisty little heart, Bee Bee lunged forward to take a bite. Wendy pulled away just in time.

"Bee Bee is one very tough bird," I told her.

Chris cleared his throat. "We're tough, but we need a lift. If you guys have a car anywhere near here, we really do need help."

"That you do," Roger agreed. He and his wife stepped away from us, apparently to discuss their options.

I turned to my companions. "Are they actually considering leaving us out here in the state we're in?" I whispered. At that exact moment a swarm of particularly vicious biting insects decided yours truly was not in enough of a state. They zeroed in for the kill, and I lost it.

I stormed over to the Harveys. "If I do not get off this damn volcano this minute I am going to die!" I shouted.

"Die!" I repeated. "Have you people not heard of the heebie jeebies!?"

I flapped my arms and took a couple more steps forward as Bee Bee commenced a sing-song round of "heeeebie-jeeeebie."

But Wendy remained unimpressed. She told me my behavior left her no choice, and pulled a cell phone from her husband's knapsack. It was hard to miss the other item she pulled out and handed to her husband. Was that really a mach—

"Stay back!" Roger shouted as he unsheathed his machete.

"What the hell?" I heard Chris say as I stumbled away from the blade.

Roger crouched into a ready-to-pounce stance. "We're armed!" he informed us.

"No shit," Chris said, and what with the absurdity of it all, I lost control yet again. But this time instead of having screaming-shouting-stomping-hissy-fit tantrum, I laughed. Oh, it was a downright psychotic laugh. But also downright cathartic. And apparently a bit contagious—Chris laughed, too.

"You might be armed," I told Roger when I could speak again. "But trust me, you are no Skylar Staggs."

"Huh?"

"Green tea and pomegranate juice," I sputtered in disgust and returned to Chris and Bee Bee.

While my back was turned the Harveys took the opportunity to hide behind the nearest banyan tree. Roger poked his machete out so we could see it. "Don't try anything funny!" he said, and Chris and I melted into another fit of laughter.

Wendy waited until we were quite finished to pop her head out from the other side of the tree. She announced she had just called the police, and they were on their way to come arrest us.

She waved her cell phone where we could see it. "I got reception!" she bragged and scurried away into the brush.

Roger swished his machete one last time. "Do not try to follow us," he warned.

"As if," Chris mumbled, and I laughed some more.

***

"You think she really got through to 911?" Chris asked after the Harveys had disappeared.

"Oh, absolutely," I lied. I limped my way over to the nearest boulder and plopped down. "And I for one am not moving another inch until help arrives." I glanced down the road. "Hopefully in a limousine equipped with running water and a shower."

Chris told me a limo was about as likely as Alexis Wynsome's white stallion, but he argued no further, set Bee Bee on a nearby branch, and sat down beside me.

Lo and behold, about ten minutes later the cops actually did arrive. We leapt for joy as two cars with flashing blue lights rolled up the road. Two police cars! They weren't limos, and in fact were funny-looking things likely suited for off-roading on places like Kekipi Crater. But this was no time to quibble.

We waved enthusiastic greetings, but once again we seemed far happier to see others than they were to see us.

Two uniformed cops, one from each car, strutted over and surveyed us from head to toe. From the frowns on their faces, I gathered we weren't all that pleasant a sight to behold.

"Names?" the female cop demanded, and we gave them our names.

"And this is Bee Bee." I gestured toward Bee Bee who was perched back on Chris's wrist.

"They fit the descriptions," the male cop said to the female cop. "Except for her hair."

My hair?

I turned to Chris, and he informed me I had a very bright, very large patch of purple hair on the top of my head. "From, umm, you know." He tilted his head toward Bee Bee.

I closed my eyes and prayed for strength.

***

And strength I needed. Because the cops, Officers Higashi and Oskeen, seemed even less impressed with our plight than the Harveys had been.

They weren't interested in our theory about Davy Atwell's killer either. We had barely begun explaining Buster's motives when Officer Oskeen the female cop interrupted. "What have you done with the Harveys?" she demanded.

I waved a dismissive hand. "They deserted us hours ago."

"It was more like minutes ago," Chris said quietly and pointed toward the brush. "They went that-a-way."

Officer Oskeen frowned in said direction, and when she told us they were taking us down to the station, we bounded for her car.

"No!" Officer Higashi the male cop yanked Chris out just as he started climbing in behind me and pointed him toward the other car. "You come with me."

"Wait a minute!" Chris and I protested in unison as I climbed back out.

"We've been through hell together," I informed the cops. "Chris rides with me."

"No." Higashi none-too-gently shoved Chris toward the other car. "We don't want you working on your story together."

Our story?

Bee Bee must not have liked the ominous implications of that. The poor thing panicked and flew off into the bushes. And meanwhile the stupid cops continued pushing and shoving us into their cars, apparently under the impression we would desert the bird.

"Nooooo!" Chris and I shouted in unison. We struggled against the closing car doors and wrestled our ways out of the respective vehicles.

We stumbled back to each other and together stood our ground. "We don't leave without Bee Bee," I said.

"Never." Chris spoke with as much authority as a bare-chested, severely dehydrated twenty-two-year-old could muster.

"So you're resisting arrest?" Ms. Oskeen asked.

"Arrest!" we shouted.

"Arrest!" Bee Bee screeched and flew back to Chris.

Chris faced Officer Higashi and ordered him to back off. "I'll get him into the car." He tilted his head toward Bee Bee. "But it may take a minute. He's kind of scared."

Bee Bee finally allowed Chris to lower him into the back seat, and the three of them drove off without further ado.

I turned to Officer Oskeen. "Are we really under arrest?" I asked wearily.

Chapter 26

Disapproving cop-eyes followed my every move as Officer Oskeen escorted me through the Halo Beach Police Station and toward what I assumed was the closed door of Captain Vega's office.

She rapped once, opened the door, and shoved me in. "Good luck," she said. "You'll need it."

I stumbled into a rather crowded office. Chris and Bee Bee were already there. And an even nicer surprise, so was Wilson. Bee Bee offered me a welcoming bob-bow from his spot on top of Vega's desk, and Vega snarled unpleasantly from his seat behind the desk. But Rye Senior was too busy hugging his son to notice me.

I smiled at Chris, especially when I saw the silly Hawaiian shirt decorated in bikinis that someone—Wilson?—had seen fit to loan him. Chris freed one arm and flapped it in my direction. "Hey, Jessie."

Wilson spun around and caught me in his arms. Eventually he let go and held me up by my shoulders. It was hard not to notice the frown—make that, the grimace.

"I have had a very rough day," I mumbled.

"What happened to your hair?"

Luckily, Vega saved me from answering. He ordered us to sit, and he and Wilson immediately dived into a heated argument about "what the hell was going on."

I had no idea, so I stayed out of it and concentrated on Bee Bee. I might have descended into a zombie-like stupor, but Bee Bee still had some spunk. He rustled around in the papers on Vega's desk making quite a mess of things. For some reason I found this most gratifying.

"I took one look at your laptop, still open and sitting out on our porch, and I knew Tessie was right to be worried." Wilson was looking at me. Evidently he was speaking to me.

"Huh?" I said.

"Tessie," he repeated and explained, perhaps for the second or third time, that my mother had been the first to realize Chris and I were missing. And by the time Wilson and Louise returned from their hike, she was in a panic.

"I left Louise with Tessie and came down here to report the latest. I've been arguing with this idiot ever since." Wilson waved an irritated hand, and I glanced at Vega.

"At least he hasn't arrested you," I said, and it occurred to me Chris and I hadn't been put in shackles either. I was gearing up to feel a bit relieved when Vega spoke.

"One of you is guilty," he snapped and pointed back and forth between Rye One and Rye Two. "I can feel it in my bones, whether or not I understand how this supposed kidnapping fits into your plans."

"Well then, your bones are as stupid as you are," Wilson said. He grabbed my mother's clipboard, which he had stashed underneath his chair, and jabbed at something for Vega's edification. "I keep telling you, it was Ki Okolo. You know Ki, Vega? The guy who does all your IT work? Your good buddy and pal?"

"You found my notes?" I asked stupidly.

"Densmore's getting a raise the minute I get home." Wilson spoke to me but kept his eyes firmly planted on Captain Vega.

But Vega refused to discuss his buddy the IT expert and reminded us once again what his bones were telling him.

Thinking we might set everyone straight, I glanced over at Chris. But the poor guy was in no shape to argue with anyone. In fact, he seemed to be in some sort of trance. I sat up and forced myself to emerge from my own stupor.

"We need water," I said firmly and tilted my head toward Chris. "We are seriously dehydrated."

Wilson took one look at his son and sprang toward the door. "Water!" he shouted. "We need water in here! Now, people!"

Captain Vega reminded us he was the one in charge. But nevertheless, two uniformed cops scurried in with two gloriously large glasses of ice water. Wilson took the glasses and handed them to us, and Chris shuffled into a more upright position.

Wilson turned to the cops. "Two more of the same, please. And keep it coming." They nodded and left, but he thought of something else and poked his head out the door again. "If there's any food in this place, bring that, too."

"I'm in charge here," Vega repeated testily, but no one was interested except Bee Bee.

He looked up from the pile of paperwork he was destroying. "I'm in charge here," he let us know, and promptly pooped.

Vega sputtered out a long string of expletives and sprang up to gather the offensive paperwork. Bee Bee obligingly repeated the expletives, waddled over to the edge of the desk, and watched as the soiled papers hit the wastebasket.

Wilson was watching also. He blinked twice at the garbage, and then at the bird, and then at my head. "Don't tell me," he said.

I set down my empty glass. "I have had A Very Rough Day," I said with a haughty toss of my purple head.

"Jessie may look like crap," Chris added ever so kindly. "But it's thanks to her Bee Bee even made it here. You should have seen her, Dad."

"No, it's thanks to Chris," I argued. "Bee Bee trusted him through thick and thin out there. Your son carried him practically the whole way."

"Believe it or not, I really don't care how this stupid bird got here," Vega muttered. While he and Bee Bee resumed cursing at each other, Chris and I were served more water and a couple of those little cellophane packets of peanut butter crackers. We ate and drank ravenously, making sure to toss Bee Bee a cracker or two.

Wilson studied us with growing dismay. "Why am I thinking your jungle adventures were even weirder than Delta Toupee's?"

"Touchette," I corrected.

Vega looked up from the mess of crumbs Bee Bee was spreading all over everything. "Excuse me?" he asked.

"My mother," I said and washed down my last cracker with some more water. The nourishment must have revived my mental acuity, and I was starting to think straight. "I need to call her."

"You can call your mommy later."

"No. Now." Wilson handed me his cell phone.

"She must be worried sick," I said as I punched in her number.

"Hello?" Mother answered after only half a ring, and when I said hello back, she started to cry.

Oh, good Lord. Mother crying always makes me cry. And after the day I had endured? Let's just say it took a few minutes to assure her I was okay. As was Chris. As was Bee Bee.

"Where are you?" I asked and was pleased to hear she was alone in her bungalow.

"Bless her heart, Louise is up at the tiki bar, trying to get some new information from Ki," she said. "But I simply couldn't face the world this evening. Not with you and Chris missing and in who knows what kind of danger. Oh, but I should go tell her you're okay—"

"No!" I said in no uncertain terms. "Please wait," I suggested in a softer voice.

With Wilson, Chris, and Bee Bee listening patiently, and with Vega looking like he was about to pop an artery, I gave Tessie a brief summary of what had happened and where I had been all day.

"In the jungle?" Mother was incredulous. "Are you alright, Jessie?"

I took stock of my bruised and bug-bitten appendages. "Sort of," I lied.

"And you say you're at the police station? I'll drive right down, Honeybunch. I'll be there in a jiffy. Aren't we glad I didn't return my rental car? Even after you and Wilson kept insist—"

"Wait!" I interrupted again, and she stopped. "By all means, go get Louise and come on down. But do so discreetly, okay? Do not tell anyone where you're going. Make something up."

She thought about what I was saying. "The culprit's here," she whispered. "At the Wakilulani."

"Exactly. So other than Louise, don't tell anyone we've been found. Anyone," I repeated firmly.

"You know who the killer is, don't you, Jessie?"

"It was Buster. Chris convinced me."

"I knew it! I've been thinking about it all day."

I frowned at the growing darkness outside Vega's window. "Mother?" I asked.

"Yes, Jessie?"

"Drive safely."

I handed Wilson back his phone. "Tessie and Louise are on their way."

"Did you just say, Buster?" he asked me.

"Did she just say her mother is joining us?" Vega asked Bee Bee.

***

I was rather looking forward to returning to a zombie-like stupor until my mother arrived, but Wilson had other plans.

"Buster Okolo?" He shook his head in disbelief. "Give me motive, means, and opportunity." He looked back and forth between Chris and me. "Convince me it was Buster."

"It was Buster," Bee Bee said.

"Why?" Wilson and Vega asked in unison.

"Means is easy," I began. "Clearly Buster knows The Big House and all the grounds at the Wakilulani Gardens like the back of his hand. He knew where to find the biggest knife, where to hide it, et cetera, et cetera."

"Opportunity is pretty easy, too, Dad. Like Jessie says, if anyone knows where everyone is at every moment around that place, it's Buster."

"It's Buster!" Bee Bee again.

"He was likely planning this for a while," I continued as my intuition began kicking in. "But he needed to have some guests staying at the resort before he did the deed—to complicate things and throw suspicion elsewhere." I nodded to Vega. "We tourists were his decoys."

"Jessie's right," Chris said. "Miss Tessie and I played right into his hand when we called in our last-minute drink order that night. I bet he was especially happy when I went up to The Big House to retrieve it."

"That was his best opportunity," I said.

"His best opportunity to make me look guilty," Chris mumbled, and Wilson and Vega exchanged a meaningful look. They didn't dispute us, but they weren't wholeheartedly agreeing with us either.

"Buster also had the means to kidnap us," Chris said. "He has that big old jeep, and he knows Kekipi Crater. He grew up here, right?"

"Right," Bee Bee said.

"But Ki also knows the volcano," Wilson argued.

"Ki Okolo?" Vega let out a snort. "Ki's about as outdoorsy as your girlfriend." Wilson raised an eyebrow, and Vega glanced up from where he was gathering the cracker crumbs on his desk into a nice, tidy circle. "Umm, maybe Ki and me are friends," he admitted as Bee Bee waddled over to again scatter the crumbs.

Wilson made sure to frown and then returned to Chris. "What was Buster's motive?"

"Jealousy," Chris answered and proceeded to explain the Buster-Davy-Samantha Dimmery love triangle.

I reached over and tapped the clipboard on Wilson's lap.

He nodded and spoke to Vega. "Rachel Tate and Samantha Dimmery are one and the same person, if you're interested."

I reminded Wilson of that raise Russell Densmore had earned, and Vega reminded him Buster's supposed motive was pretty darn flimsy. And—there's a first time for everything—Wilson agreed with Vega. They were arguing against the flimsy jealousy motive when the door opened behind us. Everyone jumped up as my mother and Louise rushed in.

"It was Buster," Mother said as we all stood up.

She tossed a jumbo bottle of Advil to Wilson, walked directly toward me, and gave me what was perhaps the most maternal hug of my life.

***

"Good heavens, Jessie," Mother said when she finally let go of me. "What happened to your hair?" Luckily she didn't wait for an answer but stepped away to hug the dickens out of Chris.

Louise also greeted us with her own brand of enthusiasm, and while Wilson divvied up the Advil to anyone in need, Captain Vega attempted to get everyone to sit down. His office had reached its maximum capacity, but we made do. Wilson gave his chair to Tessie, and found a spot at the windowsill to lean on. And Chris offered his chair to Louise, but she was happy to sit on the edge of Vega's desk and play with Bee Bee.

"It was Buster," Mother repeated when everyone was more or less settled.

"Buster!" Bee Bee wholeheartedly agreed.

"We just saw him," Louise said. "He was busy with the early dinner arrivals, but I made sure to let him know we were off in search of you two." She pointed to Chris and me.

"Wasn't that clever of Louise?" Mother asked. "She has Buster thinking we're driving all over Kingdom Come looking for you." She nodded stoutly. "It was him alright."

"Why?" Vega and Wilson asked.

"Well now, Buster was jealous of Davy wasn't he? Over the cute desk clerk that Bethany wasn't very fond of."

"I love, love, love the love-triangles theories," Louise told Bee Bee, but as usual, Wilson was not so keen on jealousy theme.

"Sorry, Tessie," he said. "But it's not enough."

Mother sighed. "I suppose not. But when Jessie came up missing this morning, I put my thinking cap on." She tapped her temple. "And I've decided Buster's problems with Davy went a bit deeper. This was about the proprietorship of the Wakilulani Gardens, wasn't it?"

"Was it?" several of us asked.

"Buster is trying so hard to give the place a fresh start, isn't he? And poor Davy Atwell was the very last remnant of the old staff under Pono Okolo." She stopped and glanced at me, as if this explanation had clarified everything.

I blinked twice. "Okay, soooo Buster wanted everything new…"

"That's right, Honeybunch. New beds, new décor."

"New pool table."

"New Christmas tree ornaments," Louise added.

"New everything," Chris concluded.

"New staff," I said and turned to Wilson. "New. Staff."

"What?" he said. "You're telling me Buster wanted a whole new staff, so he killed the old bartender?"

"Why not just fire him?" Vega asked.

"I imagine because Ki wouldn't let him," Mother answered. "Without Davy, Ki has to be the bartender, leastways until they hire someone new."

"And we all know Ki isn't happy about that," Louise said. "They should make Bethany the bartender. Someone who knows how to mix a decent pink dri—"

"Let's not forget Davy was paying Carmen Dupree child support," Mother interrupted. "Without his job, Davy wouldn't do that anymore. Ki must have instructed Buster not to fire Davy."

I thought about Derrick Crowe. "When Buster fired the old chef, the guy fell off the face of the earth, and now Carmen receives no child support from him." I offered Wilson a meaningful glance. "Buster learned a lesson from that."

"Jessie," he said impatiently. "You can't get child support from a dead guy."

"But you can get an inheritance," Mother argued. "And Buster so wants to please his big brother."

"By killing someone?" Wilson shook his head. "Sorry. I'm still not buying it."

But Rye Junior was. He helped us out. "Carmen gets happy about an inheritance from Davy Atwell, and so that makes Ki happy, and so that makes Buster happy." Chris shrugged at his father. "It kind of makes sense."

Wilson took a deep breath. "So let me get this straight. Ki wouldn't let Buster fire Davy, so he killed him instead?"

"I know it sounds crazy," Mother said. "But I do believe that's what happened."

I reminded Wilson that he himself had been insisting the killer had gone off the deep end.

"This is pretty crazy," he conceded.

"Crazy to you and me," Mother agreed. "But I'm afraid Buster isn't as logical as the two of us, is he, Wilson?"

My poor beau. He scowled, perhaps pondering the disconcerting notion that his logic and my mother's were somehow comparable.

"What about the kidnappings?" Vega switched topics and waved an index finger between Chris and me. "Why take these two?"

"Buster just wanted to confuse the issue," Mother answered. "He wanted you to think Wilson or Chris were responsible for all these terrible things. You have focused on the two Rye boys haven't you, sir?"

"But he kidnapped Chris," Vega argued, and my mother slumped.

"That does seem odd, doesn't it?"

"Yes, it does." I sat up straight as my intuition kicked into full gear. "But Buster didn't intend to kidnap Chris at all. He meant to take you, Mother."

"What!?" everyone asked at once.

"Think about it," I said. "Chris and I were both lured into the jungle with a few 'Bee Bee' calls."

"Bee Bee," Bee Bee said, and my mother jumped.

"Oh, I see!" she said. "I didn't hear anyone calling because I'm half deaf."

Chris jumped, too. "I heard it instead!" He looked at me, his eyes wide. "You and your mother were supposed to be kidnapped, not you and me."

"Exactly." I turned to Wilson. "But once Buster realized whom he had lured out there, he must have panicked and changed his plans."

Wilson groaned. "And took my son."

I studied my eighty-two-year-old mother and thought about the implications of this mishap. Chances were very good that if Tessie had been trapped with Bee Bee and me up in Pele's Prison, we would all still be there. I shifted my focus to Chris. Okay, so maybe I was starting to appreciate

Rye Junior. Maybe I was starting to appreciate him very much.

"Why was Bee Bee kidnapped?" Louise asked. "What about Bee Bee?"

"Bee Bee?" Bee Bee asked.

"Well now, I misspoke a moment ago," Mother answered. "Davy Atwell was not the last remnant of the old days with Pono. This little guy was." She reached out to the bird and he waddled over to be petted. "One last perso—I mean, one last creature to get rid of for that clean slate."

"Why not just kill him?" Vega asked, and both Bee Bee and Louise squawked.

Tessie smiled at the bird. "I do not know. But aren't we all glad he didn't?"

Wilson turned to Vega. "We need to catch this guy."

"Great idea." Vega pointed back and forth between Chris and me. "We'll use these two as bait."

Excuse me?

Chapter 27

Altogether aghast, I stared at my reflection in the cloudy mirror of the ladies restroom at the Halo Beach Police Station. The specter staring back at me was horrifying, but not nearly as horrifying as "The Plan" Captains Vega and Rye had in store for me. I whimpered slightly and set about cleaning up.

I washed my hands, face, neck and arms in the rusty sink. Then I tried doing the same to my hair. But the soap from the dispenser clearly was not meant to tackle anything so challenging, and I managed only to get my very short coif into a tangled, sticky mess. I hunched over and rinsed and rinsed to no avail whatsoever. In fact, when I looked up the purple stain at the top of my head might have actually spread.

Officer Oskeen yanked a few paper towels from the dispenser and handed them to me, and I dried my purple do as best I could. Although I was not under arrest, Vega had decided I needed an escort to the ladies room. A good idea—Ms. Oskeen was indeed keeping me from jumping out the window.

I spied her reflection in the mirror. "You don't happen to have a comb I might borrow?"

"Not on your life."

I gave up on my appearance and turned to face the cop. "I understand I'm to get one last meal before my final demise?"

She took my elbow and ushered me back to Vega's office, where a pizza party was already underway. Chris was sitting in front of an entire pie, and devouring such with little trouble whatsoever. My mother sat me down in front of another pizza, handed me a paper plate, and encouraged me to eat. She picked up a slice and no doubt would have hand-fed me if I had not taken it for myself.

Testimony to my stalwart and rugged nature, I continued eating despite the dinnertime conversation. Everyone but yours truly was excited about "The Plan," which they discussed as if it were perfectly reasonable to send Chris and me back into the jungle. Yes, you read that right. Chris and I were going back up Kekipi Crater. Back to Pele's Prison. Back to Ms. Huge and Hai—

Perhaps I should explain.

First of all, once the pizzas were gone, Captain Vega was going to call the Wakilulani Gardens and tell Buster and Ki that Wilson had been arrested for the murder of Davy Atwell.

"I'll lie and say we think he killed you guys, too, but we have yet to locate your bodies." Vega pointed back and forth between Chris and me, and I groaned accordingly.

"It'll throw Buster off guard," Wilson said. "He'll think he's off the hook." He grinned. "That is until Tessie shows up."

I groaned again as my mother and Louise chimed in with part two, their role in "The Plan." They were to take Bee Bee home. And when they got back to the Wakilulani, they would concoct a story about how they had found the bird by the side of the road, just a mile away from the resort, when they were driving around in search of Chris and me.

Of course, Mother and Louise were going to act very concerned that Chris and I had yet to be found, dead or alive.

"And we'll be shocked—absolutely and totally shocked—when we hear the terrible, terrible, terrible news about Wilson's arrest!" Louise said.

"Terrible, terrible," Mother tut-tutted, practicing her performance.

Bee Bee looked up from the pizza crust Louise was feeding him. "Terrible, terrible, terrible!" he reiterated gleefully. But of course Bee Bee could afford to be gleeful, since he was going back to the Wakilulani. Unlike yours truly.

"Y'all can count on us," Mother said. "We'll keep a close eye on Buster's actions as the dinner crowd thins out."

"Seeing Bee Bee will freak him out," Chris explained, just in case I was not following. "He'll wonder if we've also escaped from Pele's Prison. He's bound to come looking for us, right?"

"Right!" Louise answered for me. "Tessie and I will call Captain Vega the moment—the absolute moment—Buster leaves the Wakilulani," she assured me.

Knowing where this was headed, and more importantly where I was headed, I put down my pizza and tried desperately to think of a flaw.

"It won't work," I said and shook my head vigorously at Vega. "You'll be up on that mountain with us, correct? And cell phones don't work on Kekipi Crater, correct?" I threw my hands up in surrender. "It won't work," I repeated and sighed dramatically. "No reception."

"Yes, reception," Vega said. "All our cars have signal boosters." While I curled my lip he explained that his car was equipped for electronic communication, even on the mountain.

I mumbled a fantastical as Wilson, quite unnecessarily, reminded me of my role in this whole thing. Apparently Buster would come looking for us in Pele's Prison. And—I hope you are sitting down—Chris and I would be there.

Oh yes. While my mother and Louise sat at the Wakilulani bar in comfort and ease, enjoying who knows how many pink drinks without me, and waiting for Buster to make his move, I would be traipsing back up that stupid volcano with Christopher Rye, i.e. The Mountain Man. Wilson and Vega were hiking up with us in order to get us back into that stupid cave and—wait for it—tie us up again!

"We'll get lost," I insisted. "There's no way we'll find Pele's Prison at night."

But Vega assured me he was "outdoorsy," had been to Pele's Prison "a million times," and thus would have no trouble finding the stupid, stupid cave. "No trouble at all," he said.

"No trouble at all!" Bee Bee said.

"I'm too tired." I pointed to my burned-out flip flops. "I really don't see how I can get up that mountain again in these."

"I'll carry you piggy-back if need be," Wilson the ever-chivalrous offered, and Vega reminded me he'd be driving us practically the whole way. Apparently the road extended far, far up the hill, much farther than where Chris and I had found it.

"You can do this, Jessie," Wilson insisted. "And once we get you two back in the cave, Vega and I will be hiding very close by. You know I won't let anything happen to you."

"That's right," Chris said. "And when Buster shows up, we'll ask all the right questions and get a confession out of him, right?"

"Right," I mumbled.

Vega held up a tape recorder, and lo and behold I thought of another detail to take issue with. "Any confession we get on that won't be legal." I threw my hands up in defeat once again. "I'm afraid this just won't work."

"This isn't for the courts," Vega said. "It's for Ki."

"Excuse me?"

Vega insisted that, despite his lack of social graces, Ki Okolo was concerned about law, order, and justice. "It's why he does the IT work for the department. Once Ki understands what's happened, he'll make sure his brother confesses. All legal and legit." He wiggled the tape recorder at me. "You're doing the talking by the way."

"Me!?"

"You're fast on your feet," Chris said. I raised an eyebrow, and he reconsidered. "You're a fast thinker anyway. You'll talk Buster into confessing way better than I could."

I appealed to Wilson, but he insisted that I'm a great amateur sleuth, to which everyone chimed in agreement.

"You'll be perfect!" Louise said. "What with Adelé Nightingale's extensive experience at annihilating the bad guys? Just pretend you're one of your heroines, Jessica. Delta Touchette, or Ava LaTellier, or Alexis Wynsome, or Devin—"

"Jessie doesn't have to pretend to be anyone but herself," Mother argued. She turned to Vega. "My daughter is quite experienced at catching killers, you know? She's helped Wilson several times."

I sighed dramatically and spoke to Chris. "You're okay with this plan?"

"No fear," he said.

"Yes, fear," I argued. "Surely you haven't forgotten about Ms. Huge and Hairy?"

His face dropped. "Umm, she'll be asleep, right? I bet she won't even notice we're there." He tried sounding certain, but something else must have occurred to him, and his face fell a bit further. "But what about the rats?" he whispered.

"There never used to be rats." That was Vega.

"What?" Chris and I said in unison.

"It was one of our best natural phenomena. Now they've been brought in on ships. But we were rat-free for centuries."

I smirked at Chris. "Told you so."

***

Oh, to possess the skill set of Skylar Staggs, I thought to myself as I dutifully trudged through the jungles of Kekipi Crater. I mean, wouldn't it be convenient to simply swing from tree to tree and branch to branch, with wild animals smiling down upon me, until we found our destination?

But no. Unlike the brave and talented Skylar, I myself was once again flip-flopping my slow, painful way—this time uphill and in the dark—along what my companions insisted was a path. A very short path, Vega even tried to convince me as he led the way.

"Your cave isn't far from here at all," he called over his shoulder.

My cave? I had news for the guy—that cave belonged to Ms. Huge and Hairy. But I did not argue, preferring to conserve my energy for more pressing matters, such as swatting frantically at the flying insects of the Hawaiian night.

"Aren't we there yet?" I whined at some point. "It's been over an hour."

"It's been ten minutes," Wilson grumbled from behind me.

"Is she always this annoying?" Vega asked.

"Yes," the Ryes replied in unison. Wilson gave me a little push through the next patch of heavy brush and I staggered into a small clearing.

"Pele's Prison," Vega announced triumphantly and flashed his flashlight into the tunnel.

"Eeeeee…"

He jumped and dropped his light. "What was that?"

"It's just Jessie." Chris bent down to retrieve the flashlight. "It's her heebie-jeebie hum."

"Her what?" Wilson and Vega asked.

"She doesn't even know she's doing it." Chris directed the light into the tunnel and disappeared.

***

"Holy Mother of God!" Wilson, who is not much for exclamations, exclaimed.

You guessed it—we were all in Pele's Prison—and Chris had the flashlight pointed at Ms. Huge and Hairy. She was, most decidedly, not asleep. How could the poor creature sleep when she was far too busy devouring yet another Mr. Rainbow Bug?

I blinked twice. At least I assumed it was a different rainbow bug than earlier in the day. After all, Ms. Huge and Hairy looked like she had put on some weight since I last saw her.

Vega was also staring aghast. "They're not poisonous," he tried.

"Yeah, right."

"No, really." The man had yet to move his eyes from the spectacle. "At least, not very."

Wilson reached out and gave my hand a squeeze. "You guys will be fine," he said none too certainly.

"Of course we will." Poor Chris. For some reason, perhaps delirium, he actually sounded confident in that statement. He took off his Hawaiian shirt, tossed it to his father, and invited me to join him as he sat down in the gravel.

I resigned myself to my fate, and we got into position, back to back.

Wilson knelt down to tie us up. "I'm sorry," he whispered as Vega handed him the rope.

Vega had brought along some new rope in his knapsack, but we all agreed Buster should see the rope he had originally used. The hiking Harveys likely would not have approved of such flagrant littering, but Chris and I had left that scrap in the cave when we had departed earlier. Escaping with ourselves and Bee Bee alive and intact had seemed the more pressing issue.

The old rope was frayed and not in great shape, but Wilson assured us it would do the trick as he tied some sort of Boy Scout knot behind our backs. "If Buster notices it's in tatters, he'll assume you've been sitting here all day trying to free yourselves."

He guided my right hand to one of the frayed ends. "Pull this and it will come undone. But don't do it too soon. We want Buster to think you're still trapped, right?"

"Right," I mumbled unenthusiastically.

He held up two pocket knives for my viewing pleasure. And while I pondered why, he slipped one into my shorts pocket and presumably put the other one within Chris's reach.

"A pocket knife?" Chris was clearly unimpressed. "What about the gun?"

"Gun!?" I shouted.

"Yes, gun," he repeated. "If Buster has a gun and starts shooting at us, I don't care how many pocket knives we have, we'll be dead."

Silly me. Here I had been under the mistaken and altogether naïve delusion that my most pressing problem would be suffering through another simple bout of the heebie jeebies.

Wilson nodded to Vega, and a gun emerged from the knapsack.

"You guys are putting us in this situation, and you actually think Buster will have a gun?" I asked indignantly.

"No," Wilson corrected me. "We don't think he has a gun. He would have used it by now if he did. But better safe than sorry."

I nudged Chris behind me. "I assume you know how to use the stupid thing."

"I'm not Wilson Rye's son for nothing," he said. "But I've never shot at anything in the dark."

While I practiced some deep breathing, the gun and a flashlight were hidden behind our hips. Apparently, when all hell broke loose, I was to remain level-headed enough to get us untied and point the flashlight at Buster, and Chris was to remain level-headed enough to point the gun at him. The role of the stupid pocket knives? I had no idea.

Have I mentioned "The Plan" sucked?

One final task was given to yours truly as Wilson bent down and placed a tape recorder in the hiding place beside my hip. Again he guided my fingers and they found the "On" switch.

"Turn this on the minute Buster gets down here. You got it?"

"Got it," I mumbled, and Vega reminded me I was to do the talking and get a confession out of Buster. I sputtered out a few four-letter words, he wished us luck, and left.

Wilson was still kneeling next to us. He reached out and enveloped us in a bear hug. "I'll be right outside," he whispered. "I know you guys will do great."

I think he must have kissed his son on the cheek, but Chris told him to get the hell out of there. Wilson offered my own cheek a hasty but very precious peck, picked up his flashlight, and then he was gone.

And it was really, really dark.

Chapter 28

Time passed.

I listened intently, but the only sound I heard, which I hoped was a figment of my overactive imagination, was the sound of Ms. Huge and Hairy eating Mr. Rainbow Bug II. Chomp, chomp, chomp.

"Tell me a story, Jessie?"

"Excuse me?"

"How about the basics of *My South Pacific Paramour*?" Chris asked. "Dad says it's gonna be your best yet."

"Wilson?" I scowled into the darkness. "He never pays the slightest attention to my stories."

"Oh yes he does. He likes your sex scenes."

"Excuse me?"

"He says your pen name isn't Add-a-Lay Nightingale for nothing. It's how Larry broke his leg, you know?"

"Your roommate?" I scowled some more. "The guy who cancelled your ski trip?"

"Yep. After Dad told us how your books win all these prizes for being so sexy, Larry ordered a few for his Kindle."

"For his Kin—" I shook my head as it finally dawned on me. "Let me guess," I said. "Larry wasn't cramming for his chemistry final when he broke his leg—he was reading one of my books."

"A Devilish Desire. He wasn't watching where he was going and walked straight into the chemistry building."

I do believe even Ms. Huge and Hairy laughed at that.

"Well, I am sorry," I said eventually. "I assume you've been blaming me for ruining your ski trip."

"Nah. I'm having a great time with you guys. Hawaii's cool." Chris must have noticed his surroundings. "Not our cave, but generally speaking." He nudged me gently. "You're having fun, too. Aren't you, Jessie?"

Lord help me, I smiled despite myself. "Yes, Chris," I said. "I do believe I am."

"So then, tell me the story. Not the kinky parts," he hastened to add. "But the plot and stuff."

Thus I took a deep breath and filled him in on Delta Touchette's plight.

"Urquit Snodgrass, a.k.a. the Pirate of Diamond Island and the Monster of Ebony Island, has kidnapped Delta," I concluded. "He is right now holding her captive—literally holding her—over the crest of the Goochie Leoia Gorge. He's torn between ravishing her and tossing her into the depths of the waterfalls."

"Goochie Lee-O-I-A," Chris repeated. "I like that. But what's Snotgrass waiting for? Your books are all about the ravishing scenes, right?"

"Wrong. First of all his name is Snodgrass," I corrected. "And he's the bad guy. He doesn't get a sex scene—Adelé Nightingale's readers would never tolerate such a thing. He will, however, get to see our lovely heroine naked. That leaf she's wearing is about to fall off."

"Did you just say, leaf?"

"The altogether overwhelming sight of Delta's mostly-exposed bosom has left Snodgrass temporarily mesmerized. He wants to toss her into the depths of Goochie Gorge, which he imagines will surely kill her, but he can't quite tear his gaze away from her curvaceous figure."

"Why's he want to kill her?"

"Because he knows she knows about his hidden treasure. Snodgrass might be sinister, but he's not stupid. He knows if he allows Delta to go free, she'll run back to civilization and report to lawman Skylar Staggs about the gold. And then so much for Snodgrass!"

"What's Snodgrass planning to do with all the gold?"

Okay, good question. I thought about the inner workings of Urquit Snodgrass's sinister mind.

"You know what?" I said. "He just likes hoarding it. He's a hermit. He likes living all alone in the woods, and sleeping under the stars. The man really does have simple needs. But he likes power, too, and he likes instilling fear in others. He's thrilled that the inhabitants of both Ebony and Diamond Islands have begun believing in a ludicrous rumor that the pirate is in actuality a monster. The Monster of

Ebony Island! Why, that's the issue that lured Delta Touchette away from her homeland back in Dreary Old England and to her Auntie Eleanor's in the first place."

"I think I'm getting a headache," Chris said, and I admitted it was a rather convoluted plot.

"But we're just getting to the good part," I said. "The fateful scene where Snodgrass makes his decision and tosses the delectable Delta into the waterfalls of the Goochie Leoia. On her way down she finally loses that leaf and screams accordingly.

"But the despicable Snodgrass isn't the only one to witness such. Skylar Staggs has just swung into the scene—and I do mean swung. Skylar is your typical Tarzan-type hero. He can swing through the tree tops with the best of them. And just as he lights down, he sees Snodgrass snickering, and Delta falling, and he has to make a hasty decision—catch the villain or save the damsel."

"Save the damsel," Chris said with assurance.

"Absolutely. Skylar hesitates not at all before diving straight into the waterfall." I smiled at the image. "I'll spare you the details—the kinky stuff, as you say—but an altogether inspired love scene will ensue once he pulls the nubile and nude Delta out of the watery depths. They'll find themselves in a most pleasant grove of banyan trees, and, well, you get the picture."

Chris let out a slow whistle. "No wonder Larry broke his le—"

"Heads up!" Wilson called out, and we both jumped. "Buster's on his way." The flashlight shone into Pele's Prison as my beau entered through the tunnel. "Tessie and Louise just called. Buster's been on pins and needles—your mother's words—all evening. Seeing Bee Bee freaked him out—Louise's words. But the dinner crowd kept him busy. Until now."

Wilson turned to leave, but thought of something else, and stopped. "By the way, Tessie's pretty sure he left carrying a knife. A big knife, but that's way better than a gun, right?"

He gave us a thumbs up and disappeared.

I closed my eyes and prayed for strength.

But then I pictured Buster coming at me with a knife. And then I remembered how he had treated Bee Bee. And Chris. And Davy.

And then I got mad.

***

"Anyone home?" Buster called from the tunnel, all perky-like.

"What the hell do you think," I called back and switched on the tape recorder just as he emerged into the cave, flashlight in hand. Oh, and butcher knife in other hand. As Louise would say, completely and totally unfantastical.

"What happened to your hair?" he asked.

"Bee Bee."

"Huh?"

"Your bird," I snapped. "He pooped on my head."

"You're angry."

"Very good, Buster. I'm mad, and you're a murderer."

"No, it was your boyfriend. They just arrested him."

I chuckled, which apparently was not the reaction anyone expected. I could feel Chris flinch, and Buster almost pouted. "Aren't you upset?" he asked me. "Aren't you worried?"

I told him I was worried, but not surprised. "We've had all day to think about why you kidnapped us. Clearly you wanted to throw suspicion elsewhere."

"Good job," Chris added sarcastically.

"Why did you kill Davy?" I asked without further ado.

"I just told you. It was your boyfriend."

"Yeah, right. And you kidnapped Chris and me just for the fun of it. And why did you kidnap that poor bird? Did Bee Bee know something?"

"How did he get out?" Buster asked.

"He walked."

Chris jabbed me and I cleared my throat. "Or he flew," I corrected myself. "We were, as you know, in the dark." I spent a moment deciding what I would, and would not know, if indeed I had been trapped in the stupid cave all day.

"I hope Bee Bee found his way back to the Wakilulani Gardens," I said. "Do parrots have good homing instincts?"

"The Wakilulani is not his home. Bee Bee doesn't belong anymore. He was Grandpa's bird."

Grandpa's bird. I let the gist of that sink in and thought about how to proceed. "So," I said. "You didn't want Bee Bee around anymore because he was part of the old resort? I understand completely."

"You do?"

"I think so. You've been working so hard to make everything all new and fresh, correct? And Bee Bee was the mascot for the old Wakilulani. But why didn't you just kill him?"

Buster jumped. "Kill Bee Bee? Oh, no!" he said. "Bee Bee was Grandpa's bird. I couldn't kill him."

But you could let him suffer in Pele's Prison.

I took a deep breath and tried to think like a lunatic. "But you still wanted him gone, correct?"

"I'm getting a new pet. I want a puppy."

I nodded, feigning understanding. "All fresh and new," I repeated. "I guess that goes for the Wakilulani staff, too?"

Buster shifted from foot to foot.

"You may as well tell us what happened, Buster," I encouraged. "What difference will it make once we're dead?"

Chris jabbed me from behind.

"No, really," I continued undeterred. "I have had a very rough day and now face certain death by stabbing. I simply refuse to die in the dark." I blinked into the semi-darkness. "Figuratively speaking, that is."

Buster kept up with the shuffling, and my intuition told me he was reluctant to kill us. Maybe my very rough day was finally looking up.

I soldiered on. "You managed to get rid of most of the old staff pretty easily, didn't you? They all quit."

"Not Derrick and Davy."

"No clean slate with those two hanging around." I pretended to sigh. "You just had to get rid of them."

I watched Ms. Huge and Hairy continue her feast and listened to Buster complain about this, that, and the other.

He went through the whole rigmarole of Carmen, her children, their fathers, and her child support arrangements. Somehow everything ended up being Davy Atwell's fault.

I cleared my throat. "So Davy was the was the last to go?"

"He wouldn't go. That's the trouble."

"Why didn't you fire him?"

"Ki wouldn't let me."

"Why not?" Chris asked.

Buster seemed exasperated at our stupidity. "I just told you. I fire Davy, like I fired Derrick, and Carmen gets no child support. Ki would get mad at me again."

"So you killed Davy instead?" I asked.

"Well, yeah!"

Chris flinched again, and I bit my lip, and we let Buster continue.

"Now Ki will finally be happy," he said. "Carmen's children will inherit Davy's house. The place is huge! It's on all the tours, and it's worth a fortune. They can all live there, and Ki will be close by, and he can help me at the Wakilulani without getting mad all the time. We can pick out a puppy together. Carmen's children can help—"

Click.

It was a teeny-tiny sound, but I assure you the click of the tape recorder turning off reverberated throughout the cave. Even Ms. Huge and Hairy noticed. She stopped eating and shifted her gaze toward Buster.

Meanwhile, I was busy untying the ropes that bound me to Chris.

***

That bound Chris to me would be more accurate. He leapt up, gun in hand, just as Buster lunged forward.

By the time I was on my feet with the flashlight, Buster had seen the gun.

He froze in his tracks. "You miss me," he said, not taking his eyes from the weapon, "and the bullet will bounce off the walls and hit her."

He pointed at yours truly, and I muttered a four-letter word. Wasn't this just a fine time for Buster Okolo's logic to start making sense?

Buster knew it made sense. He lunged at Chris, who abandoned the gun and pulled out his stupid pocket knife.

Buster was jabbing—badly I am happy to report. And Chris was ducking—well I am happy to report, when I remembered that I, too, had a pocket knife.

It took me far too long to get the thing open, what with my hands shaking so badly. But this gave me time to rethink the plan. I pulled out the tiny blade and thrashed it upward. And the spider came tumbling down. Onto my head.

Onto my head!? My head!?

"OH MY GOD!!!!!!!" I shrieked at the very top of my lungs. I jumped up and down, and flailed my arms, and Ms. Huge and Hairy got the hint. She flew, or perhaps I swatted her, across the cave, and she landed on Buster's face.

I screamed some more, but Buster was way louder than me. That is until he fainted.

What a good idea! I caught a glimpse of Wilson and Vega at the opening of the tunnel just as I collapsed.

***

But let's face it, spending one more second on the floor of Pele's Prison was not in my best interest. I accepted Wilson's hand, and he pulled me back to my feet.

Meanwhile, Chris had a flashlight pointed at Buster, and Vega had a gun pointed at him. Buster's eyes were fluttering open, but no one was moving toward him. Not with Ms. Huge and Hairy perched his nose like that. Proof positive, boys and girls, that crime does not pay.

The spider seemed unconcerned about her mesmerized audience. She sat there until I was threatening to faint again, and then ever so slowly departed from Buster's face. While Vega and Wilson got Buster to his feet and handcuffed, Chris and I held onto to each other for support and watched our spider crawl up to her corner and start spinning a new web.

You had to admire the gal's energy.

"You think you'll use a scene like this in *South Pacific Paramour*?" Chris asked me.

I squinted at Ms. Huge and Hairy. "No," I said. "Adelé's readers would never believe it."

Chapter 29

"Who would have thunk it?" Wilson looked up from the phone as I stepped out to the porch.

No big surprise—I had spent much of the next morning washing my hair. But despite numerous and increasingly aggressive shampooings, the purple stain remained. I pointed to my head and pouted. "You're right," I agreed. "Who would have thunk it?"

"No, Jessie." He held up the cell phone. "That was Candy."

"The cats!" I jumped. "Oh, my Lord, Wilson! I forgot all about Wally yesterday! What with caves, and spiders, and jungles, and murder—"

"Will you relax?" He patted the spot beside him, and I sat down. "Wally's fine, okay? This injury was just the thing."

"Excuse me?"

"Our two females have taken to mothering him." He again gestured to the phone and summarized Candy's report. Apparently both Bernice and Snowflake had decided to nurse Wally back to health by cuddling him to death.

"Bernice wouldn't even leave him to eat her breakfast this morning," Wilson said. "According to Candy the three of them have been huddled together on your bed for the last twenty-four hours. They're even purring together. Who would have thunk it?"

He frowned at my head. "Who would have thunk it?"

I rolled my eyes and donned my new Halo Beach PD baseball cap. Then I did as suggested and relaxed. While Wilson read the newspaper, I listened to the medley of Elvis tunes wafting up to Paradise from the Song of the Sea.

"They're starting to sound pretty good," I said.

"You must have suds in your ears. Read this, Jessie." He put the paper on my lap and tapped the article about Buster's arrest.

"A local crime story on the front page?" I asked as I sat up. "Has the Halo Beach Herald changed their approach to these things?"

"Looks like it." Wilson gestured to the paper, and I read.

The summary of the interview they conducted with Chris and me was blessedly brief since the reporter had been much more interested in Bee Bee's role in the whole shebang. Indeed, a large color photo of the heroic bird adorned a good part of the front page. "Good as new!" the caption read.

"Thank you for saving me from the photographers last night, Wilson."

"That parrot might have been good as new. But you, Darlin,' looked like hell."

"Gee thanks."

"Ki called when you were working on shampoo number seven." Wilson abandoned the sports section. "He's found his brother a good lawyer. The psychiatric evaluation is already scheduled for the twenty-sixth."

I asked what would happen to Buster, but Wilson reminded me he was not familiar with the Hawaiian criminal justice code.

"Whatever happens, Buster won't be coming back to the Wacky Gardens anytime soon," he said. "Ki's in charge, whether he likes it or not."

"He doesn't," Chris called from the garden as he and the rest of our gang approached Paradise. Chris was carrying a tray of coffee and pastries, Louise was carrying Bee Bee, and my mother was sputtering that everyone, especially Chris and her daughter, deserved some sweet treats after what we had endured the previous day.

"No pancakes," she said. "But Faye was dear enough to go get these for us."

"We saw Bethany, too," Louise said as everyone pulled up seats. "She's down at The Big House."

"Ki's asked her to be the new manager." Chris set his tray on top of the newspaper, and Louise reached over to grab a treat.

"Isn't that fantastical?" she asked. "Bethany will do a great job."

"Great job!" Bee Bee agreed. He reached out a claw, and Louise handed him a corner of her pastry.

Mother pointed me to the gooiest-looking selection. "That one's for you, Honeybunch."

"And here's your coffee." Chris handed me the cup he had just poured. I accepted with sincere gratitude and tried not to act too shocked when he leaned over and gave me a peck on the cheek. "Merry Christmas Eve, Jessie."

I Merry Christmas Eve'd him back, and we all clicked coffee cups to the holiday.

Mother scowled at my ball cap. "Any luck?"

I mumbled something about my new affinity for hats while Wilson tried to take everyone's mind off my troubles. He announced our Christmas gift to the group—a helicopter tour of the island after lunch.

Mother squealed in delight. "I've never been in a helicopter before!"

Come to learn, none of us had except Wilson. But he assured us the tourist helicopters of Hawaii were far fancier than those he had experienced long ago in the Air Force. "They have six passenger seats. Six!" He shook his head in dismay.

I turned to Chris. "Which means the five of us and Emi, if you'd like to invite her."

"I would," he said, and winked at my mother. "Then afterwards she can stick around to take pictures."

I put down my pastry. "Pictures?"

"Of our surfing lesson," Mother explained. "Isn't it a shame we missed our lesson yesterday? What with you two being kidnapped and such?"

"We'll make up for lost time today," Chris reassured us.

Louise and I blinked at each other. "Fantastical," we squeaked.

***

As Bee Bee would say, "La La Land."

Oh, my Lord, Hawaii is beautiful. Our pilot guided the helicopter in and out of lush gullies, and up and down through deep gorges, while the rest of us oohed and aahed in all the appropriate places.

Far be it for me to disagree with Wilson and his son, but this was clearly the best way to see the island. I tore my gaze away from the spectacular views to smile at my beau. "No heebie jeebies," I mouthed into the din of the helicopter engine and pointed to a particularly lush patch of ferns below.

Wilson grinned, and as we leaned forward to watch the show, my imagination took off.

I pictured Skylar Staggs diving from each wondrous waterfall, and Urquit Snodgrass stashing his loot in each hidden alcove. Oh, and over there? That field of purple and pink wildflowers would make a lovely setting for Auntie Eleanor's estate. And that secluded beach? The perfect place for a picnic…and a proposal. Indeed, that would be the exact spot where Skylar invited Delta to sail the world with him. No dreary settling down for those two!

But I was getting ahead of myself. Yes, I could certainly draw on these gorgeous details as I put the finishing touches on *My South Pacific Paramour*. But what about the basics? Like how the lovers were going to vanquish the altogether evil Urquit Snodgrass?

The helicopter took a zig-zagging dive right into Kekipi Crater, and my mother squealed in delight. Or maybe that was me. Whoever it was, Adelé Nightingale decided to worry about the pesky particulars of her mandatory happy ending some other day.

***

If only her surfing lesson could have been postponed so easily.

But no. At four o'clock sharp we were out on the beach. Some of us were smiling at our surfboards, some were frowning, and the luckiest of us was taking pictures instead.

I pointed to the waves and appealed to Emi. "Make me look good out there?"

"Absolutely." She gave me a thumbs up as Chris handed me my surfboard.

"Come on, Jessie," he said. "Even you have to admit this is better than spending the afternoon with Ms. Huge and Hairy."

"With my luck, she probably swims." I winked at Emi and stumbled into the waves.

I passed Louise, who was frolicking at water's edge and clearly had no intention of getting in over her head, either literally or figuratively. But of course my mother was giving it her all. I pushed out toward her as yet another wave knocked her over. I waited for her smiling face to emerge from the depths before struggling out to Wilson.

Not that he had much competition, but he was still the star student of our group. He hung ten several times, giving Emi ample opportunity for some terrific action shots.

Boy, how I wished she could get just one shot of me being vertical. And to my credit I did manage to stand up once or twice. That is, if you count one-tenth of one nanosecond as standing up. Alas, it was never long enough for Emi to get a good picture, but Chris insisted it still counted, and that I was "doing great."

Eventually, all of us geezers gave up and sat exhausted in the sand as Chris and Emi took to the waves. They hung ten and did some general showing off—more for the benefit of each other than for those of us on shore.

Louise looked up from the camera she was now in charge of. "How can people look that good?" She was genuinely perplexed.

Mother patted her knee. "You girls give me a few days and I'll draw some nice pictures. We'll all be hanging ten by the time we leave Hawaii." She giggled. "At least on my drawing tablet."

Louise directed the camera toward us Hewitts and snapped a few pictures. "Like mother like daughter," she said. "Great imaginations and gobs of creativity."

"One draws improbable scenes, one writes them," Wilson agreed.

"We Hewitts do like happy endings, don't we?" I smiled at my mother, but noticed she was frowning. "You're thinking about Buster?" I asked, and she forced herself to perk up.

"I'm sure he'll will get the help he needs, now that the extent of his problems is understood. Ki's a good brother."

"And maybe Ki and Carmen will end up halfway happy," Wilson added. "It seems likely she and her kids will inherit Davy's house."

"So they'll get a new home," Mother said. "Won't that be nice?"

"Bee Bee's getting a new home, too," Louise said and waited for us to connect the dots. "Louise!" I cried. "You aren't?"

"Oh, yes. Oh, yes I am, Jessica! I'm adopting him! Isn't that fantastical?"

Mother squealed in delight, and Wilson offered more subdued congratulations, as Louise explained, "Let's face it, that magnificent creature is practically an orphan. Pono's dead, Buster's gone, and Ki?" She shrugged. "I'm sure he'd take care of him if need be, but there is no need. I'll take him!"

"Have you ever had a pet before?" Mother asked.

"Never, never, never!"

But even so, Louise seemed to know what she was doing. While I had been busy washing my hair, she was wading through the legalities and logistics of transporting an animal to the mainland. "Bee Bee will soon be a New Yorker!" she announced proudly.

I thought about the bird's new digs. "It will be a big change for him," I said. "Maybe he should live at your office?"

"Exactly, Jessica! Bee Bee will have lots of company since I'm almost always there. And won't he simply adore the atrium? Adore, adore, adore?"

"He'll love it," I agreed and described Louise's expansive reception area for everyone else. "It has a huge skylight, and a water fountain, and scads of plants and trees."

"Scads of palm trees, even," Louise said. "It's like the jungle itself!"

"It's far more elaborate than my rooftop garden," I added as Chris and Emi finally abandoned the waves to join us. We summarized all the good news for them.

"Looks like you get a happy ending too, Jessie." Chris pointed to me, and everyone stared aghast.

My eyes darted from person to person. "What's wrong?" I asked.

"My heavens," Mother murmured.

"I cannot believe we didn't notice before now!" Louise said.

"Who would have thunk it?" Wilson asked.

"Thunk what?" I asked.

He reached over and tugged at a tuft of my hair. "It's blond again, Jessie. Must be the salt water did the trick."

I blinked twice and turned to Chris. "Okay," I said. "So maybe I do like surfing after all."

He grinned and asked if he could fetch me a pink drink.

Epilogue

"A ukulele contest, a full moon, and a midnight stroll on Halo Beach. What better way to spend Christmas Eve?" I asked Wilson as we plopped ourselves down in our favorite spot in the sand.

"But the Hoochie Coochie Brothers didn't win." He gestured back to where we had just left the Yuletide Ukulele Jamboree.

I shrugged. "Maybe, but third place isn't so bad."

We gazed up at the moon until Wilson broke the silence.

"So, Jessie." He cleared his throat. "Chris tells me you guys talked about Dianne Calloway yesterday."

"I thought I was going to die, Wilson. And I refused to do so without knowing your deep dark secrets."

He nodded and actually admitted he was glad I knew the truth. "Dianne wasn't who I thought she was." I could barely hear him over the waves.

"That's when you moved to Lake Lookadoo?" I, too, spoke quietly. "After Dianne?"

"Once Chris got settled at college, I changed departments."

"You had too much history in Raleigh, I suppose."

"Yep. The Clarence force was organizing a new homicide squad just as I decided to leave Raleigh. They hired me to head it up."

"But you weren't about to live right in the center of things. In Clarence, I mean."

"I wanted some peace and quiet. At least when I wasn't at work."

I shook my head. If one were looking for reliable indoor plumbing, Wilson's shack on the banks of Lake Lookadoo would not be the best option. But for peace and quiet? It was just the spot.

"Will Dianne ever get out of prison?" I asked eventually.

"Hard to believe, but she's up for parole pretty soon. Her lawyer got her sentence reduced to manslaughter. I'm still convinced it was first degree murder." He shrugged. "But."

"Will she come looking for you?"

"Who knows?" He gave me a quick glance and then looked away. "But even if she does, I intend to be happily settled with someone else by then."

I put an index finger under his chin and turned his face in my direction. "Oh?" I asked.

He grinned and reached into the pocket of his Hawaiian shirt. And I blinked twice at the small sparkly thing he pulled out to show me.

The End

Cindy Blackburn is hard at work making more trouble for Jessie. She's also busy creating another series set in rural Vermont of all places. Find out how she's doing at

www.cueballmysteries.com

Just in case you've missed either of Jessie's other adventures . . .

Book One: Playing With Poison

Pool shark Jessie Hewitt usually knows where the balls will fall and how the game will end. But when a body lands on her couch, and the cute cop in her kitchen accuses her of murder, even Jessie isn't sure what will happen next. *Playing With Poison* is a cozy mystery with a lot of humor, a little romance, and far too much champagne.

Book Two: Double Shot

Jessie Hewitt thought her pool-hustling days were long gone. But when uber-hunky cop Wilson Rye asks her to go undercover to catch a killer, she jumps at the chance to return to a sleazy poolroom. Jessie is confident she can handle a double homicide, but the doubly-annoying Wilson Rye is another matter altogether. What's he doing flirting with a woman half his age? Will Jessie have what it takes to deal with Tiffany La-Dee-Doo-Da Sass and solve the murders? Take a guess.

Playing With Poison

Chapter 1

"Going bra shopping at age fifty-two gives new meaning to the phrase fallen woman," I announced as I gazed at my reflection.

"Oh, Jessie, you always say that." Candy poked her head around the dressing room door and took a peek at the royal blue contraption she was trying to sell me. "Gosh, that looks great. It's very flattering."

I lifted an unconvinced eyebrow. "Oh, Candy, you always say that."

"No really. I hope my figure looks that nice when I'm old."

Okay, so I took that as a compliment and agreed to buy the silly bra. And before she even mentioned them, I also asked for the matching panties. To know my neighbor Candy Poppe is to have a drawer full of completely inappropriate, and often alarming, lace, silk, and satin undergarments.

I got dressed and went out to the floor.

"*Temptation at Twilight* giving you trouble?" she asked as she rang me up. Candy hasn't known me long, but she does know me well. And she's figured out I show up at Tate's whenever writer's block strikes.

I sighed dramatically. "Plot plight."

"But you know you never have issues for very long, Jessie." She wrapped my purchases in pink tissue paper and placed them in a pink Tate's shopping bag. "Even after your divorce, remember? You came in, bought a few nice things, and went on home to finish *Windswept Whispers*." She offered an encouraging nod. "So go home, put on this bra, and start writing."

I did as I was told, but wearing the ridiculous blue bra didn't help after all. The page on my computer screen remained stubbornly blank no matter how hard I stared at it. I was deciding there must be better ways to spend a

Saturday night when a knock on the door pulled me out of my funk.

"Maybe it's Prince Charming," I said to my cat. Snowflake seemed skeptical, but I got up to answer anyway.

Funny thing? It really was Prince Charming. I opened my door to find Candy Poppe's handsome to a fault fiancé standing in the hallway. But Stanley wasn't looking all that handsome. Without bothering to say hello, he pushed me aside, stumbled toward the couch, and collapsed. Prince Charming was sick.

I rushed over to where he had invited himself to lie down and knelt beside him. "Stanley?" I asked. "What's wrong?"

"Candy," he whispered, and then he died.

He died?

I blinked twice and told myself I was not seeing what I was seeing. "He's just drunk," I reassured Snowflake. "He passed out."

But then, why were his eyes open like that?

I reached for his wrist. No pulse. I checked for breathing. Nope. I shook him and called his name a few times. Nothing.

Nothing.

The gravity of the situation finally dawned on me, and I jumped up. "CPR!" I shouted at the cat.

But Snowflake doesn't know CPR. And I remembered that I don't either.

I screamed a four-letter word and lunged for the phone.

***

Twenty minutes later a Clarence police officer was standing in my living room, hovering over me, my couch, and Candy's dead fiancé. I stared down at Stanley, willing him to start breathing again, while Captain Wilson Rye kept repeating the same questions about how I knew Candy, how I knew her boyfriend, and—here was the tricky part—what he was doing lying dead on my couch. I imagined Candy would wonder about that, too.

"Ms. Hewitt? Look at me." I glanced up at a pair of blue eyes that might have been pleasant under other circumstances. "You have anywhere else we can talk?"

Hope drained from his face as he scanned my condominium, an expansive loft with an open floor plan and very few doors. At the moment the place was swarming with people wearing plastic sheeting, talking into doohickeys, and either dusting or taking samples of who knows what from every corner and crevice. Unless Officer Rye and I decided to talk in the bathroom, we were doomed to be in the midst of the action.

"I'll make some tea," I said. At least then we could sit at the kitchen counter and stare at the stove. I glanced down. A far better option than staring at poor Stanley.

"Ms. Hewitt?"

"Tea," I repeated and pointed Officer Rye toward a barstool. I turned on the kettle and sat down beside him while the plastic people bustled about behind us, continuing their search for dust bunnies.

"Let's try this again," he said. "What was your relationship with Mr. Sweetzer?"

"We had no relationship."

"Mm-hmm."

"No, really. He was Candy's boyfriend. She lives downstairs in 2B."

The kettle whistled and I got up to pour the tea. Conscious that this cop was watching my every move, I spilled more water on the counter than into the cups. But eventually I succeeded in my task and even managed to hand him a cup.

"How do you take it?" I asked.

"Excuse me?"

"Your tea. Lemon, cream, sugar?"

"Nothing, thank you." He frowned at the tea. "So you knew Sweetzer through Ms. Poppe?"

"Correct." I carried my own cup around the counter and sat down again. "She and I met a few months ago."

"Where? Here?"

I sipped my tea and thought back. I had met Candy in the bra department at Tate's of course. It was the day after my divorce was finalized, and she had sold me a dozen bras spanning every color in the rainbow. Candy had even mentioned it that afternoon.

"Ms. Hewitt?"

"We met in the foundations department at Tate's."

"The what department?"

So much for discretion. "The bra department," I said bluntly. "Candy sold me some bras."

Rye's gaze moved southward for the briefest of seconds, and I remembered the brand new, bright blue specimen lurking beneath my white shirt.

My white shirt.

If there had been a wall handy, I would have banged my head against it. Instead, I mumbled something about not expecting company.

Rye cleared his throat and suggested we move on.

"Candy and I got to talking, and I told her I was in the market for a condo, and she told me about this place." I pointed up. "I took one look at these fifteen-foot ceilings and huge windows and signed a mortgage a week later. We've been good friends ever since."

"And Stanley Sweetzer?"

"Was Candy's boyfriend. He had some hotshot job in finance, and he was madly in love with Candy."

"So what was he doing up here?"

Okay, good question. I was trying to think of a good answer when one of the plastic people interrupted. "Will someone please get this cat out of here?" she called from behind us.

I turned to see Snowflake scurrying across the floor, gleefully unraveling a roll of yellow police tape. I quick hopped down to retrieve her while the plastic people sputtered this and that about contaminating the crime scene.

"She does live here," I said. They stopped scolding and watched as I picked her up and returned to my seat.

Snowflake had other ideas, however. She switched from my lap to Rye's and immediately commenced purring.

Rye resumed the interrogation. "Did you invite Mr. Sweetzer up here?"

"Nooo, I did not. I was working. I was sitting at my desk, minding my own business, when Stanley showed up out of the blue."

"You always work Saturday nights?"

I raised an eyebrow. "Do you?"

Rye took a deep breath. "You were alone then? Before Sweetzer showed up?"

"Snowflake was here."

More deep breathing. "Did he say anything, Ms. Hewitt?"

"He looked up when he hit the couch and whispered 'Candy.'" I shook my head. "It was awful."

"Could he have mistaken you for Candy?"

I shook my head again. "She's at least twenty years younger than me, a lot shorter, and has long dark hair." I pointed to my short blond cut. "No."

"Well then, maybe he had come from Candy's." Rye twirled around and called over to a young black guy—the only person other than himself in a business suit—and introduced me to Lieutenant Russell Densmore.

The Lieutenant shook my hand, but seemed far more interested in the teacups and the cat, who continued to occupy his boss's lap. His gaze landed back on me while he listened to instructions.

"Go downstairs to 2B and get them up here," Captain Rye told him. "Someone named Candy Poppe in particular."

"She's still at work," I said, but Lieutenant Densmore left anyway.

I looked at Rye. "I really don't think Stanley came here from Candy's," I insisted. "She's at work. I saw her there myself."

"Excuse me?"

"I was in Tate's this afternoon."

Rye took another gander at my chest. "That outfit for Sweetzer's benefit?"

"My outfi—What? No!"

Despite the stupid bra, only a madman would find my typical writing attire even remotely seductive. That evening I was wearing a pair of jeans, cut off above the knee, and a discarded men's dress shirt from way back when, courtesy of my ex-husband. As usual when I'm at home, I was barefoot. Stick a corncob pipe in my mouth and point me toward the Mississippi, and I might have borne a vague resemblance to Huck Finn—a tall, thin, menopausal Huck Finn.

I folded my arms and glared. "As I keep telling you, Captain, I was not expecting company."

"Is the door downstairs always unlocked?"

"Umm, yes?"

"You are kidding, right? You live smack in the middle of downtown Clarence and leave your front door unlocked? Anyone and his brother had access to this building tonight. You realize that?"

I gritted my teeth, mustered what was left of my patience, and suggested he talk to my neighbors about it. "For all I know, they've been here for years without a lock on that door."

Rye might have enjoyed lecturing me further, but luckily Lieutenant Densmore came back and distracted him. He reported that, indeed, Candy Poppe was not at home.

"What a shocker," I mumbled.

One of the plastic people also joined us. "You were right, Captain," she said. "This definitely looks unnatural."

"Yet another shocker." My voice had gained some volume, and all three of them frowned at me. I frowned back. "This whole evening has been extremely unnatural."

Rye turned and gave directions to the plastic person—something about getting the body to the medical examiner. He told Lieutenant Densmore to go downstairs and wait for Candy. Then he scooted Snowflake onto the floor and stood up to issue orders to the rest of the crowd.

I stood up also. Everyone appeared to have finished with their dusting, and I was happy to see that Stanley had been taken away. But it was a bit disconcerting to watch my couch being hauled off.

"You wouldn't want it here anyway, would you?" the Captain asked me. We stood together and waited while everyone else gathered their equipment and departed.

Rye was the last go. "I'll be downstairs if you think of anything else, Ms. Hewitt. Or call me." He handed me his card and headed toward the door. "I can't wait to hear what Ms. Poppe has to say for herself."

"She'll have nothing to say for herself," I called after him. "She's been at work all day."

He turned at the doorway. "Stay put," he said. "That's an order."

"Shut the door behind you, Captain. That's an order."

***

I headed for the fridge, desperately in search of champagne. Given the situation, this may seem odd. But champagne became my drink of choice after my divorce, when I decided every day without my ex is a day worth celebrating. Even days with dead bodies in them. I popped the cork. Make that, especially days with dead bodies.

I opened my door to better hear what was happening below and sank down in an easy chair. Candy got home at 9:30, but Rye and Densmore quickly shuffled her into her condo, and someone closed the door.

"Most unhandy," I told Snowflake. She jumped onto my lap, and together we stared at the empty spot where my couch had been.

The Korbel bottle was nearly half empty by the time Candy's door opened again. I hopped up to eavesdrop at my own doorway and heard Rye say something about calling him if she thought of anything else. Lieutenant Densmore asked if she had any family close by.

"My parents," she answered. "But I think I'll go see Jessie now, okay?"

I didn't catch Rye's reply, but the cops finally left, and within seconds Candy was at my doorstep.

"Oh, Jessie," she cried as I pulled her inside. She stopped short. "Umm, what happened to your sofa?"

"We need to talk," I told her. I guided her toward my bed and had her lie down.

The poor woman cried for a solid ten minutes. I held her hand and waited, and eventually she asked for some champagne. Like I told Rye—Candy and I are good friends.

I went to fetch a tray, and she was sitting up when I returned to the bedroom.

"Do you feel like talking, Sweetie?" I asked as I handed her a glass.

She took a sip, and then pulled a tissue from the box on my nightstand and made a sloppy attempt to wipe the mascara from under her eyes. "Those policemen told me what happened, but I could barely listen."

"They wanted to know why Stanley was here tonight. Do you know?"

She shook her head. "They kept asking me where I was. I was at work, right?"

"At least you have a solid alibi." I frowned. "Which makes one of us."

"Captain Rye was real interested in you, Jessie. I think he likes you."

I rolled my eyes. "Would you get a grip, Candy? Rye's real interested because he thinks I killed your boyfriend."

Her face dropped and she blinked her big brown eyes. "Did someone kill Stanley?"

Okay, so Candy Poppe isn't exactly the fizziest champagne in the fridge. Even on days without dead bodies.

"It looks like Stanley was murdered," I said quietly and handed her another tissue. "Did he have any enemies?"

"That's what Captain Rye kept asking me," she whined. "But everyone loved Stanley, didn't they?"

I had my doubts but thought it best to agree. I asked about his family, and over the remains of the Korbel, we discussed his parents. Apparently Margaret and Roger Sweetzer did not approve of Candy.

"They think I was after his money," she said. She put down her empty glass. "They don't like my job either. I swear to God, his mother comes into the store twice a week to embarrass me in front of the customers. And every time Mr. Sweetzer sees me, he asks how business is and stares at my chest."

While Candy blew her nose, I stared at her chest. The woman is my friend and all, but I could see how people might get the wrong impression. On this particular occasion she was wearing her red mini dress—and I do mean mini—

and had accessorized with a truckload of red baubles and beads that would have fit better on a Christmas tree than on Candy's petite frame. An unlikely pair of red patent leather stilettos completed the ensemble.

I stifled a frown. Hopefully, Captain Rye understood she had not known her fiancé was about to die when she wiggled her curvaceous little body into that outfit.

I mumbled something about trying to get some rest. If I still had my couch, I would have slept on it and let Candy drift off on the bed. I lamented such as she got up to leave, but she assured me she would be fine and teetered out the door in those ridiculous red shoes.

About the Author

Cindy Blackburn has a confession to make–she does not play pool. It's that whole eye-hand coordination thing. What Cindy does do well is school. So when she's not writing silly stories she's teaching serious history. European history is her favorite subject, and the ancient stuff is best of all. The deader the better! A native Vermonter who hates cold weather, Cindy divides her time between the south and the north. During the school year you'll find her in South Carolina, but come summer she'll be on the porch of her lakeside shack in Vermont. Cindy has a fat cat named Betty and a cute husband named John. Betty the muse meows constantly while Cindy tries to type. John provides the technical support. Both are extremely lovable.

When Cindy isn't writing, grading papers, or feeding the cat, she likes to take long walks or paddle her kayak around the lake. Her favorite travel destinations are all in Europe, her favorite TV show is NCIS, her favorite movie is Moonstruck, her favorite color is orange, and her favorite authors (if she must choose) are Joan Hess and Spencer Quinn. Cindy dislikes vacuuming, traffic, and lima beans.

www.cueballmysteries.com

www.cueballmysteries.com/blog

@cbmysteries

Made in the USA
Lexington, KY
27 February 2014